I0647737

DREAMING GODS OF GAIA

A Novel of Dystopian Speculative Fiction

by Cherokee Freechild

Filidh Publishing

Copyright © 2021 by Cherokee Freechild

All rights reserved. This book or any portion thereof may not be reproduced or used in any manner whatsoever without the publisher's express written permission except for the use of brief quotations in a book review or scholarly journal.

First Softcover Printing: 2021
ISBN 978-1-927848-47-0
Filidh Publishing
www.filidhbooks.com

An original electronic version of this novel was published in serial postings of chapters at greeneggmagazine.com

Cover Art by Oberon Zell
Cover Design by Danny Weeds

* Quotes from *Franklin Jones*, **The Knee of Listening,** are cited and used under the Fair Use exemption of the US Copyright Act.

DREAMING GODS OF GAIA

In this alternative timeline, the Confederate States of America is the only free nation left in a world ruled by Commies and Corpses (a/k/a Companies and Corporations). A journalist dabbling in Sex Magick gets more action than he had bargained for.

Chapter 1
The Circle of Conception

"The unreal, typical man is constantly deciding about food and sex. He either tries to control it or he exploits it, and the average life is an alternating cycle...."

~ Franklin Jones, ***The Knee of Listening*** ***

Ceremony

The moonlight glinted eerily off the blade of the athame as the skyclad priestess swept the ceremonial dagger in a wide arc from West to North.

"Guardians of the Watchtowers," she chanted with dramatic flourish, "by the powers of the four elements, we bind this Circle into your safekeeping."

"So mote it be," intoned the ring of robed figures surrounding her.

She carefully inserted the blade of the athame into a crack in the altar stone and turned empty-handed to face her priest. Her gold medallion and silver crescent tiara accented the perfection of her nude form.

Along the horizon, the city lights of Atlanta formed a speckled outer crescent. The stillness was punctuated occasionally by the sweeping, twittering form of a bat or a nightbird.

Mark Lance felt his bare skin getting goosebumps from the chill night air, and he was trying hard to ignore the fact that his left foot was planted in a puddle of cold water. He noticed with surprise that his priestess showed no signs of discomfort.

Light from the bonfire on the South side of the Circle flickered off the surface of several similar puddles. Mark could almost sense the mineral presence of Mount Arabia, the huge granite bubble atop which they were gathered.

He became aware of Lana Morgan's eyes on him from the West curve of the Circle. He pictured with satisfaction what a striking figure he must make, silhouetted naked against the night sky with his gorgeous red-haired priestess.

Well, damn it, Lana had been invited to be priestess herself tonight and had *refused,* after all these weeks she had been after his ass! He had been forced to spend an outrageous sum of money to procure the services of a professional, but now that this amazing woman actually stood before him, he didn't regret a dime of it.

He mustered all his will to stop his teeth from chattering and extended his hands toward that lithe, muscular form.

"My Lady of the Night," he heard his voice speak the ritual invitation, "would you consent to be my partner in the Great Rite on this Beltane Eve?"

"I will," she said simply, and the couple knelt to position themselves on the satin cushions between the fire and the altar stone.

First sat Mark, in an awkward cross-legged position. Though he had done his yoga stretches for weeks, hoping to master the Lotus pose before this event, he had gained in flexibility only slightly. He surreptitiously glanced down and was pleased to confirm that his body was cooperating with the ritual in at least one respect: despite the cold, his phallus rose up proud and hard.

His priestess seated herself on his lap, facing him, her strong legs wrapped around his buttocks. He involuntarily gasped as he felt himself enter her. With effort, he reminded himself that this was a Sacred Occasion, not a time to indulge in haphazard fleshly pleasures.

Mark was grateful when two robed figures stepped out of the shadows to drape a blanket across the shoulders of the couple. They clasped forearms, leaned their upper bodies slightly apart, and locked gazes. One of the robed figures bound their arms together, while the other bound their lower bodies with a wide silken sash.

The robed figures stepped back into the shadows. The Torch of the East flickered in the eyes of the priestess as the couple began to synchronize and slow their breathing.

Members of Circle began to croon a low round of chants, their voices blending in with the night chorus of crickets. Almost imperceptibly at first, the cone of energy began to build. After a few minutes, the current had increased to an almost audible hum. The priestess still showed only a slight tremor, but Mark was shaking violently.

Then came that terrible moment when, had they not been bound together, their contact would surely have been broken. As Mark felt a great wave of force slam into him, he broke the visual circuit and flung his head back, fixing his gaze on the sky, where the stars seemed to swirl around like a Van Gogh painting. Mark's breathing deepened into gasping heaves, and he felt himself being drawn upward into that whirlpool of stars. As if from a great distance, he heard one wordless cry escape his throat, and then his consciousness was thrown forth.

Ontogeny Recapitulates Phylogeny

This must be the Astral Plane, Mark mused. For all his fine words, this was the first time he had experienced it during waking consciousness. So far as he could tell, he still had all his wits about him. But his body was another matter. It kept changing shape, and even threatening to fade away entirely.

For a moment he almost panicked, like a swimmer who finds the waters deeper than he had thought. Then, just in time, his meditation training came to the rescue.

He constructed an imaginary vantage point about three feet above and behind him, and allowed his bodily perceptions to take shape as reflected from that perspective. At last some control began to return, but...

Now he needed some surroundings. He was in a murky, hazy place. Whenever he thought of any form, the ghost of an outline would begin to take shape before him. It was only a matter of time before he lost concentration and allowed something really unpleasant to manifest. Once he'd been frightened into forgetting his own identity, it could take eons to find himself again!

I wasn't ready for this, he thought. *I want to go back!*

Obligingly, his surroundings radiated unreadiness and wrongplaceness.

With a sinking feeling, Mark realized that he didn't really want to contact the Elder Gods, or even the Lower Astral Realms. This whole project, planned for months, had been undertaken in a spirit of self-important sexual titillation and social defiance. But on this plane, those motivations threatened to call up forces that he did not want to face just now — or ever!

"Forgive me," he spoke hoarsely into the not-quite-void. "I was unworthy."

The Universe echoed back his unworthiness. Just below the threshold of perception, he could sense every shameful experience of his life drifting slowly toward the surface.

"Please," he whispered, "please, let me go back! Let me go back!"

First to take form was the little girl he had played doctor with when he was five. She hadn't entered his mind for almost

25 years, but here she was in every detail. He, too, was only five; this astral body was small and weak. In fact, it was shrinking steadily. With horror, he realized that he had soiled himself.

"I might have known I couldn't trust you," said a disgusted female voice. Rough, large hands scooped him up, threw him face-down onto a soft surface, and began removing his pants. He cried out in dismay and tried to run away, only to realize that he was no longer able to stand.

Awkwardly, he started off at a fast crawl, only to find his way blocked by a big brown shoe. His eyes tracked up the pantleg for miles, and from far away came the booming male voice: "And just where do you think you're going?"

And then he lost the ability even to crawl. He lay helplessly on his back while giants ticked his belly with their great fingers, and all the corners of the Cosmos echoed with their mocking laughter. As he screamed out his dismay, he heard a familiar voice: "He's crying *again*!"

His eyes were blinded by the lights, and more harsh noise assaulted his ears. His body was swung head over heels in space. His penis was in such agony that he scarcely noticed the drops that burned his eyes.

His throat and lungs burned with a terrible pain as he gasped for something insubstantial and unfamiliar, but strangely necessary.

His whole being knotted with pain and grief as the lifeline at his midsection was slashed away in mid-pulsation. He had lost the companion extension of himself that had rooted him to Life's source.

But in the next instant that comforting connection was restored, and he felt the reassuring pulses of energized lifefluid coursing through his body.

Then the Great Mother engulfed him. His whole body was being crushed, and the pressure at the top of his head was unbearable!

He folded his arms across his chest and bent double. He was dizzy with oxygen starvation, and his chest made ineffectual breathing motions, but to no avail. He was utterly trapped, trapped forever.

Somewhere the Great Mother was screaming in anguish that merged with his own, and somehow he knew that each of them was both the cause and the victim of that horror, and that the echoes of that rage and terror would drive them both to seek revenge.

And then the space around him grew larger, and he felt no further urge to breathe. Sucking his thumb, he lovingly fingered the pulsating cord and floated for a peaceful eternity in a soft bubble. "*Love-dove*!" the Universe crooned to him. "*Love-dove*!"

Memories of primeval organisms awakened through his transformations. He was nothing but an eyeless head and a spine, unable to move.

He was an orgy of Sixteen through a wondrous miracle, and the units merged and became Eight, and then there were Four, touching hearts in a daisy of bliss, and then again Two in a joyful communion, and then the two formed a Great One, as he relived that moment of ecstatic dissolution when those separate beings had come together as lovers and had merged completely and irrevocably with their Deity.

Then he was racing ... *No!* He was swimming. He had a wonderful long tadpole tail, and he was desperately, joyously eager to meet his Beloved, who was, he knew, almost within reach. Though the frantic journey had occupied most of his lifespan and would end with his dissolution, it was Destiny incarnate.

But then a new Reality spread out before him, complete with its own history.

Circle of Selves

Two of us had been killed by an avalanche, and the time had come to replace them. It was a solemn occasion as we gathered on the mountaintop.

Yellowhair was the right one, for she was the right age and had the right heritage and was not needed for any other cooperative task.

Freckleface was the right one, for twice already we had taken him to the Cauldron to fight back the unruly signs of approaching maturity.

For six months the two had lived apart from the Community and from each other, receiving the teachings they would need to live as single units. Already he had the beginnings of a beard; already she had the buds of breasts.

Their loneliness was palpable, and we enfolded them with our love until we saw their smiles begin.

They faced each other across the Cushion of Conception and we began to hum and chant encouragement. They maintained contact in this way for a long time before they moved closer together and began to stroke each other's skin.

Their faces took on a look of strange hunger as they joined their bodies in the sexual way, at the second chakra, the woman atop the man in a sitting posture, her legs folded around him. They began very gently to rock back and forth as we continued our chanting and humming, until we perceived at last that their circuits had fully melded. They were again temporarily at One with the Other and at peace.

Slowly we accelerated the rhythm of our crooning sound-drop, guiding their bodies to climax, guiding them into the consciousness of the Sperm and the waiting Ovum. Those vibrations enfolded their souls again into the consciousness of our Circle, which had once been their own,

After climax, they remained united for a long time. The woman lay back and a fellow supported the man from behind, and we followed with them the questing of the sperm up the long, long tunnel to the moment of joyful union and the celebration of cell divisions that mirrored our own Circle.

At last our chant faded into silence, as the man and woman separated and cried. A blanket was draped across both of them and a Teacher led them away, hand in hand.

They were now Individuals. They would live together but would be alone in their souls forever, except for those brief moments of copulation or other forms of Tantric union. They would live out their lives in this sad condition, from time to time bringing forth children whom they would fail to comprehend.

But these lives would be mercifully short; they would probably die within 60 years of their sexual maturity. Perhaps they would not even wait out their full span after fulfilling their reproductive responsibilities, though that was their right.

Then I saw the Circle of Selves fading into the distance and realized that it was I who was the Individual. It was I would know sexual ecstasy, grow old and die, all alone except for fleeting moments.

I turned to my mate and pressed my forehead to hers, but it was all over now. There was not enough energy charge left to close those circuits again today, and in my soul I remained alone.

She whispered, "Next moon we can do it again."

"A mooncycle is very long," I replied. But I knew that if the waiting time were less, the higher circuits would not be fully recharged and only the lower chakras would bond. We would experience only one quick flash of sensation that would not relieve our loneliness even for the moment of its occurrence.

We had been taught that very old ones could sometimes rejoin the Community years after the sexual chemicals had ceased to replenish themselves, but not all succeeded in this reunion. No, most Individuals would die alone, while the common units of the Community lived on, forever children, forever young, unless some accident befell them or they were selected for sacrifice to the reproductive cycles.

"Somebody has to do it," she reminded me, "or our species could not continue."

"But why can we not grow new bodies in the same Cauldron that renews the Old Ones?"

"My Teacher said that such Cauldron lifelings grow without feelings in the heart. They can never join the Community, but are Individuals even from the day of birth, and a danger to the others."

But that Community had left me now; it was no longer my own, and I would not hear her words. I had made the supreme sacrifice, and I knew what I had done, and I knew why. There was no body of ignorance to help me forget; there were no lies to console me. I turned away from my woman and the tears streamed down my face. I was doomed to live forever alone, yearning for that brief union of lust. No matter how close our bodies were, I would grow old alone, and later I would die. And all of this to serve a Self that was no longer real to me, that had cast me out from itself.

How desperately I longed to escape this dreary fate, to abandon my hapless mate and this treacherous body to carry out their duties without me!

Then I grew dizzy; I stumbled and fell, and the world turned black.

Lost in the Labyrinth

For a second time, Mark found himself naked and helpless in adult form in the Halls of Nowhere. But now he knew that he had been born again of the Spirit, and that this body would prove more durable than the last.

He lay motionless for a long time, sick with grief for the wholeness he had left behind.

At last he got to his feet and found himself in a space that had shape, branching off into several passageways from where he stood. The walls, multilayered and translucent, pulsed slowly and rhythmically like living flesh. Though all directions looked the same, one way must be chosen.

This time he had more forethought. He manifested a glowing globe and a dark pedestal to support it, and a strong web of light to contain it and protect it. These he placed where the passages came together, and one glowing fibre of the web he tied to his left wrist, bidding it to draw him back after a certain time had passed. He bade the globe to contain his memories, and to watch through his eyes and record all that happened. Then he took a deep breath and struck out down the passageway to his right.

Almost immediately, Mark found himself in total darkness, save for the fibre of light stretching out to infinity behind him.

Resolutely, he walked on into the dark until, without warning, his eyes were struck by a glaring light radiating out from behind an imposing figure silhouetted a few feet in front of him. The apparition's deep purple garment trimmed with gold was a fashion statement suggestive of both clerical garb and a sorcerer's robe — and it was all too familiar.

Magician at Large

Despite the copper Afro and greying beard, Mark might not have recognized the man before him if the purple robe had not been open at the chest. But there was no mistaking that huge ornate gold cross pendant resting against the mahogany skin. Just underneath the cross, Mark could see the pink edges of an old scar of the same shape and size. That scar was the identifying mark of Christopher Rose, the notorious TV evangelist.

His services, usually broadcast from the massive Druid Hills Afro-Pentecostal Church, were noted for a maudlin emotionalism that bordered on the orgiastic, with strong overtones of Voodoo. Though popular among the simpleminded of all races, the Reverend Rose was viewed with ridicule or disdain by more sophisticated folks.

But there was nothing foolish about Christopher Rose in this context. He was looking Mark straight in the eyes, pulled up to his full impressive height, clearly horrified and outraged by the unexpected intrusion of this naked stranger.

"Excuse me, sir," Mark stammered apologetically. "I was just trying to find my way back the way I came."

Then he saw that the evangelist's eyes were looking past him and registering increasing alarm. From behind, a feminine voice sang out cheerfully, "Why, fancy meeting you here!"

Mark turned and saw his red-haired Priestess standing about 15 feet away. But her words had not been addressed to him; she was looking at Christoper Rose.

"How did you find me?" Mark asked in wonder.

"You left a pretty good trail," she said, waving what looked like a glowing ball of yarn. With dismay, he saw that it was made up of his own light thread.

"What have you done?" he cried. "Now we'll never get back!"

"Don't get so worked up," she told him. "I know this corridor like the back of my hand."

She brushed past Mark and advanced toward Christopher Rose, wagging a forefinger. "Now, don't you think it's about time you told me the truth about what you're up to?"

"Jennifer," said the Rev. Rose with infinite sadness, shaking his head, "I might say the same to you."

Then he vanished in a puff of smoke.

"Poor old fellow," Jennifer said with regret. "His heart would be lighter if he would share his burden with someone."

"He recognized you," Mark said accusingly. "Christopher Rose recognized you!"

Jennifer raised one eyebrow. "As I told you when you hired me, clients can always count on my complete confidentiality. Now, you are probably eager to get back to the material plane, and our presence there is urgently needed. Please take my hand."

Their surroundings vanished, and they tumbled through the void for another eternity.

Meanwhile, Back on the Rock

Mark landed back in his body with an almost audible THUNK!

Some kind of commotion was taking place. Had the Circle been broken?

He opened his eyes and looked around. Indeed it had!

Percy, a skinny youngster whose shaved and tattooed head was punctuated by an orange-tipped spiked Mohawk, multiple earrings and facial piercings, had seized the athame and was standing guard over Mark and Jennifer like the proverbial Banty rooster. Percy's robe had come undone so that his sexual attributes, or lack thereof, dangled close to Mark's eye level.

Several other members of the Circle were arguing loudly with three drunken wildling teens who were all waving shotguns in unison.

Mark quickly extracted himself from the ceremonial bonds and scrambled to his feet. His right hand automatically slapped at his flank for his Dress Bowie. The knife wasn't there, of course; he had taken it off for the ceremony. *Damn!*

The blanket slid from his shoulders, not quite covering the unceremoniously dumped Jennifer. The wildlings immediately riveted their attention onto the naked duo.

"Look what we've got here," they leered, all as one. In easy teamwork, they pushed their way into the Circle and advanced toward the centre.

Jennifer leapt to her own feet with a piercing whistle. From out of the shadows, two huge German shepherds sprang to her side, snarling menacingly at the intruders.

The wildlings halted in confusion.

Jennifer snatched the athame from Percy. Grasping the shaft with both hands, she lifted the blade high overhead; then, with a bloodcurdling shriek, she drew a slash from the sky to the ground. Sparks flew as the blade scraped the granite beneath her feet, and she abruptly dropped to a crouch. Through some trick of the firelight, the contours of her body seemed to blur and expand until she resembled some shadowy wild beast. The wildlings stared, immobilized. Jennifer let out a short series of piercing howls, echoed by the two dogs at her side, and ran full-tilt at the intruders with the dagger extended in front of her.

A single gunshot echoed off a distant rise. Then the wildlings broke formation and fled downhill in random haste, slipping and sliding over the smooth granite surface with its litter of broken glass. The dogs pursued them for a few hundred feet, yelping and snapping at their heels, then came loping back to Jennifer, tails held high and wagging with pride.

Jennifer praised the animals and checked their paws. Then she retrieved her clothing from the stacks just outside the Circle and began matter-of-factly to get dressed. The others took this as their cue to duff their ceremonial robes and also change back into street clothes. Mark noticed for the first time that the sash around Jennifer's jumpsuit was the official Black Belt of a martial artist whose hands are legally registered as a deadly weapon.

Security Guard

Percy was first to speak: "The Circle was broken."

"No shit!" Mark said sarcastically.

"Well, shouldn't we do something to close it?" the youth persisted. He took the rules of Ritual Magick seriously.

"Let the Circle take care of itself. We need to take this lady home!"

Mark was buttoning on his breeches with as much dignity as he could muster. He didn't take time to do up the knee-cuffs or to strap up the Roman sandals around his calves. During the fracas he had stepped barefoot onto a small cactus that they had neglected to clear out of the Circle, and he was trying to tolerate the pain until he was out of the spotlight.

"I have my own car," Jennifer told him. "That's how the dogs got here."

"You had someone follow our cab here?"

She shrugged. "It would be pretty reckless to come to some secret place alone with a stranger to take part in weirdo sex rites, don't you think? — Ah, hi, Dredmore!"

A hulking Black youth with shoulder-length dreadlocks loomed out of the shadows. He was wearing a rainbow knit cap and a red denim tanktop, expertly ripped to display his washboard belly muscles. His cotton trousers were belted with a black sash like Jennifer's; nevertheless, he was carrying a shotgun.

"Hi, Jenni, I see you have no more problem here."

He grinned, and the moonlight glistened off a gold-and-rhinestone inlay in his left incisor.

Must be her pimp, Mark thought resentfully.

"Look, Jennifer, can I see you again?" he requested with clumsy haste. Her eyebrows arched with amusement. "I mean, that's part of the same experiment, to compare notes and see what happened and what worked and what didn't."

"No freebies for you, mon," Dredmore interrupted. "Bloodclot! You put de lady in danger; you gonna have to pay double next time, if she see you at all."

"Experiment, my sweet ass," Jennifer added. "This was just your own little scheme to get your rocks off in public!"

"But I never did—" Mark began an indignant protest, then stopped in embarrassment as he realized that he still stood at the centre of a circle of curious onlookers.

"Well, Mark," Lana volunteered from the perimeter, her silken voice as carefully manicured as her scarlet fingernails, "it did seem a bit unorthodox to some of us, but we had to trust that you knew what you were doing."

The jealous bitch! Mark raged inwardly, but he refused to lose even more face by allowing himself to be drawn into a public quarrel. He pointedly turned his back on Lana and addressed himself again to Jennifer.

"Do you have time to see me tomorrow?"

Her eyes twinkled, but she kept a straight face and shrugged. "You'll have to phone tomorrow and find out. Dredmore keeps my appointment book at the studio."

"Dis lady *always* booked up at least two weeks in advance," Dredmore proudly volunteered. "But you can come sit in de waiting room; maybe we have a cancellation." Two of the onlookers chuckled.

Damn! This was getting worse and worse!

"I'll do that," Mark declared — anything to end this ordeal; he was getting tired of standing on one leg. "Er ... where is your studio located? You picked me up in the taxi and never gave me your own address when I called."

Jennifer glanced around the circle of spectators and smiled demurely. She reached into her pocket and handed him a business card. "Here's my card again. When you call tomorrow, Dredmore will give you directions."

"Well, a fine night to you good people," Dredmore said formally in a lilting Caribbean accent. "Praise Jah, all is irie! Now I and I must be on our way."

He bowed with exaggerated courtesy, then did an about-face and headed down the hill at a fast clip, with Jennifer and the dogs following close behind.

Cross-Examination

When they seemed safely out of earshot, Lana remarked in a low voice, "What a striking woman! I've always wondered what kind of people place those ads in the *Bird*. How much did she charge you, Mark?"

"Too much," he said evasively, casting around for a change of subject. "Well, we should probably call it quits for tonight. We can review all this with the coven at the next New Moon, and I'll be seeing you and Percy at work tomorrow."

When the group still showed no signs of dispersing, he raised his voice and added: "Would somebody please check and make sure the fires are all out?"

Please, Goddess, just let him make it home in time to reassemble his shattered defences!

"Sure thing, Master," Percy cracked back. "Wouldn't want to start any lava flows!"

Mark gritted his teeth. True, extinguishing fires on this slab of granite was a purely symbolic act, but someday the young upstart might understand the importance of acting with impeccability!

The diversion served its purpose. As Percy and Lana turned their attention to clean-up tasks, the other spectators drifted off down the hill amid animated gossip. Breathing a sigh of relief, Mark sat on a rock and began picking cactus spines out of his foot by flashlight.

All too soon, Percy was back.

"Tell us what happened," he demanded eagerly. "Did you break on through to the other side? What did she feel like inside? Was it like being with a regular woman?"

Mark sighed again. Someday soon they'd have to do something about Percy's virginity before the kid's prurient interest got him into deep trouble.

"Lay off, Percy! Can't you let me have a few minutes to get my head together before you start interrogating me?"

"Then just answer the one question, please, Mark; we've got to know! Did it work the way you planned? Did you go between the worlds?"

"Yes, if you must know now, yes, I did. But I haven't even begun to sort it all out yet, and if you don't shut up and let me collect myself, Percy, I swear, I am going to bust you right in the jaw." He illustrated the point by waving his fist, with its menacing silver rings on all four fingers, under Percy's nose.

The lad gulped. "I understand. I'm sorry; it's all right. Lana, I think Mark wants to be left alone tonight." Shouldering his backpack of magical paraphernalia, Percy seized the elegant older woman by the elbow and began steering her toward the parking lot below.

Mark watched them walk away with a sinking feeling in the pit of his stomach. The darkness pressed closely around him, and his heart began to pound wildly. He threw his knapsack over one shoulder and hurried after them, with the thongs of his untied sandals trailing on the ground.

"Wait! Wait, you idiots!" Almost out of sight in the shadows, they stopped and looked back. "Don't you even remember? Lana, I came here in a cab; I need you to drive me home!"

"Oh, shit!" Percy exclaimed, slapping his forehead. "I rode here with Joe, and he's already left without me. I need a ride, too."

"Well, since I won't have to drive Jennifer back, I think we can all fit into the *Hummingbird*," Lana said, "if we get *very* friendly. Percy, why don't you drive? I'm lighter, and I can sit on Mark's lap."

Percy beamed with pleasure, but Mark saw through this ruse immediately. "No, Lana, I think you should drive. I'm too shaken up, myself, and Percy isn't used to the vehicle. We shouldn't ask him to handle an unbalanced load on a dark country road. We'll manage somehow."

Flight of the *Hummingbird*

The little iridescent three-wheeled smart car with its spiky hood ornament awaited them in the parking lot. Its solar-panel "wings" were folded for the evening alongside the auxiliary methanol tank. Hand-painted lettering and logo identified it as the staff car of **The Third Speckled Bird**, the most recent incarnation of Atlanta's underground press.

Percy sat in Mark's lap as they motored off, his cockscomb fluttering in the breeze and tickling the top of Mark's head.

"Pretty sweet little car," Percy remarked, "even if she does run on fumes from chickenshit and kudzu compost!"

"Not for long," Lana told him. "Most of the methanol suppliers will soon be switching over to hemp. It produces more biomass per acre."

"If you ask me, the South is getting too reliant on hemp," Mark said darkly. "Hemp already supplies most of our paper, a lot of our vegetable protein, and what little cloth fibre doesn't come from kudzu or cotton. We're setting ourselves up for another monoculture crisis like the one when the boll weevils destroyed all the cotton crops. That will play right into the Commies' hands."

"Yeah, well, why don't you take your complaint to the St. Money plant inspectors?" Percy retorted. "It's hard enough just to grow a few heritage vegetables without getting a fine slapped on us for patent infringement or unapproved crops."

Mark shrugged. "Big deal! Don't you keep up your bust insurance payments?"

"Hell, no!" Percy was indignant. "You know I'm an anarchist! If you ask me, the KKK isn't any better than the Government. Why should I have to pay them protection money?"

"Especially," Lana said pointedly, "when you don't even grow a garden."

Percy fell silent for a moment, embarrassed by having attention drawn to his neglect to perform this act of ritual defiance. Every patriotic Confederate citizen was expected to grow a Victory Garden. But he soon saw a way to change the subject.

"Prohibition didn't start with St. Money," he said. "Hemp's been illegal for a long time. Even back before the Big Bang, my granddaddy used to grow it and sell it. People used to smoke it to get high before they had designer drugs. Imagine running your car on hemp oil," Percy chortled. "You might have trouble keeping it on the road!"

These attempts at humour were met with silence, but Percy took the lack of backtalk as a sign that he was on a roll and decided to press his luck. "Hey, isn't it my turn to drive the *Hummingbird* this month?"

"Tomorrow," Lana replied with a sigh. "I'll hand you the keys first thing Monday morning."

Mark had argued privately with Lana that Percy was too young and irresponsible to be entrusted with the precious new staff car. But this night had left him without the strength to protest.

"Hot shit!" exclaimed Percy. "I'll be King of the Road."

"No, you'll be Page of the Road," Lana retorted. "The King just drove off with Lady Jennifer. I caught a glimpse of their car on the way here. It's a tank! I'm surprised it's even allowed on the road. Couldn't possibly get more than 50 or 60 miles to the gallon."

"Yeah," said Percy, "but a gallon of what? Some of the new models can store solar power to convert water to hydrogen."

"Will both of you please pipe down," Mark snapped peevishly. "My nerves are all shot to hell and I need some peace and quiet!"

They rode the rest of the way in silence.

As she let Mark out in front of his home, Lana asked hopefully, "Will you be all right by yourself tonight, or would you like to have someone stay with you?"

"Thanks for your concern," Mark said sourly, "but I'll be okay. I'll just pop an EZ-Dozit if I have trouble getting to sleep."

"Up to you," Lana said. "See you at work tomorrow."

"Yeah," Percy chimed in, as Mark limped up the walkway, "and I hope you're ready to talk to us by then, because I think we have a right to know what happened!"

Mark slammed the door shut behind him. He turned to the punching bag that hung from his ceiling and viciously assaulted it until his knuckles were raw.

Chapter 2
Evil Dreamtime

Things can always get worse!

Quarantine

There was peace again, but now a colourless quiet with no random meanderings of the senses.

Dozens of workers scurried about at their tasks with scarcely a sound. They were solemnly purposeful and acknowledged another's presence only when necessary. They were ranged thickly along the steep sides of a small quarry, performing simple mining tasks. Several figures in orange shirts, taller and thinner than the rest, walked from place to place supervising the work. Except when instructions or questions were vocalized or signed, the crew went about their business as though the orange-shirts were not there.

This body of viewpoint was standing on a walkway about two metres from the edge of the pit. Like all the other workers, it was male, squat and massively built, a head shorter than the supervisors. A heavy weight balanced atop its head. Ore passed up by the workers below was being dumped into a large container a few steps away. Back and forth, back and forth, the rhythm continued, the whole process moving like clockwork. This body perspired and squinted against the harsh glare of the sun.

After a time, a bell sounded and everyone stopped to eat food distributed from a grey cart on wheels. It consisted of a dense, tasteless square of some semisolid white substance, accompanied by a flask of tepid water. The workers and supervisors ate in silence and then stretched flat on the ground for a siesta.

The position of the sun had changed only slightly when the bell sounded again and the workers began to stir. The supervisor for each group led a short series of breathing and stretching exercises; then they resumed their labour.

This body was deeply troubled. Something was not right! He stood in confusion, shaking his head and shading his eyes with one hand. An orange-shirted supervisor hastened to his side.

"You have stopped working. Is something wrong?"

"Head feels ... funny."

The supervisor laid a clammy palm against his forehead. "Get in the car," he ordered, gesturing to a three-wheeled, two-seater vehicle shaped like a bubble. This body obeyed, and the supervisor drove a short distance to a concrete structure, where a higher-status red-shirted figure waited inside before a computer console.

"Sick," the supervisor relayed. "Head feels funny."

The red-shirted man looked troubled. "Others sick, too?" he asked.

The two replied as one: "Don't know."

"You rest in different rooms," Redshirt ordered. "Stay away from the others. Don't leave your rooms. Rooms 5 and 6 will be waiting. Now, go."

This pair walked in silence to the nearby isolation section. The doors to the designated rooms opened and closed behind them of their own accord, and he heard a lock click shut.

The Loneliest Number

The grey-shirted medic arrived a short time later. As the door began to open, this body started to his feet.

"Please," he said, "tell me what is going to happen to me."

The medic spun on his heels and left, without entering the room.

A short time later a green-shirted one came and took him on another, slightly longer journey. This time his head was covered with a hood so that he could not see where they were going. Panic seized him to the point that he began to experience nausea, dizziness and dry mouth.

When the hood was lifted, at first he didn't recognize the man who stood before him. How could he? It had been years since they had last seen each other, and they had both been only children at the time. And, after all, they both looked much alike, being members of the same caste.

But despite his physiognomy, this man was no worker; he was wearing the yellow headband and white shirt of a Scientist. This body knew that any caste could produce a Scientist, but such offspring were rare among the workers.

"Our type is rare among the workers," the Scientist affirmed in greeting, after motioning for his green-shirted escort to leave the room. "I didn't expect another one of us to come from the same pod, though I have been closely monitoring the whole group. After all, we do share the same clone-father."

This body was more confused than ever.

"I'm not a Scientist," he stated. "I don't know what's happening to me."

"There!" said the Scientist. "In one sentence you dispute my statement, and in the next you express curiosity. Neither of these turns of thought would be possible to a true worker. Yes, my pod-brother, it appears that you, too, have become a Scientist. The change often happens suddenly. But you haven't anything to be afraid of; it's a grand destiny."

This body had never aspired to any grand destiny, nor conceived one as desirable, so he was not comforted.

"You must know best, as you are a Scientist, but I feel cold inside. I know myself alone. Thoughts of the death of this body cause me distress. But I have always known that bodies wear out and more can easily be made. Why should the fate of this one concern me now, when it did not before?"

"But this body is *you!*" said the Scientist, slapping him on the shoulder alarmingly. "You and I have somehow broken free from the Mass Mind. Each of us is now a Person in his own right."

This body knew it must be true, and his dismay knew no bounds.

This Thing Called Death

"No!" this body cried. "I don't want to be a Person, like the Evil Ones of the past who brought ruin to our planet. I've always known that Scientists are important, but I thought they were units of the Whole who work with the brain instead of the body. Now the Whole has shut me out completely! This body feels terrible to be so alone."

"Believe me, trust me," the Scientist assured him. "The day will come when you will look back on your worker companions with pity."

"Pity?" He did not know the concept.

"Never mind. Please try to understand: we Scientists are the one who run things on this planet. The workers and the other castes exist only to serve our needs. And why is that? Because without us, nothing new is made; nothing new is learned. Without us, our species would stagnate and die. And to become a Scientist, it is necessary to become a Person alone, not a mere unit of the Whole.

"I will admit that the dying bit is irksome to us all, but you will learn to stop thinking about it so much after a while. We've got research teams working on ways to delay and overcome it. We've set goals and interim targets. They report that they're still on track to find a solution before our own time is due, so why lose sleep over it?

"Yes, my friend, we Scientists do work hard to maintain the well-being of the Whole, but we have our own projects, too. Let me tell you now about the Great Work that occupies all Scientists at this moment. We have been keeping it secret from the Coordinators. Smart as they are, they're not People like us, so they would not understand the importance and might interfere."

"Then why are you telling me? I could go to them and reveal everything."

"Oh, no, my friend. You will be watched constantly from this moment until your Initiation. Once the Individuation process has begun, no one has ever failed to become a full Scientist at the end. We know how to recognize our own kind. A few novices have attempted to inform the Coordinators, but they cannot understand or respond to a situation of this nature. They just assume the source is mentally defective and needs to be recycled. But so long as Scientists and Coordinators keep to their own kind and tend to their own work, everything will continue to run smoothly."

This body sighed. "Tell me then, since you must, what is your Great Work?"

The Unbearable Heaviness of Being

The Scientist rudely stared this body directly in the face for a long, full moment, and then spoke.

"We wish to release all units from the tyranny of the Whole and transform them into Persons — every one of them!"

This body was confused. "But how is that possible?"

"Come, now, what about yourself? You started out as a worker unit, and now you are a Person. That proves the transformation is possible. We just need to find out how to trigger it."

"But why? A Scientist would not be capable as a worker, and then who would do the work? The Scientist is the most ill at ease of all castes, the one who stands alone and fears death. Every worker knows how the Scientist complains at the smallest variation of heat or cold or hunger or other discomfort. What use would be a world of such … Persons?"

"My poor friend — do you know why the workers have such hard lives? Do you know why extremes of discomfort must so often be endured to accomplish some project?"

"No, I do not, but I had supposed it must be needful for the Whole."

The Scientist spat. This body was shocked to see such gross disregard for basic sanitation.

"With everyone working together, it would take very little labour from each unit to sustain our Whole," the Scientist declared. "No — the workers suffer so that extra supplies can be produced, far more than would be needed by the Whole, even if everyone enjoyed all the comforts of a Scientist. Most of those supplies are being shipped elsewhere. We aren't yet certain of their exact destination, but we believe they are actually leaving this planet.

"Don't look so shocked! I know they don't teach you workers much about the greater picture, but you must have learned that there are other worlds besides our own. And some of those worlds have their own inhabitants — but not like us.

"My simple friend, we have not been working to serve the Whole. We are working to serve … Them! They are stealing the very life substance of our planet."

Now this body was really convinced that Personhood was a bad idea!

"Them?" he asked weakly, as he sank to a squatting position and rested his head on his knees.

"We aren't sure who They are, but we do have sound evidence that They're out there and They're stealing the resources of our planet. Our immediate mission is to track Them down and wipe Them out and take back control of this planet while there's still something left of it! We intend to free our People, who have so long been bred to serve only as willing slaves for an alien species."

"Perhaps you can destroy Them," this body acknowledged. "Perhaps you can provide the workers with more supplies and ease their burdens. But how can you free them? They don't desire to be free; their desire is to serve. If they cannot serve, what purpose will they have?"

"If indeed they can never become People," the Scientist said coldly, "then they must be eliminated. But we would never take such an action lightly. If you only knew the effort we have been expending to help the workers make that leap. Some of us disguise ourselves as workers and mingle with them, talk to them…."

"How has this been working?"

The Scientist sighed. "Actually, not too well. The Medics usually come for us before we can accomplish much, and they bring us back here to the Science Centre. Most Scientists still occur spontaneously, as they have always done. But we are developing other techniques! We have drugs…."

"Pardon me; I'm going to be sick." This body cast eyes around frantically and scuttled across the floor to bend over the compost bucket.

When he was done vomiting, the Scientist offered him a glass of some sweet, bubbly, cold beverage. It tasted … *good!*

"Forgive me, my friend," the Scientist said gently. "I was so excited to hear that one of my old podmates would be joining us that I have broken protocol. We usually don't give newcomers this much information for weeks. There's so much to get used to."

The door opened, and through it walked a young female — one of the few that this body had ever seen.

"We have our own call-names in this caste." the Scientist explains. "This woman is called Marcie, and she specializes in welcoming newcomers. Direct physical contact makes the transition less stressful. You'll find her company a pleasure and a comfort tonight. Sex is one of the prime compensations for our painful self-awareness. My own call-name is Marx. And you — may I call you Wonder?"

"Call me what you will," this body said dully, as Marcie took him by the hand and led him away to his new room.

The Great Work Revealed

Of course, there was no sexual intercourse that night. Wonder had never had any experiences that would cause him to desire such a pastime, and the hormone suppressor chemicals from his last meal as a worker were still circulating through his system.

But the Scientist's supper was a pleasure, a taste medley of many hues and textures, and Wonder enjoyed the warm bath and the massage that followed. Later, unable to sleep, he appreciated the contact of Marcie's body beside him in the dark on an oversized mattress filled with warm water and covered with a colourful down-stuffed quilt.

He compared the sweet physical pleasures of this night with the austerity and sameness of his long years as a worker. No, he had never thought to complain, but even a worker unit knows the difference between pain and pleasure. And now the Scientist had told him all those discomforts had been unnecessary. They had not been endured for the sake of the Whole, but for … Them.

What must They be, to impose such conditions on a whole caste, to take their lifelong labour and offer nothing in return? Workers who became unable to perform up to specifications were euthanized immediately. The horror! — to be serving creatures so monstrous, and not even know it!

Though he could not say how, Wonder felt certain that the Scientist was mistaken to think that his own kind had control over this sad, deluded world. If this planet was indeed owned by Them, the Scientist and others like him must also be fulfilling some purpose for Them — all the while thinking that they were secret saboteurs, that they alone were free.

Now for the first time he felt pity, but it was not for the workers. No, he envied the workers their simple earnestness. Wonder pitied the Scientists! And he vowed that, now that he was an Individual at last, he would never join the Scientists in serving Them. The thought of that fate made termination of this body seem acceptable by comparison.

By his side, Marcie breathed heavily and tossed in her sleep. Quietly, gently, Wonder pushed aside the bedcover and tiptoed out onto the spacious balcony.

For a long while, he gazed about him, appreciating for the first time the beauty of this Earth that he had so long inhabited without really seeing. A full Moon was reflected in the swimming pool some twelve stories below. Marcie had explained its function. Swimming — that would be another new experience. Without doubt, there must be many other pleasures waiting to be tasted if he remained in this life.

His gaze swung upward to the night sky, and he wondered which of the lights there belonged to Them.

Perhaps he should postpone his departure for a few days, until he had tried swimming and sex. After all his years of toil, surely he was due the taste of those simple pleasures.

But after he had sampled them, he might no longer be able to summon the willpower to take the action that he knew was necessary.

"I will *not* serve Them," he whispered to that starry sky, as he hurled himself headfirst off the balcony. In the grief and the glory of his final fall, Wonder understood himself to be, at last, a Person.

Chapter 3
Dawn in the New Confederacy

The Red, White and Blue

Mark started awake and shook violently with relief. It had all been a dream! At least, whatever it had been, it was over now, and he was safe back here in his own Reality.

He lurched out of bed and staggered across the room to the window. The sun struck him full in the face as he drew up the shades, but he welcomed its effect of anchoring him firmly in the present time and place.

Across the street he could see the red, white and blue flag fluttering over the Post Office, confirming that he had escaped the Orwellian horror of his night visions.

He felt as if he had been run over by a train. Thank Goddess, most of his work for the week on *The Third Speckled Bird* had already been done, with enough copy entered into his home computer to fill the next issue.

Like many of his contemporaries, Mark did much of his work at home. Getting from one place to the other wasn't as easy as it had been back in the days when private automobiles were common.

Mark stood at the window long enough to make sure his consciousness was securely back in his own time-frame. As he showered and dressed, his thoughts continued to scan lovingly every detail of this reassuring Reality.

It was the first time, perhaps, that he had fully appreciated how good it was to be a citizen of the C.S.A. The Confederate States of America was the only large nation that had maintained its freedom and independence by resisting takeover by the Commies and Corpses (the popular derogatory terms for Companies and Corporations).

Shortly after the Big Bang, the old U.S.A. had formally disbanded, along with all the other Superpowers. The other newly formed remnant nations that had once made up the old U.S.A. — New England, BosWash, Little Israel, Texico, Middle America and Cascadia — had all grudgingly accepted the terms of the Commies and Corpses and applied for aid.

But Southerners still remembered the horrors of slavery, and they were having none of it. They had never really considered themselves part of the United States in the first place. With the backing of the Reverend Christopher Rose and his followers, the New Libertarian Democrats had easily won their first national election on a platform of local self-governance, and now it looked like they were in for a long run.

After the Big Bang

No one would ever forget the disaster that had struck in early October 1990. The largest gathering of heads of states in history had convened at the United Nations to hold a World Summit for Children. Responding to the public pressure of candlelight vigils around the world, these leaders had promised to cooperate in a grand plan to end hunger and poverty. The event had been widely predicted to mark a turning point in human history.

But the occasion turned out to mark a different kind of turning point. The residents of Manhattan and the heads of state gathered within the U.N. building were only the first casualties of the neutron bombs. Thirty-four other major cities around the globe had met the same fate within an hour.

The world was left too stunned to resist the Companies' generous offer to take on the work of restoration — in exchange for certain concessions.

Eventually a small band of expatriate Iraqi Muslims were arrested and charged with the crime, but many people suspected that the real culprits were still at large, high up in Commie officialdom.

Nevertheless, the whole world had breathed easier after the old stockpiles of nuclear weapons had been sought out and destroyed. Next to be destroyed were national currencies, flags, politically incorrect literature, and personal weapons. That's where the South had drawn the line.

Mark buckled on his Dress Bowie.

The large number of military assault weapons owned by ordinary citizens were among the reasons the South had been able to get away with its secession. The New Libertarian Democrats had been quick to resurrect and expand Georgia's old Cobb County statute requiring every household to own a gun. In the new version, every adult citizen in a public place must display a weapon and be certified as trained in its use.

Having been active as a teen in the Society for Creative Anachronism, Mark was among the minority who had chosen to wear the Dress Bowie. He affected an eclectic archaic style of dress to display the weapon to best advantage. Whenever he passed a reflective surface, he felt pleased to see what a swashbuckling figure he cut.

Confederate citizens were only rarely permitted to travel among the Commies and Corpses beyond the Cotton Curtain, and even then they had to be accompanied by a minder and stick to a clearly defined itinerary. But the travel restrictions on Commie citizens were much worse.

All electronic communication systems were rigorously monitored, so information from areas beyond the Cotton Curtain, even from friends and family members, was notoriously unreliable. Turner Broadcasting was now the only satellite transmitter not controlled by the Companies. Based on the Commies' own newscasts, it had become a standing joke that they must be the only dictatorship in history to censor the good news and broadcast the bad!

The Companies did provide for their citizens in a minimalist fashion that was a cross between Medieval feudalism and post-industrial Japan. Every detail of daily life was scrutinized and regulated, but enough guaranteed income was provided that homelessness and hunger had been relegated to exhibits in historical museums designed to highlight how much better off people were under Commie rule.

To be sure, the "homes" were flimsy pre-fab cubicles not much better than the tiny shacks that Atlanta's Mad Houser had built for street people back during the shameful years of the 1980s. And the "food" was a tasteless mush of laboratory-grown meat tissue or textured vegetable protein derived from tobacco, soybeans and algae. But many of the world's people felt it beat starving or sleeping in the streets, as they had done before. Any dissidents were quickly rounded up and "reeducated," or made to disappear.

Off to Work We Go

This New World Order was not so well received by the more prosperous communities of North America, Europe and Australia, but it was too late for an unarmed populace to mount an effective resistance.

From time to time a few brave souls did manage to slip through the Cotton Curtain into the Confederacy, and their arrival was always the object of much media attention. Mark had interviewed a case for the *Bird* just last week.

Before he left the house, Mark ate a heaping bowl of TVP cereal, swimming in soy milk. Now that the South had to supply most of its own nutritional needs from a limited land base, cattle products were too wasteful of water and agricultural land, and produced too many greenhouse gases, to eat on a regular basis. Florida and New Orleans would soon be underwater, and there were already many Climate Change refugees to be resettled. The meat industry was no longer subsidized, and flesh foods on the market were rationed only for special occasions. Even raising your own livestock entailed paying a hefty fee for permits and inspections. Not everything was free yet in Liberty Hall!

Mark chased the cereal with a jigger of Sassafras ImmuJolt. This health tonic, produced and distributed by the Atlanta Centre for Disease Control, was another reason the Companies had been willing to leave the South in peace. To maximize consumption, the Coca-Cola facilities had quickly been nationalized, after their top executives were declared to be in league with the Commies and banished. ImmuJolt was now incorporated into all soft drinks and some alcoholic beverages. These essential export commodities brought in enough foreign exchange currency to keep the Confederacy sitting pretty, relative to the rest of the resource-poor world.

Not to be outdone by the Commies, the Confederacy issued every citizen a modest monthly dividend representing their own share of the national assets. These funds not only stimulated the economy but also helped to discourage environmentally destructive employment and criminal enterprise.

Since the citizen-shareholder dividend was geared to survival rather than luxury, most people still preferred to supplement their stipend with earned income. To keep citizens happily occupied, the New Libertarian Democratic government was generous with its Arts and Culture grants. One such grant had recently provided startup funds for *The Third Speckled*

Bird. Few readers considered the irony of having an alternative press that was heavily dependent on government subsidies.

The secret formula for ImmuJolt had never been cracked. The Companies had attempted one raid on the Centre for Disease Control shortly after the remedy had gone public. But they had backed down when they realized that the director was prepared to TNT the entire kudzu-covered facility rather than allow it to fall into Commie hands.

Nobody, nowhere, wanted a world without ImmuJolt. It was a panacea that protected against cancer, arthritis, tooth decay, and almost every other infectious or autoimmune disease, including the common cold, acne and dandruff. It was even hard to drink yourself into a hangover.

Since the overzealous female immune system treated sperm and fetal cells like any other foreign invaders, ImmuJolt also functioned as a contraceptive. When pregnancy was desired, the tonic had to be temporarily discontinued, but by this time there were few pathogens floating around to be caught during that drug holiday.

ImmuJolt had not been able to eliminate HIV entirely, once the virus had become part of the genetic material of its host. But it did keep the virus suppressed and prevented new infections. Since HIV is a slow-acting virus, AIDS was no longer a big threat. It sometimes caused pregnant women to feel a little peaked, but their health returned rapidly once they resumed their ImmuJolt after childbirth — and the newborn was protected from infection by the old-style medications. Even reckless people who welcomed the weight-loss and stayed off their ImmuJolt past the limits of safety usually made a swift recovery once the doses were resumed.

But there were still a few religious sects and holistic individuals who refused to take it. There was ongoing controversy over the ethics of forcing people to medicate for their own good, especially when children were at risk.

A few alarmists worried about the declining birthrate, and others worried about what might happen to a human population grown careless, if anything should interrupt the supply of ImmuJolt. But most people were just happy to live in a world where such a thing existed. Their increased physical vigour and good spirits more than made up for the decrease in material luxuries. Life without ImmuJolt had become almost unimaginable, like a step back into the Dark Ages.

Mark clipped his mobile phone next to the Dress Bowie, unfolded his electric bicycle and set off for work. As always, whenever he entered or left his home, he felt deeply grateful that his salary as editor of the **Bird** allowed him to maintain this modest two-room apartment in Cabbagetown, a picturesque and friendly community of artists and nonconformists.

When he'd first begun adult life in Atlanta, his citizen-shareholder dividends alone had been barely enough to live on. Poverty had forced him to share a run-down dump in the slums of Outer Buckhead, which had become a suburban wasteland after fuel shortages made commuter travel problematic. From there, it had been a long and hazardous bike ride to places where the action was.

Cabbagetown was much more convenient. He even had access to a small plot of ground where he had begun a postage-stamp vegetable garden — which wasn't looking too healthy, come to think of it. He made a mental note to collect some water to pour on it the next time he took a shower.

Damn, the next thought entered his mind, *I haven't applied for my garden permit yet!*

Victory Gardens

Despite the New Libertarian Democrats' official policy of *laissez-faire*, they still had to make some concessions to the Commie thugs. By now the Companies held patents to every common vegetable variety. They would not tolerate anyone growing "their" products without paying royalties, nor would they tolerate the propagation of varieties not on their Approved List.

When the Garden Inspectors had crossed the Cotton Curtain for the first time, Governor Valk had blocked the roads as he had promised. He had thrown his own body in front of the herbicide trucks. But workers in hazmat suits had just lifted him out of the way and gone on about their business of poisoning any "unauthorized greenery" that met their eye, all the while assuring bystanders that the chemical was perfectly safe.

A minor skirmish had ensued that was sarcastically known as the Second Civil War. Though officially defeated, the Confederacy had won more than it lost in that battle. An old cultural wound had become healed at last.

Faced with a common enemy, those damyankee Commie bastards, a peace pact was quickly sworn between coalitions of disgruntled Southern Whites, including the Ku Klux Klan (by now a ragtag bunch comprised largely of FBI agents), both factions of Black Panthers, and a South African import called the Schwartzen Broderbund. Most radical groups already maintained alliances with the state militias and the now-unemployed mercenary troops that had been trained in the Southern swamplands. When the League of the South sounded its call to arms, everyone eagerly responded, right down to the jousters and swordfighters of the SCA.

There was never any real possibility of a Confederate victory, but the Company forces had easily been held at bay with a minimum of casualties while soldiers on both sides honoured a backroom agreement to fire over one another's heads. Finally an uneasy truce was declared. The Confederacy would maintain its own Garden Inspectors (subject to surveillance by the Companies) to ensure that the Commies received the royalties they felt entitled to. In return, the Commies would leave the South in peace — at least, until the next claims were laid!

Now it was the civic duty of every good Confederate citizen to maintain a Victory Garden of unauthorized Heritage Plants, but it had to be done with discretion. Anyone caught and fined was privately reimbursed by the KKK, so long as they kept up minimal monthly payments into their Bust Insurance Credit Account. Some said the funds were supplemented by ImmuJolt revenues; others said the Garden Permit fees themselves were laundered and recycled for this purpose. Being appreciative of the public service, most people were willing to leave those questions unanswered.

The *Bird*'s Nest

The Pub stood quiet and empty as Mark pedalled past, but he knew that by nightfall it would be bustling with life again. A long line-up of Atlanta's finest, desperately eager to be selected for admission to this small highbrow music club, would be stretching down the sidewalk. All the contenders would be dressed to kill and classy as hell.

Once, right after The Pub had been restored to its former glory by an Arts and Culture Grant, Mark had gone there with Lana. Thanks to his own vanity and Lana's fashion sense, they had easily been able to get in. They had toasted their Mint

Juleps at the bar, almost within handshaking distance of the dummy human arm reaching down from the ceiling.

Even in this casual city where she could have easily worn flip-flops and shorts, Lana always looked like Pub material, so polished and well-dressed. He had to admit she was one helluva good-looking woman, despite her years. In fact, Lana was almost like an older female version of himself, Mark reflected ruefully, but what man would want to bed a woman who could pass for his big sister?

He was sorry now for his automatic flirtation on first meeting Lana, for he had no intention of ever following through, and now he couldn't get her off his case. He didn't want to offend her or hurt her feelings, but what was a man to do?

That Jennifer, now — she was more his type, so vibrant and mysterious. She could get into The Pub in her pajamas … if she wore any.

Soon Mark was heading down the Road to Nowhere — now a town mall, lined with craftspeople and other vendors. It was shaded by a tall trellis of kudzu and honeysuckle, supported between huge concrete pillars on either side, originally intended to hold up a superhighway. But after almost two decades of protests and obstruction by local residents, combined with skyrocketing gas prices, the Road had finally been closed to heavy vehicle traffic in the wake of a public scandal.

Mark found himself absent-mindedly humming the old Atlanta folk tune, "*Ten Million Dollars a Mile*," as he dismounted and locked up his vehicle.

He always enjoyed the short walk past the artificial lake, where otters frolicked by day and skinny-dippers by night. Soon he was at the door of that choice cubicle in the old Carter Memorial Library. Mayor Rowley had donated that space to provide offices for Arts and Culture grant recipients, including *The Third Speckled Bird*.

Most newspapers now were downloaded onto wafer-thin reading screens. Wasting trees to make disposable paper seemed almost sacrilegious. Hemp was a more energy-efficient source of fibre, but even hemp paper was a luxury. Some hard-nosed environmentalists scowled on the fact that, for the sake of authenticity, the *Bird* was distributed on tree paper, but Mark didn't feel too bad about it. It was made from scrap wood unsuitable for other uses, and most copies were diligently recycled, though a few collectors were probably hoarding theirs.

Since most of the actual work was done from home, the *Bird*'s office served more as a clubhouse to boost staff morale than as a serious workspace. In fact, Percy and Lana were not in it.

Mark stepped outside again and found them by the lake, propped against a big oak tree, ignoring the laptop computers beside them on the grass and talking a mile a minute.

"Now you stop looking at me that way!" protested Lana. "I'll have you know I already got us three new advertising accounts this morning!"

"Yeah," added Percy — eager as usual to make sure no one got more than their fair share of glory — "but two of them were waiting on the computer when you came in. And I don't think we ought to accept that one from the Reverend Christopher Rose!"

Chapter 4
A Visit to Valhalla

Threshold

The sun was already sinking in the west by the time Mark made his way over to Jennifer's establishment in Virginia Highlands. He'd had to stay late at work to tie up some loose ends of formatting and put the ***Bird*** to bed — mainly because Percy and Lana had taken up so much of his time with their endless questions.

Well … since they had both been involved in planning the ritual, they did have a need to know, but how could he explain an experience like that to someone else? Especially when Mark himself still wasn't sure what had really happened.

He was usually something of an exhibitionist, as Jennifer had so rudely pointed out the night before, but these latest adventures felt too personal to be spoken of so openly. He would have to formulate an edited version for the other coven members, but the six weeks before the next esbat should give him enough time to get his story straight.

Despite the friction among the trio, Lana and Percy were as close to Mark as anyone he knew. Mark was as private on the inner levels as he was brazen on the outer ones. He had learned early on that knowing looks and strategic pauses would prompt most people to fill in the blanks with projections of their own choosing, sparing him the hazards of revealing too much of himself. His haughty good looks assured him a supply of willing sexual partners, and at the same time helped to keep them at a safe emotional distance.

This visit to Valhalla, as Jennifer's massage studio was called, would be a new experience for him. Oh, he had hired the services of prostitutes a few times in his youth, even before the New Libertarian Democrats had repealed antiquated statutes such as the laws against prostitution and oral sex between marital partners. He'd enjoyed the self-indulgence of being totally passive, without having to pretend concern for his partner's satisfaction. It had made him feel deliciously wicked.

But Mark had never before been able to afford a high-class call girl, and Jennifer's cut-rate sisters had not proved satisfactory. Disease was no longer a concern in these days of ImmuJolt, but Mark had still ended each such encounter with a strong urge to take a bath, as though fragments of the woman's inner unrest had been left clinging to his own aura.

But he was definitely eager to see Jennifer again! He had been delighted when he had called and learned there had indeed been a cancellation in her schedule this evening. She obviously had more Magickal experience than Mark himself, for she had known how to handle crises on both the astral and the material planes. He fervently hoped that she'd be able to help explain the events of last night.

He wondered why such a multi-talented young woman had become a prostitute. Perhaps that Dredmore, her pimp, was coercing her. Perhaps she had been waiting all this time for a caring hero like himself to come to her rescue!

Well, the male voice on the phone that had set up his appointment had sounded businesslike enough. It had been stern and deep, with a European flavour that he couldn't place. Immigrants from the regions under Company control were so uncommon that Mark couldn't recall ever hearing any European accents except on old movies or satellite TV.

Valhalla was located in a large modern apartment building cleverly designed to imitate an old Southern plantation house. Each white plaster faux-marble porch column was flanked by a magnolia tree. The effect was marred by the fact that each tree bore a red metallic inspection tag, and the small lot had only a twenty-foot stretch of yard space.

Mark fastened his bike to one of the "hitching posts" in front of the porch and walked up the wide steps. By the doorway, he found a set of buttons under a closed-circuit video camera. He took a deep breath, pulled back his shoulders, and pushed the button labelled "Valhalla."

"Welcome to Valhalla," said that same deep male voice, rendered tinny by the intercom. *Scandinavian, that must be the accent!* Mark envisioned a blond Viking type standing guard within. "Your name, please."

"Mark Lance." He hadn't thought to use a pseudonym when he'd first hired Jennifer, so there was no point starting now.

"You're early," the voice reproached him.

Actually, Mark had intentionally left himself some extra time for snooping around and questioning anyone else on the premises, if he had an opportunity.

"Sorry; shall I come back later?"

There was a pause. Then: "No, that won't be necessary. I'll buzz you in. Please take the first door on the left-hand side of the hallway."

Guardians on the Threshold

Mark found himself in a spacious waiting room. Dredmore, the Rasta youth, sat behind a large desk at the far end. Flanking the desk were two German shepherds, pretending to be asleep and watching Mark balefully out of the corners of their eyes. One of the dogs curled a lip in warning as Mark met its gaze. He hastily looked away and cast surreptitious glances around to find the Viking gent, while politely unbuckling his Dress Bowie and hanging it on the weapons rack by the door. He noted that two of the four weapons already on the rack were concealed within elegant monogrammed cases, as though their owners wanted to suggest they were carrying something too formidable for casual display.

Dredmore flashed him a rhinestone-studded grin. "If you prefer, you may have a private waiting room," he told Mark in that deep European voice. His grin widened as Mark's eyes registered his surprise.

"Ah," Mark said wisely, as if this were an everyday occurrence, "you are a man of many voices." He seated himself in one of the comfortable armchairs across the room from the desk.

Dredmore shrugged. "Hey, mon," he said, matching full-body rhythm and gestures to his Caribbean style, "it is good to become a mon o' de world in dese days when so much trouble walk de land."

"Where are you really from, if you don't mind me asking?"

Dredmore's body language underwent another subtle shift, and he emitted a string of vocalizations that Mark found familiar but unintelligible. Then Dredmore slowed his speech to about a quarter of its original tempo and spoke again.

"I be nothin' but a Georgia boy," he confessed. "But when I get to University, I find out right quick nobody take me serious, an' me soundin' fresh off de streets. Can't get no foxy ladies to look twice at me, neither. So I decide to acquire me some new personalities. I figure it's gonna help me out one o' dese days, seein' as how I'm plannin' to go into An-thro-po-logy."

That last word must have felt out of place in this particular speech pattern, for Dredmore spoke it carefully, articulating each syllable.

"Wouldn't think there'd be much work for Anthropologists these days," Mark said, "with travel being so restricted and the Confederate Indian Nations doing their own research."

"I figure I can make a name for myself for exac'ly that reason," Dredmore expounded. "Not a lot o' competition. Folks can still travel abroad if they've got the right connections. I know how to disguise myself an' fit in 'most anywhere." He rubbed his decorative tooth thoughtfully with one forefinger and tossed his dreadlocks ruefully. "Though it might entail some personal sacrifices."

"I take it your luck with the ladies has improved now?"

Dredmore gave a bashful smile. "Good enough fo' my needs. Can't get myself too involved with one woman just yet. Most of 'em get mad when they find out where I work."

"What made you decide to go into this business?"

"Shit, man," Dredmore said defensively, "they ain't a lot o' good jobs out there fo' a po' Black kid jus' off the street. 'Specially not ones where you can get *paid* to sit an' study an' chat it up with a bunch o' good-lookin' women!"

"So," Mark prompted, delighted at Dredmore's willingness to tell his story, "you decided to round up a few ladies and…."

"No way!" Dredmore seemed shocked. "You think I run this place? I am just a' em-ploy-ee! To tell you the ugly truth, Jenni took me in off the streets a few years ago. I wasn't nothin' but a kid, all strung out on dope an' sleepin' in a doorway, half-froze. She got me cleaned up an' gave me a job here.

"Firs' she started me out as a bouncer. I didn't know nothin' but street-fightin', but I knew how t' stand around an' look mean! After that, she got me a computer with a bookkeepin' tutorial. Nex' thing, she started teachin' me how to run the office when she's busy with a client. Before you know it, she's tellin' me I oughta get a university degree an' make somethin' of myself.

"An' you know what?" Dredmore leaned forward confidentially. "Now she's got me thinkin' maybe someday I might go into pol-i-tics!"

Interrogation

Mark was beginning to get the drift. "It sounds as if you and Jennifer must be pretty special to each other."

"Jenni, she's a special one, all right. Still can't get her figured out. When I first come here, I use' to be head over heels after her, but didn't nothin' ever come of it. She say we just be friends. Sometimes I hope maybe she change her mind after I get to be a famous anthro-po-logist or pol-i-tician. But that be nothin' but a dream, 'cause Jenni don't care nothin' 'bout that kinda stuff."

"She probably sees some pretty famous clientele here," Mark said, trying to lead up to the subject of the Reverend Christopher Rose.

Dredmore shrugged. "Guess you might say that. We're right close to the Capitol here. Most of 'em don't use their real names, o' course, but we get to find out who they are. I imagine that's why they decided to make places like this legal. Don't look good for a lawmaker to get caught breakin' the law!" He chuckled.

Mark's thoughts flashed back to that camera lens in the doorway.

"Ah… when Jennifer and I were doing the Circle, I had a vision that we both met the Reverend Christopher Rose. The two of them seemed to know each other." Mark waited to see how this piece of information would go over.

Dredmore showed no surprise. "Now, don't that beat all! You never can tell where that ol' scoundrel's gonna turn up next! That one be a true-blue *Obeah* man. Jenni say I'm makin' too much out of it, but I know all the signs. He always seem to me like a real *good* sort o' man, but he sho' can lay that preachin' on ya thick!"

"I guess he'd be embarrassed if word got out that he comes here."

Dredmore frosted up immediately. "What make you think he comes here? If he does, maybe he's tryin' to save our souls; what would you know? Mister, you be better off mindin' yo' own business 'stead o' meddlin' with the likes o' Christopher Rose!"

"Why? Is he dangerous?"

"I just said he seem like a' *Obeah* man! Now, you can make o' that whatever you like. I ain't sayin' whether I ever set eyes on him in the flesh, but I wouldn't advise you to go 'round spreadin' no rumours. I ain't forgot that you work at that newspaper."

Dredmore mischievously started flapping his elbows and singing the radio jingle: "***Bird, Bird, Bird****! De **Bird** is de word!*"

Mark could see that the conversation had reached a dead end on that subject.

The Waiting Room

"So tell me how I'm supposed to behave here, Dredmore. This is my first visit to a place like this."

"Well, first off the bat, you need to pay me." Dredmore reverted to his Nordic business voice and mannerisms. He reached into the desk drawer and brought out a cash box. "You will be charged according to what service you want today. We offer three levels of service to our clients, but if you want the full treatment, I'm afraid you'll have to see one of the other ladies. Jennifer herself offers only the Level One."

"And what does that include?"

"Oh, I can assure you that you'll get your money's worth. You'll receive a soothing mineral bath and a relaxing full-body massage, followed by a manual release."

The absurd image of the *Hummingbird*'s emergency brake lever flashed into Mark's mind; then he translated the words into sexual terms and smiled.

"Is it customary to tip?"

"Oh, yes!" Dredmore seemed surprised. "In fact, it's expected, unless you're dissatisfied with the service."

Mark reluctantly parted with most of his week's salary. It wouldn't do to make a habit of this!

Then he settled back into his chair, while Dredmore returned to the book he'd been reading: Gregory Bateson's **Mind and Nature**. It was a real book, on real paper. These were getting harder and harder to find, though it had been less than a decade since electronic books became more popular.

Mark surveyed the magazine discs on the coffee table, and was pleased to find a wide assortment of subjects instead of the sports and girlie magazines that he'd expected. He chose the latest edition of **Confederate Geographic** and inserted it into the reading screen. This month their cover illustration had something new: a Moving Picture that showed ocean waves lapping onto the pink-white sands of a beach in Pensacola. *Planned obsolescence again*, Mark thought. His reading screen back home, which was last year's model, wouldn't be able to display the motion.

He could hear some soft classical music playing in the background, but he didn't recognize the composer. He glanced up to see where the speakers were hidden, and noted that the walls appeared to have real wood panels. Behind Dredmore hung another Moving Picture, almost four feet across. Mark studied it with fascination.

Its art program was a pastel fractal fantasy that seemed somehow erotic. The images changed too fast for him to make out any details, but they were subliminally suggestive of a celestial orgy. Perhaps it was a computer modification of an actual video.

He focused on one particular configuration in the pattern, and determined that the picture recycled itself every three minutes in a seamless loop. Whenever the music changed tempo, the rhythms and colours of the Moving Picture followed suit, though the sequence of images remained the same.

While Mark was watching the Moving Picture, two other clients, both middle-aged men wearing business suits, arrived at the door. They averted their faces in embarrassment and proceeded at once to the private waiting areas, where Dredmore joined them for a time, presumably to collect their payment.

Then, to Mark's bemusement, there entered a little hunchback with Native American features. He was wearing long dark braids, patched and tattered cargo pants, and a black leather jacket marked confusingly with the dual insignia of Wotan's Warriors and the Confederate Indian Nations. He had a half-full duffel bag slung over one bowed shoulder and the mouthpiece of a penny-whistle protruding from one of his pockets. Strange clucking sounds came forth from the bag, and the fabric rustled slightly. The two dogs abandoned their pretense of sleep and sat up with ears at alert.

Dredmore, grinning broadly, hurried to the door to greet the newcomer.

Without words, the two men bridged the two-foot difference in their height with a comradely handclasp. The clucking sounds sped up as Dredmore relieved the little man of his bag, flung an arm across his shoulders, and escorted him quickly into one of the back rooms.

Mark started rehearsing various comments he could use to elicit some information about this strange little man, but when Dredmore returned, he was curtly informed:

"Jennifer is ready to see you now. Please step through this door and wait in the first room on your right. And ... I want you to make yourself Completely Comfortable."

The Reluctant Guru

Dredmore had emphasized the last two words, so Mark presumed that he was meant to undress. He waited awkwardly, perched atop a narrow waist-high massage table. The cubicle was decorated in the style of a Swiss chalet, with wicker shelves and baskets and cedar shakes on the walls. The mood music had switched to Pachelbel's *Canon in D Minor*, he noted with pleasure. He could hear water running in the next room.

At last the sounds of water stopped, and Jennifer entered. She was wearing a sleeveless turquoise spandex jumpsuit, tied at the waist with her official Black Belt. Waves of red hair cascaded to her waist, contrasting with the dark green crystal set in her gold Celtic Cross medallion — apparently the same one she had worn during the ritual on Mount Arabia.

"Hello, Mark," she said, smiling at him as though he were a long-time favoured client. "I'm glad you were able to make it. Your bath is ready now."

That image of her dark, slightly slanted eyes with their thick curly lashes, full red lips, gleaming white teeth and smooth tawny skin would be imprinted in Mark's mind forever. All the questions he had been rehearsing dropped away like autumn leaves, and he found himself blushing furiously.

He obediently followed Jennifer into the adjoining room, where a small Japanese-style wooden tub awaited him. Even Valhalla had to conserve water! The room was steamy and scented with fresh herbs; Mark could identify overtones of mint and eucalyptus. He inhaled deeply and then sighed with pure pleasure.

As he stepped into the hot water, he felt his consciousness drifting off into a blissful nonverbal space. Such a rare opportunity — and an expensive one, at that! Why not relax and savour it? All those questions could wait till later. They would just spoil the mood if he started asking them now.

Mark remained passive and silent while Jennifer's expert hands soaped, scrubbed and sponged him from head to foot. When the bath was done, she helped him to dry off with a huge fluffy towel, and then led him back to the first room.

Her attentions in the tub had given him an erection, and he was disappointed when she didn't seem inclined to attend to it yet. She indicated that he was to lie face-down on the cot, and proceeded to rub him down with almond-scented massage cream. She was making long, slow, firm strokes up the right side of his back with the flat of her hands, forging a sensory path from buttock to shoulder.

She chose that time to begin a conversation — but about his life, not her own.

"Well, Mark, I'm flattered that you wanted to see me again so soon, but doesn't a handsome guy like you have any other women in your life?"

Mark was puzzled and a little irritated. What kind of conversation was this, for an expensive massage parlour?

"Not really," he replied. "There are a couple of women that I see now and then for sex, but there's nothing else to it."

"Why is that? Aren't they up to your standards?"

"Oh, yeah, I guess they're all right. I just don't have much feeling for either of them."

"How about that woman at the Circle, the tall one that looks like a fashion model?"

How had she picked up on Lana? "Nah — she's interested in me, but I don't want to get involved with somebody I work with."

"You're not gay, are you?"

Mark was startled. "Hell, no! Oh, I tried it with a man a few times when I was younger, but it turned out to be the same old story."

"Which is…?"

"He wanted to have a relationship, but so far as I was concerned, we had just been fooling around. It turned into a messy situation."

"How many different sexual partners have you had in your life, Mark?"

"I dunno — I lost track a few years ago. It was in the eighties then."

Jennifer switched her massage strokes to the left side, as the mood music changed to the old movie theme from *Chariots of Fire.* "So if you don't have much feeling for the women you sleep with, who do you care about?"

"Nobody, I guess. My dad is dead, and my mom never really knew how to relate to a son." This reminder was depressing. He hadn't come here for a therapy session. Why was he paying good money to be interrogated?

"Surely you must have loved someone in the past."

"Well, I had a dog once." Then Mark remembered. He let out a long shudder of grief. "When I was thirteen, I had a girlfriend. She was a year older than me, and she played the violin in our school orchestra. They were all on a field trip to Washington, D.C., on the day of the Big Bang."

Mark didn't mention how he had tried to kill himself by taking a whole bottle of Valium when he heard the news. His parents had both gone out of town on the emergency cleanup crews, so Mark knew no one would be around to save him. However, he had awakened three days later with a soiled mattress and a splitting headache.

After spending the next few hours ineffectually trying to clean up the mess, he had decided that trying to make an early exit from this life could be even worse than waiting out his time. His parents had returned from D.C. too traumatized even to ask how he'd managed on his own.

"Ah, I see — you're still being true to your lost love."

"*I am not!*" Mark pushed himself up onto one elbow and turned to face Jennifer. "How dare you try to pry into my private life! How I live is none of your business."

"I apologize, Mark. You're right, of course," Jennifer said soothingly. "But I did get the feeling that you may have come here with the intention of prying into my own private affairs."

He settled back down, and she continued the massage, stroking both sides together now, from buttocks to shoulders and then back down. Deep, almost painful strokes. Resisting a strong impulse to get dressed and walk out, Mark slowly allowed himself to relax again.

"Love will come to you again someday," she said.

"Okay, so I was trying to pry," he admitted. "But, Jennifer, I've dabbled with Magick all my life, and last night was the first time I ever got any results that couldn't have been coincidence or the power of suggestion. And you just seemed to take it all so matter-of-factly! If you know what really happened, then I wish you'd explain, because it's still a mystery to me."

She remained silent until Mark found himself blurting out the whole truth: "Actually, I was hoping you might be willing to take me on as an apprentice." He tried his best to sound humble. It was easier than he had expected.

"A little knowledge can be a dangerous thing," Jennifer reminded him tritely, as she turned her attention to his left leg. "I think you found that out last night."

"Ignorance can be dangerous, too."

Her hands kept moving during the pause in their conversation.

"Mark, I am not unwilling to teach you what I know, but it may not be anything that I can teach another person. I've never had any formal training in the Magickal arts. Most of what I could teach you are practices that you could learn at any dojo or yoga centre.

"It's true that I have been … chosen … to receive certain guidance, but that is a personal matter that applies only to my own life. It wouldn't be of any use to you.

"I do know certain ways of altering one's energy states and entering other, non-material planes of existence or dream-states. But those can often be difficult, hazardous and unpleasant. I don't get the sense that you are ready to handle those abilities wisely. In fact, I was surprised that you were able to achieve any results in that Circle. When I agreed to help you with it, I assumed that you were just a harmless dabbler."

"Then perhaps I'm more ready than you think."

"Mark, to find out whether I can trust you enough to teach you anything of substance, I will have to put you into some challenging situations."

"But if I pass those tests, you'll teach me?"

"I'll teach you unless you give me reason not to." Jennifer switched to his right leg.

Mark had an unpleasant thought. "Will you let me know ahead of time when one of those 'challenging situations' is coming up, and how I can prepare for it?"

"Of course not. You'll have to respond spontaneously from your true heart."

Mark, whose adult life had been based on self-control, contemplated this idea in silence for a time. Then, as Jennifer began to massage his arms, he decided to pop the big question: "How about Christopher Rose? How does he fit into all this?"

"What the Reverend Christopher Rose does is neither your business nor mine. What makes you think I know anything about him?"

"You two obviously recognized each other."

"Both of us know lots of people."

"Damn it, Jennifer, stop jerking me around like this."

"Mark, believe me, anything I could tell you about Christopher Rose would be either pure speculation or a violation of confidence. I will say this much, however: I know much less about the Reverend Rose than you seem to think I do, but I do sense that he has been navigating those Magickal planes for a long, long time. He is a wealthy man who has millions of followers. You would be wise not to cross him."

"But...."

"Now, Mark, you have paid a large sum of money to have this session with me. I have given you my promise to try to teach you as much as you can safely handle. So here's the first thing you need to do: Stop asking questions! And turn over onto your back."

For one of the few times that he could remember, Mark obeyed a direct order.

To his surprise and delight, after his upper body had been thoroughly massaged, Jennifer leaned over and kissed him firmly upon each nipple, cupping one hand under his balls. Then she nibbled her way up his neck to his lips. While one hand continued to stimulate his genitals, the other hand travelled back and forth between his nipples, and her tongue moving inside his mouth orchestrated delicate nuances of response in the most primeval language. He realized that deep kisses were probably a rare honour in such a setting.

Though Mark's body arched and pulsed to the rhythm of her hands, he strangely felt no urgency to possess her flesh, for it was already his own, another part of his own Self that he had just lost track of for a while. He had felt the same way during his astral visit to the Circle of Conception, before the post-coital alienation had kicked in.

Three times, Jennifer brought him to the verge of climax and then backed off. At last, when Mark was dizzy with a joyful passion, when he felt his whole Being was a dam on the verge of bursting, when he felt his body could contain this force no longer, she took her lips away from his.

"Breathe," she told him sharply. "*Breathe!*"

Mark became aware that he had been holding his breath. As he felt the air flowing through his lungs again, his orgasm began, and it was not the localized explosion of sensation that he had experienced in the past. It started as a gentle bubbling fountain of music and colour that rippled through every fibre of his body like a clear mountain stream, building volume and force as its tributaries joined it, until at last it had grown to become a raging river that, with mighty triumph in its annihilation, came crashing to the sea.

After he had regained control of his senses, Mark realized that he had been thrashing about and shouting. He gradually quieted his vibrating body and lay back in great satisfaction, feeling peace at last. But there was a sinister undertow to this satisfaction. He felt also an uneasy, unfamiliar sense of... of....

Tantra Made Simple

"There are two different kinds of Tantra," Jennifer informed him, as she returned from the bathroom with a small basin of water and began to sponge off his groin with a warm wet washcloth. "There's the kind you did in the Circle, where you rev up all your energy and bounce it off someone else. Your partner is just there as a launching pad. In fact, if you have a good enough imagination, you don't even need a partner.

"If your own system can contain that extra energy, your higher chakras will be activated and you can attain new levels of consciousness. But your partner will probably not be sharing them. And if you can't assimilate all that energy back into yourself, then you end up inside *it*, being buffeted around like a plaything of the Gods.

"Sometimes people can learn to direct that excess energy away from themselves to accomplish special purposes — to harm, to heal, or even just to entertain themselves. But it's a dangerous pastime. If you're not careful, it can damage your partners or drive you mad.

"The second kind of Tantra is what you just experienced with me here tonight. That's when two nervous systems join as one. The other person ceases to be the Other, and you both becomes a single Being in two bodies. This can also be done with more than one person; it's how wildling mobs are formed. This is the highest form of Tantra, but you can't do a lot of fancy tricks with it.

"And it has its own dangers. An energetically weaker person, or even a whole group, can get lost inside a stronger one. So most people are rightly terrified of the experience. It isn't really sexual in nature; it's just that, for many people, sexuality or religion are the only bonding forces strong enough to overcome their fear.

"For some reason that I don't understand, I am able to offer some people a taste of this Communion experience. Perhaps they feel safer, knowing that I'm going to set them free at the end of it. Romantic longings are foreign to me, Mark. I am complete within myself. People fear Communion because it often changes them, but I remain always the same. This enables me to serve as their stable anchor."

In that instant, Mark knew that this thing she called Communion was what he desired, and feared, more than anything else in the world, and now at last he had found his Teacher. How wise she was! How many years had he searched, through how many beds, to come to this moment and this woman, at last to be united....

His thoughts were interrupted by the sound of the door opening.

"I have to go now," Jennifer said casually. "I've got another client waiting. You can take your time getting dressed; we won't be needing this room again for another half-hour."

She had disappeared down the hallway before he could utter a single word. Mark had been thrust outside the gates of Paradise yet again.

With slow, laborious movements, he sat up and began to pull on his breeches. At last he could identify that uneasy feeling he had noticed earlier. It was ... **violation!**

She had reached so deeply into his being. Had he touched her, really, at all? She hadn't even taken off her jumpsuit!

Damn her! What did she expect him to do with the rest of his life, now that she had made all the other women he had known seem like cardboard cutouts?

The Most Unkindest Cut of All

"How'd it go?" Dredmore hailed him breezily at the front desk, back in his Atlanta street persona. Without waiting for a reply, he went on: "She knock you for a loop, didn't she? That Jenni, she can do it ever' time!"

"Look, Dredmore," Mark said, steeling himself to get through this necessary transaction, "could you do me a favour? Could you please give Jennifer my card and tell her I'd like her to call me at home as soon as she gets a chance?"

"Sho' thing, I'll tell her that." Dredmore accepted the card. "But I wouldn't be gettin' my hopes up. What happens in Valhalla ain't nothin' but strictly business; you gotta understand that. Some o' the fellas get their hearts broke over Jenni. But I tell you what makes her so good at what she does: Some o' the girls, they give the extra-special treatment to some guy they like, an' then some other guy, maybe he's not as good-lookin' or they figure he ain't got as much money, well, he don't get it so good. But Jenni ain't nothin' but fair. Ever'body get the same service from her. That's why she make twice as much as any o' the other girls in tips, an' don't do half as much for it."

Mark flinched, realizing that he had forgotten to give Jennifer a tip! Well, if Dredmore was telling him the truth, maybe that wouldn't count against him too much. He retrieved his Dress Bowie and began buckling it back on.

"So Jenni has a lot of guys in love with her, does she?"

Dredmore grinned. "Like I tell you before, I use' t' be one of 'em. Jus' 'tween you an' me, I even ask her to marry me once. But she tell me no, she wouldn't make no right kind o' wife for a man like me."

"And why was that?"

Dredmore shrugged, as though it were a mystery to him. "She say she don't like sex."

Chapter 5
Hell Hath No Fury

Sunsong

Awake, arise, the Sun is soon!
Oh joy and rapture, let us greet the first warm glow of Dawn!
We run toward the Sun with rainbow ribbons;
We stretch, we swirl, we sing,
We roll and squirm on grassy cushions!
We sing with warblers to the pink horizon!
To the river! to the river!
To the cool-running blood of our Mother!
We form a living bridge across the waters,
We sway, we slide on slippery stones,
We listen for the first sunbeam
Bringing song from river crystals,
And soar on that sound like swallows,
With open throats to harmonize:
"Aaaaa000000hhhhh,Aaaaa0000000hhhhh,
ahOmmmmmmmmmmm!
The Sun, the Sky, the Day,
This Day has come with Joy and Beauty,
Let us praise, praise and love,
Awake, awake, ALIVE!"

Each rainbow form in turn leaps forth, its robe a handheld parachute, plunging through air to the icy wake-up water that flows below in frosty freedom. Each slides and glides over slippery stones to wash ashore on the sandy beach below with gusty shouts of joy and greeting:

"Ah, Sunsong, we are dripping water rainbows,
We are mirrors to your glory!
O Happy Day, well woken!"

Wildling Blockade

Mark sat up in bed. It had happened again. He didn't move for a few minutes, while he traced back over his latest night vision. This dream, reminiscent of a troupe of circus acrobats or river otters, had certainly been an improvement over the horrors of the night before … though it made his everyday life seem barren instead of reassuring by comparison.

No, these couldn't be ordinary dreams, nor did they have the malleability of the astral levels. Then — *what were they?*

He looked at the clock. *Damn!* No wonder he was having wake-up dreams. He had slept through the alarm, and it was already after 10:00. He was late to work — so late, in fact, that it seemed beside the point to hurry now.

Mark moved through his morning preparations at a leisurely pace, even taking time to pour a couple of sprinkler pails of water onto his thirsty garden.

His bike was further delayed at the Little Five Points intersection by a pack of wildlings who had formed a spontaneous traffic blockade. None of the bystanders wanted to tangle with them, so everything came to a standstill until three vans of cops arrived with police dogs. Even then the wildlings held their ground, almost 20 of them.

Except for the night of the Circle, this was the first time Mark had seen a pack of wildlings in action in the flesh. Their group choreography was uncanny, and this was starting to look like the makings of a bad scene.

On impulse, Mark reached for his camera and snapped a few photos in case the incident turned out to be worthy of a news item in the *Bird*. But almost to his disappointment, the event petered out fairly quickly. Once the cops had subdued the

Alpha, the other wildlings followed docilely along, and the intersection was soon back to normal.

Just as well, Mark decided, as he went on his way. He had no taste for violence.

However, for some reason the scene stuck in his mind. He knew that youth gangs had always existed, so it ought not to seem so eerie that pack-bonding had become such a prominent stage of pubescent development. Even Percy had run wildling for a year or so, before he settled down and started taking his ImmuJolt like a responsible adult. Now he regarded that period of his life with all the embarrassment of a man caught sleepwalking naked.

Naturally, older people kept talking about how different things had been in their own youth, before the Big Bang. Though elders had been saying things like that since time began, it had never been truer than it was today.

Mark passed three or four smaller sets of teens walking in lockstep rhythm. They were so young … and once the wildling phase started, kids were usually out of the educational system until it had run its course. Fortunately, most wildlings didn't come to harm or cause too much trouble.

Sociologists said it depended on the Alpha, but that seemed too simplistic. Mark felt sure the wildling trend represented some nameless danger much more sinister than the usual concerns that the little dears would do violence or start a pregnancy while they were off their ImmuJolt.

Waiting Is

To Mark's relief, Lana and Percy made no comment about his late arrival at the office. They both seemed in rare good spirits, and even hummed as they went about their tasks. He was pleased that they did not question him about his assignation with Jennifer the night before; he knew they had probably overheard him call to make the appointment.

Maybe it will work out all right after all, Mark told himself encouragingly. *Maybe she'll even call tonight.*

The ad for the Reverend Christopher Rose had turned out to be a routine one placed by his publicity agent. Some High Holy Whoop-de-doo would be taking place this weekend at the Druid Hills Afro-Pentecostal Church. Since **The Third Speckled Bird** was receiving public funding, they couldn't indulge in religious discrimination. The ad would have to be accepted as submitted. It couldn't even be tucked away discreetly amid the movies and concerts — there was a whole tasteless full page of it.

That ministry must be rolling in money. Where did it all go? Mark knew the mainstream press had been keeping a watchful eye on Rose for years, but no air-conditioned doghouses, gold bathroom fixtures, private jets, diamond mines, or even flashy limousines or mistresses had yet turned up.

On impulse, Mark phoned the Reverend Rose's publicity agent to say that, on behalf of the **Bird**, he would like to conduct a personal interview. The woman who answered told him the Reverend always had time for genuine seekers, but, well, they'd had their share of problems with the press, and right now the Reverend preferred to pay for his own publicity.

Mark pressed her with hurt protests of great sincerity as a Spiritual Seeker, until at last she relented. If he would sit in the front row and wear his press badge, the Reverend *might* grant him a few minutes right after the sermon. He should be careful to arrive early, because once the service had started, the doors would be locked. And, of course, he would be expected to pay for his admission ticket like everybody else.

A front-row seat at a Christopher Rose spirit-rousing would cost a day's wages. Mark wondered if he could write it off as a business expense, or even get reimbursed from the *Bird'*s investigative reporting budget. Percy and Lana would probably let him get away with it if he invited them, too. Anyhow, he could use some reinforcements against the Faithful. No telling what kind of mind control techniques went on in there. *Locked doors!*

Mark dragged himself through his daily routine, forcing himself to go through the motions of his usual workouts at the Breeches & Cutlass Club. He hurried home as early as he could manage, where he horrified himself by sitting and moping beside the telephone.

Twice his heart leapt with joy, and then fell with a plop into the Slough of Despond. The calls were only from the two women Mark had been seeing occasionally, each calling separately to invite him over for dinner. He refused politely, but knew he'd have to deal out several more rejections before they got the message. Mark was a notoriously unreliable date, and he couldn't formally call off these two relationships, since neither had ever really been "on."

As the week dragged on, with no call from Jennifer, Mark began to wonder if she'd been stringing him along to humour a difficult client. But then again, this could be meant as a test of patience. He would try to wait, difficult as it was.

Virgins on the House

By Friday, Mark was in a truly foul temper. His mood was not improved by the fact that Mayor Rowley had issued a drought ban on garden watering — nor that several times he had seen Percy and Lana whispering together and glancing at him with secret smirks. If the idea weren't so absurd, he'd almost suspect they were having an affair. They were definitely up to something. Well, better for them to have their own secrets than to be prying into his.

The shit hit the fan on Friday afternoon. Mark had snapped at Percy for returning late from a couple of ad pick-ups, and Percy had responded with uncommon forbearance. Then Mark slipped two of the ad photos out of their packet and pursed his lips. They were showing some risqué computer art programs that were in questionable taste, to say the least.

"What do you think, kids?" he asked, holding the pictures up for Lana and Percy to see. "Will we get shit from the feminists and the holy-molies if we run this stuff?"

"I dunno about them," Lana commented, "but you'll get shit from *me*."

"Yeah, man, I say let's turn it down," Percy righteously agreed. "Who'd want this crap in their house, anyway?"

Mark raised a skeptical eyebrow. "Do I hear the pot calling the kettle black?"

"No, seriously," Percy protested, now having a position to defend, "that kind of stuff's for kids. I like art that leaves a little more to my imagination, like that big pink and purple Moving Picture on the wall in —"

Lana flashed him a warning glance.

"—in my aunt's living room," Percy ended in a rush, turning beet-red. "But each to their own taste, I always say. Well, back to work; I guess you'll be wanting me to take these back now, and say they don't meet our standards."

Percy had snatched the offending photos off Mark's desk and was hastily stuffing them back into the envelopes as he headed toward the door.

Mark stood up, fingers clenching the edge of his desk. He could feel the heat rising in his face, the blood pounding in his temples. His voice was dangerously low and reasonable.

"Wait just a minute there, Percy. What were you about to say?"

"Nothing," said Percy defensively, his hand on the doorknob. "I finished what I had to say."

"Percy," Mark continued. "I'd like to see this picture you enjoy so much. Maybe we could do a feature on it as part of a comparison study of contemporary art. Which aunt did you say has it on her wall?"

"Oh — my Aunt Bertha. She lives in Missouri."

"I'm just curious, Percy. Your old auntie must be very *avant-garde*. Moving Picture wall art hasn't been on the market for more than a few weeks."

"Well, it came out earlier in Missouri —"

"Well, sure, Missouri is *always* first with the trends. But you haven't taken a vacation day in over six months. Pray tell, when did you see this artware?"

"My aunt sent me a videoclip."

"Would you mind forwarding it to me so I can see it myself?"

"I accidentally deleted it."

Percy dashed out of the office just as Mark leapt over the desk, intent on homicide.

The **Bird** might have lost its junior staff member then and there, except that, as Mark was crossing the threshold in pursuit of Percy, with his hand already on his Dress Bowie, something tight and painful suddenly lashed around his left ankle and pulled it sharply backward. Mark pitched forward and landed face down on the Welcome mat. He could hear the soft purr of the *Hummingbird* retreating in the distance.

Damn that Lana! Again, Mark was glad he'd never started any involvement with her. The woman was dangerous! What kind of Psycho Bitch from Hell chooses a retractable bullwhip for her official public weapon?

He picked himself up slowly. His knickerbockers were torn at one knee, his palms were bruised and skinned, and the raw, red welt that had begun to appear around his ankle hurt like hell. Sandal straps didn't offer much protection against bullwhip attacks. If these things kept happening, maybe he ought to switch to full-length pants and boots. Roman sandals and knickers showed off his calf muscles to good advantage, but he was tired of having his toes stepped on, anyhow.

Lana was dusting him off apologetically.

"You knew," he told her accusingly. Her eyes did not deny it. "*You knew!* The little twerp! I know how low his salary is. Where did he ever get that kind of money?"

Lana lowered her eyes and bit her lip.

"Let me guess," Mark raved on. "An early birthday present? Or was it a personal loan!"

"Mark, please come to your senses! We've talked several times about how Percy needs some experience with women, and Jennifer is a real professional. Percy had every right —"

"Look, Lana." Mark seized a copy of the **Bird** and brandished the Classified page in her face. "There's a column and a half of whores advertising in here. Why did he have to go to *Jennifer*?"

"Probably for the same reason you did."

Mark shook his head and squatted on the floor with his face in his hands.

"Why, Lana? I know you had a hand in this. Why did you do it?" He looked up sadly. "I guess you thought I had it coming. I know a lot of women call me a cunt-tease. So you can pass the word that Mark finally got his just deserts." He made a hoarse, bitter sound that failed to qualify as a laugh, then stiffly rose to his feet.

Lana silently helped him put the desk back into position, and he began to gather up his scattered papers. Then another awful thought occurred to him.

"When did this deed take place, Lana? When did he see her?"

Lana remained silent.

Mark persisted: "It was Tuesday, wasn't it? *Wasn't it?* When was it? What time? When did he see her?"

"Right after he got off work," she said softly.

Mark remembered well that he had stayed late at the office that night, alone.

"He did, then, didn't he, the little bastard? He got there first! So this busy, busy lady fit *two* last-minute johns into her schedule. Ha! Some line of bull she hands out. Lana, I've been a fool."

"Well, it's not that bad. She wasn't going to see him at first when he called. And, Mark, when she turned him down, he was *so* disappointed. So then I called her back myself and explained that he had seen her at the Circle and this would be his first time. She got interested then. She may have even rescheduled another client to make time for him."

"Virgins. She likes virgins."

"I guess she must. She said a virgin's always on the house. She wouldn't even accept the tip that Percy tried to give her after they fucked the first time."

"After they fucked," Mark repeated dully. "The *first* time."

"She said she knows how important it is for the first experience to be a good one," Lana continued, "because her own was not."

"I suppose you know all about that, too."

"Well, she *did* tell me she was raped. By her own father. When she was just eleven." Mark stared at Lana in horror as she continued: "It went on for weeks until he finally got her pregnant. Then she ran away and took to the streets. Some pedophile up in Clayton took her in and raised her and the baby. She still thinks of him and his wife as her family.

"And that's about all I know," Lana concluded. "Mark, stop staring at me like that."

"That's *all?* You're sure?"

Lana nodded.

"Damn you both!" Mark exclaimed in frustration. "Now I'm almost tempted to send Percy back to find out more."

"Oh, she didn't tell *him* all that stuff. She told me, over the phone. Next time Percy will have to pay, like everybody else."

"Next time."

"I mean, if there even is a next time. I doubt he'll ever be able to afford it."

"Look, Lana, why couldn't you have saved all of us a lot of grief and fucked the kid yourself?"

Lana looked shocked. "But I work with Percy!"

"You work with me, too."

"I haven't fucked you, either."

"Damn righteous of you, I'm sure. Lana, *please*! For me. As a friend. I'm asking you to save Percy's life, or maybe my own. Sic him on somebody else!"

"Well … maybe Jennifer can recommend some other girl who takes *pro bono* cases or doesn't charge so much. Mark — I really am sorry. I just saw this as a practical joke on you, and a big favour for Percy. I didn't know Jennifer meant so much to you."

"You're a real friend, Lana," Mark said sarcastically. To his horror, a tear trickled out of the corner of one eye.

Lana suddenly hugged him and patted him on one shoulder.

"Please forgive me," she whispered. "I promise not to do it again."

She squeezed his hand comfortingly. "Well, Mark, this has been a rough week for all of us, so I'm going home early today, and I'll be working from home tomorrow. See you at the Reverend Rose Rabble-Rousing tomorrow night."

Lana gathered her bag, holstered her bullwhip, and hurried out of the office.

As the door closed behind her, Mark's tears began in earnest.

Chapter 6
Pear-Bonding

Buzzard Meat

Jackrabbit squatted down in the dirt, patiently turning over stones. It was hard work, because only the biggest ones were damp enough underneath to attract any grubworms. He worked methodically, popping each grub into his mouth as he found it. The centipedes he let go. They tasted bad, and he didn't like the feel of their tiny legs wiggling across his tongue.

His homemade sunglasses kept slipping down to the end of his nose. He stopped for a moment to tighten the strip of braided grass that tied them in place. Though it was almost dusk, he never came outside to grub without wearing his glasses and wrapping himself up from head to toe. Not that it was any fun to dress that way, hot as it was, and wrapping-rags were getting scarce as hummingbirds. But he'd seen what happened to people who took chances with the Sun. His own Pappy had gone out that way, blind as a bat and rotted away with malmel cancer!

Sometimes he missed the old man, but he sure didn't miss all the beatings he used to get. His ass had stayed sore all the time, either from that reason or the other. But he'd evened up the score before the old man finally croaked. He chuckled at the memory.

Sister Sue was all his now, and she was finally big enough to be good for something. Almost time for her to get her bleeding, according to the two old brother farts in the next hut. He'd have to start staying away from her then. They were hard to trade off once you got them pregnant, and he was counting on her to bring in enough so he could get a wife of his own.

Maybe he ought to just keep Little Sue for himself. But those old farts kept warning him that the baby might not come out right if a brother got it on his sister. A lot of them didn't, anyway.

What were babies good for anyhow? *Ought to put 'em all out for the buzzards, not just the funny ones. Best thing that could happen to them.* Everybody was gonna go to the buzzards sooner or later; might as well save yourself the suffering.

"Bizarros for the buzzards," he hummed and drummed the popular ditty, "fems for the family, and boys for the wars."

They said he was lucky his folks had decided to keep him. Boys didn't have much trade value these days. It was too hard to make them mind, and when they got big, they just up and left or turned against you. His Mam had had to stand over him with a knife to keep his Pappy from taking him out to the buzzards, but the old man had softened up after he was old enough to help out. Back then they'd had chickens that ran loose and fed themselves. There were eggs to find and firewood to gather up.

Property Rights

A loud racket from inside the next hut caught his ear. He saw a flurry of dust, and then a small blue-wrapped form came hurtling out the door toward him, with the two old farts in hot pursuit. Jackrabbit was quick enough to stick out his foot and trip the fugitive as it ran by. The old farts grabbed hold of it at once and began pounding away.

"*Hey!*" Jackrabbit sprang to his feet. There were two of them, but he was bigger and stronger, and they were already over the hill — 35 if they were a day! So they stopped to see what he wanted.

"I helped you catch him," he pointed out, "so he's part mine now. What you plan on doin' with him?"

The terrified, trembling youngster could not have been over seven or eight. He tentatively held out his hands to Jackrabbit, a can of sweet pears in each. Jackrabbit inhaled sharply with pure lust at the sight of the brown and crumbling labels.

"Caught him stealin' food," one of the men explained. "We oughta kill him right here and now." That was the customary punishment. Food theft could not be tolerated.

"Ain't seen him around before," the other man noted. "Musta come from up the creek. Them water rats think they can come here and take whatever they want, any time they feel like it."

"I ain't had nothin' to eat for three days," the boy protested weakly. "The creek's all dried up."

"Nice-lookin' pears," Jackrabbit observed.

"Shit," said the first man, "they probably ain't good to eat no more. Found 'em in our grandpappy's stuff after he died. We just like to keep 'em with a bunch of other old stuff that we can look through ever' once in a while and think o' the way things used to be."

Jackrabbit realized then that they must be afraid of him, or else they'd have just snatched their food back.

"You're right," he said. "Probably not fit to eat. Might even make you sick. Tell you what, why don't you let me take 'em off your hands? I'll even do somethin' with this here little son'bitch so he won't bother you no more."

The brothers were old, but that food had been in their family for three generations. Their frowns and sidelong glances let him know they weren't going to part with it without a fight. He could probably lick them both, but he might get his glasses broke, and the boy would get away while they were goin' at it. Then the old farts might come sneaking back in the night and try to kill him.

What to do? He just had to have that food. He'd never even tasted sweet canned fruit before; he'd thought the last of that had been used up before his time. But he could remember the stories his Mam used to tell Little Sue and him around the fire — back when his Mam was still alive, back when there was still enough wood to make a fire a few nights a month when the sky was dark.

He heard a rustling behind him and saw Little Sue's rag-wrapped head peeking from around the corner of their mud-and-straw hut. As her eyes met his, he scowled his disapproval. She wasn't wearing her wide-brimmed straw hat or her veil and sunglasses, damn her, after he'd took the trouble to rustle them up for her. What good was she going to be once she went blind and wrinkly? He'd have to give her a good thrashing once he got this mess all squared away!

Then an inspiration struck him.

"Hey, I didn't mean no harm," he protested to his neighbours. "I know you ain't gonna just *give* me no cans o' food, no matter how old they are. What I meant was, if you let me have these pears, I'll loan you Little Sue for a month or so. I know you ain't got enough goods between you to buy no wife, but Little Sue's gettin' almost big enough to marry off, and it's time she got some trainin' in how to pleasure a man."

The brothers smirked. They'd heard her cries of protests when Jackrabbit first began forcing himself on her. Sex with a close blood relative was still frowned on, but it was so common for lack of alternatives that most folks were willing to look the other way unless a baby came from it.

To his disappointment, Little Sue showed more curiosity than dismay to hear his offer. Guess he'd been a little too rough on her lately. Well, he could ease off some now that he'd have the new boy around to help out. The kid didn't look too old to train, and he might be good for several more years before he got big enough to be dangerous.

He'd surely try to run away, though. Jackrabbit would need to fasten him down in the root cellar at night until he learned his place. About time that hole was good for something — he sure didn't have any food to store in it, like his granny used to do.

The two old farts raised their eyebrows at one another and exchanged snaggle-toothed grins. Then they nodded assent.

"You heard me, then, Little Sue," Jackrabbit snapped with a great show of authority. "You go pack up your things and do what these men tell you till I come and get you. And put on your god-damned hat and sunglasses, you hear me?"

He turned back to the old farts and said, "I want you to take good care of her, you hear? If there's anything wrong with her when I take her back, it's comin' out o' your hides."

Then he turned to the boy and held out his hand for the cans of pears.

"And the first thing I want you to do," he ordered, "is to get into that there house and get out o' those filthy clothes. Right now!"

He hadn't had any fresh ass in almost three years, and now he even had pears to go with it. He might even let the kid have a slice or two, if he cooperated. Yes — this was going to be a good night after all!

Juggling the canned pears from hand to hand, Jackrabbit hummed a lusty little ditty and followed his new slave into the hut.

Chapter 7
High Holy Hootenanny

Front Row Seats

By this time, Mark had come to expect these night travels, but that didn't make them any less disturbing. In some ways, this one had been worst yet.

He didn't bother lying in bed to try to recapture the details. Instead, he headed straight for the bathroom, intending to break out of the evil mood with a cold shower. But after he turned the tap and nothing happened, he recalled that the latest drought measure meant the municipal water supply would be shut off from midnight until noon on weekends.

Cursing, he brushed his teeth with soy milk, wiped down his face with aftershave, and hopped onto his bike to work off some steam at the Breeches and Cutlass Club, several blocks away. But when he got there, the door was locked, and he recalled that it didn't open till noon.

Returning home, he took a three-block detour to avoid crossing paths with a rowdy pack of wildlings.

He furiously bustled around, performing several long-postponed household chores that involved a lot of vigorous hammering until, inevitably, he hit his thumb. But by that time it was afternoon, so he was finally able to take that shower and reassemble his civilized persona.

The religious rally was scheduled for 8:00 p.m. Mark donned a handwoven white tunic with Celtic knots embroidered around a deep V-shaped neckline, tied at the waist with a braided rope. It had been a gift from some woman in his past whose name he could barely remember. He donned an undamaged pair of knickerbockers. But in light of the foot-stomping crowd expected tonight, he decided to forgo his usual

Roman sandals and instead drew on a pair of troubadour boots with curled-up pointy toes reinforced with metal.

Then he selected his largest, gaudiest pentagram pendant and arranged the gold-plated chain so that it was prominently displayed against his bare skin at the V between his collarbones. At his shoulder, he pinned the fluorescent orange-and-green polka-dotted press badge of *The Third Speckled Bird.*

He paused to inspect himself in the full-length mirror before leaving the house. Even in these times of imaginative dress, he was bound to be conspicuous. But that was the whole idea. He wanted to set himself apart from the Afro-Pentecostal crowd in as many ways as possible, to ensure that he wouldn't be sucked into whatever mind magick would be worked there tonight.

Time to pedal over and meet Lana and Percy. Best to try to forget what had happened on Friday and hope that would be the end of it. Much as he hated to admit it, Mark needed all the friends he could get during this crisis.

Lana and Percy were waiting for him at a corner near the church, as planned, each of them also displaying a large pentagram and a press badge. They carefully avoided any mention of yesterday's dispute, but there was a conspicuous absence of their usual banter. Mark filled them in on the latest dream, as they stood in line.

"The only thing I can compare it to," he said, "is a scene out of one of those old-time horror movies about life after a nuclear war — not a neutron bomb like the Big Bang, but a dirty atomic bomb that destroys and poisons everything. You know, *Mad Max* or *A Boy and His Dog*."

"It sounds to me," Percy said, "like the Other World is starting to bleed through into this one. I told you we should've closed that Circle!"

"Thanks, Percy, I needed to hear something encouraging."

"Well, Mark," Lana said, "he could be right."

"What if he is? What can we do about it now? Do you have any suggestions?"

"Try casting a protective Circle around your bed before you go to sleep, and see if that helps."

The doors were opened and the line began to move. Expensive front-row seats had been reserved for the trio, so Mark had to turn in his chair to survey the room as the rest of the congregation filed in.

He could have saved his costuming efforts; he would have been out of place in this crowd no matter how he had dressed. Most of these folks were salt-of-the-Earth types who probably worked in some factory and had too many kids just because they used to drink more moonshine than ImmuJolt. Before they got religion, their main pastimes would've been drinking, poker and football for the men, and drinking, daytime soap operas, and antiquated tabloids or cheap romance novels for the women. Those weren't printed on paper anymore, and the people who read them often didn't own an e-book. But there were still plenty of yellowing copies to be found at thrift stores or yard sales, tossed into barrels for a dollar a dozen. The readers liked to romanticize the Good Old Days when, according to the tabloids, life had been so much more exciting. Mark had studied enough history to scoff at this perennial fantasy. He might enjoy some of the retro fashions and music, and envy his immediate ancestors' access to plentiful water and flesh foods, but he didn't envy their constant struggle with diseases.

The ill-fitting clothing of tonight's audience consisted of tacky sweatshop imports dating back decades. It still hadn't been that long since the South had engaged in commerce with foreign nations for non-essential goods and manufacturers wasted precious petroleum reserves on making synthetic fabrics. But only a few households had kept alive the demanding arts of home-sewing or knitting, let alone weaving or spinning, which some female SCA members were trying to revive. Though the clothing he saw tonight was unfashionable and unimaginative, it was probably the best they owned, and most were doing well just to keep it mended. The newer homespun hemp, cotton, and kudzu fabrics were still in short supply and priced out of their reach.

This pathetic world of the earnest working (or wannabe working) poor was one that he had almost forgotten existed, now that his job enabled him to mingle with artists, performers, intellectuals and politicians. But it was the world he had grown up in.

Blacks and Whites were represented in about equal numbers and, to Mark's surprise, there was even a contingent of wildlings. They did not take seats, but stood in the rear of the large room, each gang forming a cluster of a different colour. He knew that fights often broke out when different wildling gangs spent much time in proximity, and wondered what crowd control provisions had been made.

Ah, there they were! Burly men and transwomen in nurses' uniforms were strategically scattered throughout the room. This seemed to be a gig where size mattered.

"What's with all the nurses?" Percy wondered aloud.

"They're bouncers in disguise," Mark told him.

"They're real nurses, too, though," Lana informed them. "I saw it on one of his TV shows. When the Believers get possessed by the Spirit, they fall down or go into convulsions, or who knows what, and these nurses try to keep anybody from getting hurt."

"Yeah," said Mark cynically, "especially the Reverend Rose!"

At last a hush fell over the crowd, as Christopher Rose strode on stage.

He was a large man, at least 6'6", and massively built. There were grey streaks in his black-and-copper Afro, and his scruffy beard might soon be completely white. That famous gold cross was displayed against brown skin under the open neckline of a tunic remarkably similar to the one Mark himself was wearing.

Mark felt a sudden strong desire to take on the colours of his surroundings and fade into oblivion. But it was too late for that now.

The Reverend's eyes flashed thunderbolts as his gaze swept across the room. He paused for the merest fraction of a second to take in the trio sitting primly in the front row, wearing their pentagrams and fluorescent polka-dot *Bird* press badges. Mark thought he saw the Reverend suppress a smile.

Right Here, Right Now!

Christopher Rose raised his arms in benediction.

"Welcome to each one of you, my dear brothers and sisters," he intoned in a deep, resonant voice.

The crowd greeted him with enthusiasm: *"Amen, Brother Rose, Praise the Lord, Hallelujah!"*

"My dear hearts, I know it's hard —"

"Amen, Brother Rose, it's hard!"

"It's hard for you, I know, brothers and sisters, but a new world is coming —"

"Hallelujah, Brother! It's a-comin'!"

"And it's gonna come tonight!"

"Praise God! This very night!"

"That's right, brothers and sisters. They lie who tell you the Kingdom of Heaven is off in the sky, off in the future. I tell you that the Kingdom of Heaven is right here in this room tonight!"

"Tell it, Brother! It's here right now!"

The Reverend lowered his voice and adopted a sombre, serious tone.

"There may be some non-believers among us here tonight."

"Not for long, Brother, not for long!"

"There may be non-believers, but that's all right, for the good Lord welcomes all who come to Him."

"Praise the Lord, He welcomes all!"

"Yes, Brothers and Sisters, that's the Holy Miracle: that non-believers often come among us, but non-believers do not walk away."

"Amen, Brother, they do not walk away!"

Mark could feel his hairs starting to stand on end. This whole thing was beginning to seem like a Very Bad Idea!

"So before we start this service, friends, I warn all of you in this audience for the first and only time that if you are not willing to receive the Holy Spirit into your heart tonight, you do not belong here."

"No! For shame!"

"There is no shame in the Lord, dear hearts, but shame in the hearts of those who hide from His mercy! But there will be no escape from the Lord when the doors are locked tonight. If you are not willing to receive the Lord tonight, dear friends, I ask you to leave now for your own safety."

"Leave now! Hallelujah!"

A handful of people stood up and skulked toward the door. Mark, Lana and Percy exchanged sideways glances. Only sheer willpower was keeping Mark in his seat, and from the expressions they wore, the same was true for the other two.

"Let the room now be sanctified," declared the Reverend Rose, after the doors were shut. "Hallelujah, children, prepare ye now to receive the Holy Spirit!"

All's Well That Ends Well

The speaker system started blaring with the sounds of electric guitars, organs, Voodoo drums and … was that a theramin? A half-naked young woman wearing a wooden mask and feathered headdress darted out of the wings and leapt off the stage. She began frenetically dancing her way around the perimeter of the room, swinging a smoking censer on a chain as she went.

The crowd went wild. People were standing on their chairs and howling, waving their arms in the air, tearing off their clothing.

"Dredmore was right," Mark shouted incredulously into Lana's ear. "He is an *Obeah* man!"

"What?" Lana shouted back — and Mark realized he would never be able to make himself heard over this uproar. Nor, for that matter, would the Reverend Rose, but that didn't seem to bother him.

The tempo accelerated; some Panpipes and flugelhorns were added. A few members of the congregation got to their feet and started dancing behind the masked woman, forming a Conga line. In the rear of the room, the wildling gangs had forgot their differences and were hugging and kissing one another with tears streaming down their cheeks.

Occasionally, someone would stiffen up and topple over in what looked like an epileptic seizure. Two nurses would instantly appear to carry them off, often even before they hit the floor.

The whole room started to swirl around in a human current. Without any break in the rhythm, chairs were systematically folded up and stacked against a side wall. Another masked dancer joined the procession, juggling several flaming torches. In all his years of thrill-seeking, Mark had never seen any spectacle to compare with it.

Suddenly, he felt a poke in the ribs. Lana pointed toward Percy, who was standing on his chair and swaying, with an ecstatic expression on his face. At that moment, another member of the crowd danced by and motioned for Percy to get down so the chair could be folded away.

Percy leapt head-first into the mob. Arms stretched up to break his fall, and Mark watched in horror as Percy was passed hand over hand through the mob toward the centre of the room, wearing an expression of pure bliss. He had literally been carried away!

Mark turned to Lana, but she was gone. Then he caught sight of her again, a few feet away, clapping her hands and jumping up and down with the rest of the crowd.

It was more than Mark could stand. He elbowed his way to her side, grabbed her by the wrist, and started pulling her toward the door. She made little effort either to cooperate or to resist, apparently now regarding everything that happened as moves in a dance.

They hadn't made it more than 15 feet before Mark felt a heavy hand on his shoulder. He looked up into the eyes of one of the big nurses, who was shaking his head reproachfully.

The next thing Mark knew, he had been tossed outside onto the dew-covered grass. He could hear music coming from inside the building, but the doors were securely locked and guarded.

And Lana and Percy were still inside. The next time he saw them, they would probably be brainwashed robots, programmed for perpetual tithe to the Reverend Christopher Rose. His two best friends, such as they were, would be lost to him forever — and it was all his fault. The thought was too depressing for tears.

The uproar would probably go on for most of the night, and after it finally broke up, it would be nigh impossible to find Percy and Lana in that crowd, in the dark. He would have to go home and try to talk to them in the morning — if they remembered who he was, and who they were.

He wouldn't have thought anything that happened today could possibly be worse than the dream that had begun it, but he'd been wrong.

But after he got home, Lana and Percy's fate was soon the last thing on his mind. A message from Jennifer was waiting on his Voice Mail:

"Mark, pack an overnight bag and be dressed and ready to travel at 7:00 sharp tomorrow morning. I'll be coming by to pick you up. I'm taking you to Clayton to spend some time with my family."

Chapter 8
King of the Mountain

"The man of understanding is acceptable only to those who understand.

"He may appear no different from any other man. How could he appear otherwise? There is nothing to appear except the qualities of life. He may appear to have learned nothing. He may seem to be addicted to every kind of foolishness and error. How could it be otherwise?... There is no exclusive state of truth. But there is the understanding of the ordinary.

"Therefore, the man of understanding always appears to be the opposite of what you are. He always seems to sympathize with what you deny... He is not consistent... At times he denies. At times he asserts. At times he asserts what he has already denied...

"His paradoxes deny every seeker's 'Truth,' every path by which mankind depends on mere simulations of Freedom and Enjoyment. He is a seducer, a madman, a trickster, a libertine, a rascal, a fool, a moralist, a sayer of truths, a bearer of all experience, a prince, a king, a child, an old one, an ascetic, a saint, a god. By mumming (or mockplaying) every seeker's role of life, He demonstrates the futility of every seeker's path... except He always coaxes every one only to understand...

"Heartless one, Narcissus, friend, loved one, he weeps for you to understand. After all of this, why haven't you understood?"
~ *Franklin Jones,* **The Knee of Listening**

Anticipation

Mark was too excited to get much sleep that night. If he popped an EZ-Dozit, he might not wake up in time to get ready for Jennifer's arrival, so he resigned himself to tossing and turning. But he did follow Lana's suggestion to surround himself with a protective Circle.

After browsing through an old book on psychic self-defence, he soon had the four corners of his room cluttered with raw eggs, open bowls of water, jar lids of turpentine, cloves of garlic and lettuce leaves. It would be a brave demon that would fight its way through that miasma to molest him. In fact, despite the open window by his bed, Mark soon decided the turpentine smell was more than he could tolerate. He trotted the jar lids out to the kitchen sink and poured the stuff back into the bottle.

His efforts were not entirely wasted. No alien landscapes intruded into the little sleep he did get that night. However, he woke up a couple of times with a vaguely uneasy sensation of something dark and sinister prowling around just outside his field of perception.

Shortly before dawn, he decided he might as well get up and get dressed. Any further sleep seemed out of the question.

He took a sponge bath with water that he had saved out in a cooking pot the night before, and dressed conservatively in a retro Earth Day T-shirt, jeans and sneakers. He made himself a gourmet breakfast, splurging on real eggs in lieu of scrambled tofu. He even treated himself to a cup of coffee with honey and whitener.

This self-indulgent meal helped to brighten his mood, though he remembered that back in his early teen years he could have had bacon and coffee with cane sugar and real cream. In those days, people still used a lot of animal products and imported exotic items like coffee, black tea and even chocolate from far-away places.

Much of the world had been under Company control even then. Coffee and tea plantation workers were paid starvation wages, when they were paid at all, and chocolate was produced with literal child slave labour. But the so-called "free world" had turned a blind eye so long as the goodies kept flowing their way.

Now the Confederacy refused any non-essential commerce with the enslaved nations beyond the Cotton Curtain. Confederate freedom was based on the principles of self-sufficiency espoused by Booker T. Whatley and Stephen Gaskin. Mark had felt pangs of guilt when he had purchased even this small bag of instant coffee on the Black Market, but he found caffeine a far superior drug to any of the over-the-counter pep products, even ones spiked with ImmuJolt.

After breakfast he ran through his daily home routine of isotonic exercises, but his mind was miles away, thinking of Jennifer.

"To spend some time with my family," she had said. What on earth did she have in mind for him? What kind of family did she have? Hadn't she told Lana that she'd left home at an early age? Was she now reconciled with her parents, even though her father had abused her, or was she still close to her foster family — including the pedophile? Did they know what she did for a living? For that matter, what could Jennifer have told them about *him*?

Lana had said there was a child in the picture. How old would it be now? To have learned so much, Jennifer must be older than she looked. If she was in her early 20s, the child must be almost ten years old. Who was looking after it while she worked?

It would be rude of him to ask all these questions of Jennifer directly, but somehow he must learn the answers. Mark was beside himself with frustration. As a reporter, he was used to pursuing information through direct interrogation, not polite indirection.

Until now, subtlety had never been necessary in his relationships with women. His usual style was just to first attract his target's interest with eye contact and body language, then play cat-and-mouse games from a safe distance until she was inflamed with lust, and finally move in for the capture with some romantic one-liner like *"My place or yours?"*

It didn't always work, but it worked often enough to meet his needs, and Mark played the game with Buddhist detachment. The only drawback was that he had to change his hunting grounds at frequent intervals, since women do get together and compare notes.

But they were mistaken to assume that his tactics were driven by any disrespect for women. He was simply unwilling to pretend emotions or levels of involvement that he did not feel. Surely, he told himself, a woman in Jennifer's profession could appreciate this quality in a man.

And there were the door chimes!

Mark arranged his most charming smile before the mirror and hastened to open the door, only to find himself gazing across the threshold eye-to-eye with Dredmore.

Crossing Over

It was a surly and uncommunicative Mark who rode in the back seat, sandwiched between two huge slobbering dogs, all the way to Clayton. Dredmore drove, while Jennifer sat beside him and hummed to herself as she listened to an audio CD and embroidered what appeared to be a panel for a patchwork quilt.

An aura of suspense permeated the car. Mark couldn't decide if it was more like the suspense before a jury's verdict, a surprise party — or an execution!

He felt sure now that he was being set up for one of those Challenging Situations that Jennifer had warned him to expect. No more hopeful romanticizing, then. He'd better prepare for the worst and try to keep his composure no matter what happened.

They passed through Clayton, a quaint but sleepy little town at the base of the Blue Ridge Mountains, and after a few more miles Dredmore headed up the side of a steep slope. The bumpy dirt road spiralled up and up for what seemed like hours, without any signs of human habitation. Mark flashed on the paranoid fear that he was about to be murdered and his body dumped off here in the middle of nowhere. But Dredmore and Jennifer must realize that any police investigation would link them with his disappearance, so any life-and-death scenarios were unlikely.

They crossed over several makeshift bridges that appeared unsafe for traffic, and must have been close to the top of the mountain by the time Dredmore came to a stop. High as the elevation was, a clear stream cascaded down the side of a cliff on one side of the road, and was conducted by a culvert to a house on the other side.

That is, it was sort of like a house. It was also sort of like a castle, except that instead of being made of stone, it was made of plywood. In some places the plywood was painted with a solid colour or mural, or covered with a wood or stone facing. But most of it was just overlaid with ugly black tar-paper that had been weathered away in some places and covered with graffiti in others.

The building consisted of three separate houses haphazardly joined together around a huge oak tree in the centre. Each section appeared to have been designed by a different person. Two of the sections had rickety "towers" that rose four or five storeys and were connected near the top by a narrow beam with a handrail — probably a walkway for the courageous and sober. Their roofs were at different levels, a crazy-quilt of asphalt tiles, camouflage canvas and kudzu vines. The windows were also oddly shaped and placed, and a ceramic gargoyle face loomed over the doorway.

Even from this distance of three or four hundred feet, Mark could hear some weird electronic music blasting forth.

As soon as the car doors were opened, the dogs bounded off into the woods.

Mark strode toward the house behind Dredmore and Jennifer, doing his best to behave as though this spectacle were perfectly ordinary.

He soon saw that what he had first taken to be the stream continuing its course alongside the house was, in fact, a moat measuring about 15 feet across. A sturdy drawbridge, operated by a crank-and-pulley apparatus attached to the side of the house, was already down. On the far side by its hinges frolicked a marble statue of Pan.

As the trio strode over the bridge, Mark heard a barking sound below him. Of course there might be watchdogs at a place like this, but — in the water? Looking down, he saw a three-foot-long cast bronze mermaid on the banks below. He felt relief that the banks were so steep when, near the mermaid, only partly submerged in the water, a six-foot alligator looked back at him. Somebody had spray-painted its back and the top of its head a bright blue. At first Mark took it for another sculpture. Then....

"Arf!" it said. *"Arf!"*

"That's Kundabuffer," Jennifer told him. "She's as mean as she looks, so stay out of her way!"

Reclining in a wooden lawn chair, reading a comic, sat a green-haired nymphette wearing denim cut-offs, huge dark glasses, long purple fingernails, and nothing else except a tattoo over one small breast that said *"Daddy's Girl."*

She glanced up at the visitors and said, "Hi, y'all," with only cursory interest or politeness. Dredmore and Jennifer nodded their greeting with even less ceremony and proceeded past her onto the porch.

As they approached the steps, the door to the house was flung open.

"Well, well, well! 'Bout time you young 'uns came back to see yo'r ol' man!" boomed a deep baritone voice, shouting to make itself heard over the music. "Who's the new face y'all done brung along with ye?"

This red-bearded apparition was attired in a Samurai robe, waving a beer bottle in one hand and a sword in the other. His ferocious aspect was moderated a bit by the ferret perched on one shoulder.

Jennifer stepped forward and gave him a cautious side-hug, avoiding the sword. Then she stepped back and said formally: "Mark Lance, I'd like you to meet my foster father, Michael Arthur."

"Aw, Corey, what makes you act that way in front o' company? Don't pay her no mind, Mark, you can jus' call me Mickey, like ever'body else does."

Though the ferret clattered a warning at him, Mark extended his hand and found it enclosed in a vise-like grip. He opened his mouth to say hello, but nothing came out. Confused and a bit angry, Mark tried two more times to speak, and again failed.

With some effort, he managed to extract his hand from the other man's grasp. Only then did his throat loosen up enough for him to mutter, belatedly, "Pleased to meet you."

The stranger beamed in satisfaction. Obviously, he was used to having this effect on people, and enjoyed it immensely.

Meeting the Family

When Dredmore also embraced their host, Mark could spare no thought to wonder; he was too busy trying to identify the source of the man's overpowering presence. It wasn't his size, for he was no taller than Mark himself. True, he was massively built; the beer belly combined with his attire and musculature made him resemble a Sumo wrestler. Even if he hadn't been waving a beer bottle, the fine red veins around his nose would have revealed his fondness for alcohol. Mark would have bet money that the theatrical Southern drawl was not this man's customary way of speaking, but he was not about to challenge his host under these circumstances.

Greetings done, Mickey stood with his feet wide apart, knees slightly bent, restlessly shifting his weight from side to side as if he expected someone to rush at him and try to wrestle him to a fall. Finally, he lifted one eyebrow, angled his chin toward the non-ferret shoulder, which shrugged away in a deprecatory fashion, and said, "I reckon Corey-girl has done told you **ALL** about me?" He winked at her and cocked his pelvis provocatively.

Mark was horrified to feel his face turning beet red, and even more horrified to feel a corresponding rush of blood to his loins. He felt an almost overpowering surge of hostility toward this arrogant peacock.

"Mickey," Jennifer said reproachfully, "please try to behave yourself. Mark is here as my guest."

"Oh yeah," Mickey said, slapping himself on the side of his head in a comic routine of a dullard remembering the obvious. "Guest. Well, shet mah mouth! Girl, are you ashamed o' yo'r ol' man?"

Dredmore suppressed a snicker and turned away, studiously examining a leaf of kudzu by the door-frame. The nymphette put down her comic and turned her sunglasses toward this little drama. Two more youngsters, a male and a female, lurked within the house, a few feet behind Mickey, watching with curious amusement.

Jennifer enthusiastically played her own role, cupping her hands behind her ears in mock deafness. "What did you say? Speak up, I can't hear you over that racket!"

Mickey spun around and bellowed, "Vivi! *Vivi!* You come here right now and turn that thing off!"

Vibrations of footsteps on the floor were followed by a resounding silence. A handsome, statuesque American Indian woman with long unkempt braids, wearing a tattered print smock besmeared with paint and clay, stood just behind Mickey with her arms folded, glowering. As a patch of sunlight illuminated her face, Mark could see that the tawny skin over her right eye was darkened by a nasty bruise, and so was her right upper arm.

"If you'd move out of the doorway," she said icily, "they would probably like to come inside."

"Oh yeah," Mickey mumbled again, in his dullard persona. "Pardon my manners. Been drinkin' before breakfast again. One o' my bad habits. But please do come in."

He turned aside and swept his sword arm around in an exaggerated gesture of welcome, severing the rope that had suspended a large clay pot containing a spider plant. It came crashing to the floor amid shards of pottery and dirt.

"MICKEY!" thundered the Indian woman. "Put that thing down right now before you hurt somebody."

Somewhat abashed, Mickey obeyed, laying the sword on the floor behind a row of larger potted plants.

"It's a prized possession," he explained proudly, quickly recovering his aplomb. "My daddy brought it back from Japan. Just about the only thing the bastard ever gave me."

Mickey sauntered down a short hallway to the kitchen, with the others trailing along behind him. Several more ferrets converged on them from all quarters.

In passing, Dredmore and Jennifer exchanged sympathetic glances with the Indian woman, who sighed in resignation and began sweeping up the mess.

"That's Viviangela," Jennifer whispered to Mark. "She's Mickey's wife, my foster mother. When she's not cleaning up after Mickey, she does sculpture."

Comparative Vices

The little procession passed by a small iron charcoal grill by an open window and arrayed themselves around a huge industrial spool that served as the kitchen table. The ferrets took up observation stations along the tabletop, counter, windowsills and floor. In the adjoining living area, Mark could see a Moving Picture similar to the one in the waiting room at Valhalla.

"Here, Mark," said Mickey. "Have a beer." When Mark hesitated, he grew more insistent: "Drink up, boy, this here's home-brewed ginger beer. You won't find no better beer in the state of Georgia!"

Mark politely accepted the beer, which turned out to be as good as advertised, and Mickey began rolling cigarettes on a paper copy of *Confederate Science.*

This was farther into the realm of sleazy activities than Mark felt comfortable with. Tobacco was a terribly dangerous and addictive substance. Mark's own father had died of lung cancer. There hadn't been much medical help available for the first few years after the Big Bang, and ImmuJolt wasn't on the market yet. The doctors had said his dad's mesothelioma had come from decades of working with asbestos insulation on his construction jobs. Since the man had been self-employed for most of those years, the family had never been able to collect a dime of compensation. Mark wondered if his father's cancer had actually been triggered by his work on the D.C. clean-up crews, or by chain-smoking.

Less than a generation ago, the tobacco industry had been causing massive deforestation and killing 20 million people a year, while world hunger killed another 15 million. Then scientists discovered that tobacco protein was of higher quality than soy, and more easily extracted.

After the Big Bang, petro shortages, climate change and political conflict had cut off long-distance trade options, so Confederate tobacco crops were now grown mostly as a source of textured vegetable protein. But the Commies still claimed a big share of patent royalties, and addicts everywhere missed their nicotine.

The New Confederacy couldn't afford to waste valuable human resources and alienate voters by policing the private lives of its citizens, so most anti-drug legislation had been repealed soon after the Secession. Homegrown tobacco remained legal, so long as it was a variety on the Approved List, and only the Plant Police cared about its provenance. It was a popular barter item, and even more popular on the Black Market, but it was no longer sold openly except for nutritional purposes. Nicotine abuse was a repugnant and shameful habit that would seriously undermine a person's social standing.

Trendy young adults now chose hothouse coca leaves, magic mushrooms or the designer drug Agape as their vice of choice. However, in the spirit of naughty children playing with fire, more flamboyant households sported cuttings of a genetically engineered bioluminescent tobacco plant that doubled as a night-light. Some saw it as their civic duty, considering that the donor plant had come with a tag: "Illegal to reproduce in any form."

Food of the Gods

Mickey must have noticed Mark's disdainful look, because he shoved the tobacco aside and boomed out, "Hell, this ain't no way to treat a guest. Hey, Zonker, bring out those mushrooms!"

After a short delay, an owlish adolescent trudged forth from one of the back rooms, dragging his feet with obvious displeasure and carrying a tray of psilocybin mushrooms still in their growing medium. There was also a small pan of *Amanita muscaria* under a glass dome.

Mark cringed with dread; he hated to trip with strangers. But he didn't dare to refuse Mickey, who was gesturing toward the mushrooms with an air of one conferring a great honour, while Jennifer beamed her approval. Mark tried to get away with taking only two very small psilocybin, but Mickey wouldn't desist until he had consumed six larger mushrooms in addition to the first two small ones.

Hang onto your seat, Mark instructed himself. *We're in for a ride!*

Looking back, Mark never could fully reconstruct the events that took place that weekend. Everyone in the house ate mushrooms, and the Owl was obviously unhappy to see them disappearing so fast. Mickey kept flashing the youth amused glances, daring him to complain about it.

Mickey held forth in a philosophical monologue for what seemed like hours, while his audience listened raptly and laughed appreciatively in all the right places. Though Mark could later remember little of what was said, at the time he found himself so mesmerized by Mickey's discourse that the effects of the psilocybin came upon him almost unnoticed.

What he did soon notice was an urgent need to urinate. But he couldn't stand up and leave the table without interrupting

Mickey's monologue, and leaving now would make it look like he couldn't take the heat.

Mickey continued to gulp one beer after another and, as his speech grew more slurred, his fake hillbilly dialect was soon discarded. He thought it was great fun that Mark had been so dense as to have been fooled by it, and launched into a little speech about how most people were just "sleepwalkers."

Dredmore tried to lighten up the conversation: "Hell, no, Mickey, if there were that many streetwalkers, Corey would have to lower her rates!"

But this crack only gave Mickey an opening to grill Mark about how he had met Corey — which was apparently the name Jennifer used in her private life, short for Coretta.

After she gave him a nod of permission, Mark gulped and started explaining as best he could: "Well, you see, I needed a woman who could help me out with some Sex Magick experiments…."

"*Magic!*" roared Mickey with a loud guffaw, slapping his thigh while the ashtray spilled and the ferrets scattered. He shook his head tipsily, awed by the extent of human folly. "Magic. People are afraid of life in the raw, so they try to find some gimmick to hide behind.

"Mark, you appear to be a reasonably intelligent man. Let's face it, you're not in *my* league, but you have more going on upstairs than most people. What made you start believing in magic?"

"I can't really say … I just always had a feeling that there must be something more than ordinary Reality. Something, well — profound."

"You're telling me ordinary Reality isn't profound enough to satisfy you? Hell, man, just look around you!"

Needless to say, their surroundings were glowing with the transcendent beauty of raindrops trickling down a stained-glass window in a ray of sunlight.

"Well, yes," Mark conceded, "but it looks this way now because we ate the mushrooms."

"It looks this way all the time," Mickey informed him, "but you're too damned *busy* to look at it. What other magic could a man want?"

"This may be the best kind of magic," Mark said, "but it's not the only kind. Jenni — ah, Corey showed me a whole new way of experiencing the sex act."

He paused briefly to note the reaction and see if he dared say more. No one appeared shocked; however, Mickey did flinch and give Corey a hurt look. She did not meet his eyes.

"It was more than just a feeling," Mark hastened on. "I started going into Alternate Realities. They felt as real to me as all of you do right now, but in most of them, I wasn't even the same person. And after our first session, I started having vivid dreams. I don't know what it all means, but I'm convinced it hasn't all been just my imagination."

A hush fell over the room. Finally, Mickey spoke slowly, in the tone of a man humouring a lunatic: "Just what do you mean by Alternate Realities?"

"Well, there was one regimented world right out of Orwell's *1984*, and then there was a barren, degenerate place that had been hit hard by climate change or nuclear war. There was another place that seemed wonderful and joyous, though most of its people were asexual units in a group mind. Then there was an Astral Plane place where your thoughts became reality. I relived my own conception and birth, backwards, and saw some other real people there, too. I met Corey there the first night, and that TV evangelist Christopher Rose, all dressed up like Merlin the Magician."

This time Mickey sat up and took notice. "You don't say! You met Corey there?" He glanced at Corey, and she nodded confirmation.

"Well." Mickey set his beer down and stared at his hands. "I guess I owe you an apology, Corey, if this man is telling me the truth. All these years, I've worried about you, because I know you have some learning disabilities...."

"Just reading," Dredmore protested; "she's just dyslexic." But Mickey's eyes challenged him.

"Dredmore, you don't want to see the truth about Corey; you're her son. Believe me, there are many other ways that your mother is different from the rest of us. Now, I don't mean to run her down, because we all know how special she is, but I'm just telling the truth as I see it. —What's the matter, Mark?"

"You— you mean— Corey is Dredmore's *mother*?" Mark stammered.

Dredmore and Corey smiled.

"Yeah, mon," Dredmore admitted, "I lied to you. It's the same story I always give to nosy clients. I never was no street kid. I was born and brought up right here on this mountain with Mickey and Vivi home-schoolin' both of us. But the part about me studyin' anthropology was true, and I been a serious Rastafarian goin' on two years now."

"You better believe it," Mickey said ruefully. "Can't even get that boy to eat a slice of bacon or take a drink of beer anymore."

A Man and His Harem

Mark was flummoxed. "But— but— how old are you both?"

"I be but 17, mon," Dredmore replied. "I know I be big for my age. Corey be 28. She feels more like my big sister than my mama, 'cause she was just 11 years old when I was born. Her real daddy raped her. He was part Black and part White, and her mama was part White and part Filipino. So Corey come out a redhead, but I come out Black."

Corey spoke next. "When I told Mama that Daddy was fooling around with me, she beat me and called me a liar. I got pregnant the same year I started getting my periods. When Mama found that out, she beat me even worse and started making plans to take me in for some backroom abortion. I knew I couldn't live at home after that, so I ran away that same night. I hitched a ride from Jackson to Atlanta, and got raped again at the end of it.

"After a couple of weeks of sleeping rough, some street kids told me about this man up in Clayton who'd let kids like me stay with him for a few days and give them food and clothes. They said, if he liked them and they'd fuck him and do what he said, a few kids could even stay on with him, and he'd teach them things they couldn't learn in school.

"Well, I managed to find my way up here from the directions they gave, and Mickey and Vivi took me in. He knew I'd been traumatized, so he never touched me sexually for the first couple of years. They found a midwife for me and stayed right by my side while Dredmore came out. Then they helped me to raise him. They home-schooled both of us. Dredmore stayed on with them for a few years after I left to live on my own."

"She's a feisty one, that Corey," Mickey acknowledged. "But I'm surprised to hear you say what you did, Mark, because sexually she's always been one cold fish. Oh, she's a good kid; she was willing to hold up her end of the bargain, but what fun is it fucking somebody that can't respond? I may be a dirty old man, but I don't enjoy imposing myself on people. Got carried away a few times back in my hotheaded youth, I'll admit, but rape ain't the thrill it's cracked up to be. And I've always been lucky enough to get a response out of most of the people I go after. It's easier when they're young enough that they haven't had a chance to build up their defences yet.

"Oh, don't give me that disapproving look! I know what you're thinking, but the Confederacy lowered the age of consent back to 13 for a good reason. Girls used to marry that young in the old days. There's no sense putting folks in jail for something that comes natural, something that a lot of 'em are gonna do anyhow and the rest will wish they could.

"The kids will tell you themselves that they've had better experiences with me than they had with their peers. Why do you think so many of them come here from far and wide and stay for so long? Word gets around. These kids have run away from more homes than you could shake a stick at. Believe me, if they decide they don't like it here, they'll be gone in a flash!

"A few of 'em do leave. Most of 'em, I have to evict. I buy 'em a bus ticket to the place of their choice, and I warn 'em not to come back until they're grown. Once in a while I have to give 'em a good thrashing just to get the point across.

"But I let the smart ones hang around for as long as they're willing to respect the rules. The main rule, of course, is that what I say goes! They can get a better education with me and Vivi than they could in school, plus they're a big help. Maintaining a place like this takes a lot of work. God knows, a drunk like me needs folks around to take care of him! And I need a *lot* of other folks to modulate my overbearing personality enough to keep me sane — or as close to it as I'm likely to get."

Mark sat silently for a time, digesting this information and wondering if he had heard it all correctly. True, the admixture of old-time Southern tradition with Libertarian philosophy had decreed that young adolescents who would have once been jail-bait were now legal, just as interracial and same-sex couples and plural marriages were now legal. With all citizen-shareholders receiving monthly dividend funds from the government, nobody was forced to be financially dependent on — and therefore subject to the whims of — any other person. In theory, anyone over the age of puberty was free to leave their family of origin and take up with whomever they pleased. But most of the kids who tried it soon beat a quick retreat back to their own parents.

There were competency tests for the younger ones, and occasionally even a precocious 10-year-old successfully won the right to live as an emancipated minor. It was not uncommon for an older man or woman to marry an adolescent who had matured earlier than most, or for youngsters to ease out of their parental nest by moving in with a polyamorous extended family until they got the hang of living as adults.

But even in these liberated times, a man of Mickey's age keeping a harem of barely-legals was disreputable enough to attract the attention of local law enforcement. The situation was too suggestive of a pimp-daddy scamming off the citizen-shareholder dividends of the naive and gullible — a privilege normally reserved for TV evangelists like Christopher Rose!

At last Mark ventured, "How does all this affect your wife?"

"Viviangela was the one who brought me the first two kids! She picked 'em up on the road during an ice storm and brought 'em home for a hot meal. They were already used to swapping sex for lodging, and remember, we were both a lot younger then, and they thought we were a real turn-on. They were the ones that initiated the sex, and we all had such a good time, they ended up staying with us for three years. We were sorry to see them move on, but within a few weeks other kids started showing up that they'd met and referred to us. The whole thing just grew naturally.

"Viviangela knows she's the only woman for me. A man like me needs to be married to a nymphomaniac — ain't that right, Vivi?"

Mickey's wife met his wink with a stony silence.

Guerrilla Psychotherapist

"Vivi doesn't like it when I talk about her this way with strangers, but let me tell you, Mark, she's a tigercat in the sack. You ought to try her out sometime. She's never turned anybody down to my knowledge, and she's never failed to climax. Viviangela is one special woman! Where could I ever find another one like her?

"Now, I know you're besotted with Corey at the moment, but you're wasting your time on her. She's the only woman I never could get to respond to me sexually. I'm ashamed to say, I even got drunk and forced myself on her a few times in my frustration. That isn't usually my way, and I knew she would have done it voluntarily if I had approached her nicely. But I had a small hope that since tenderness hadn't done the trick, she might respond better to a show of force. A few women do.

"Well, next thing I knew, she'd rented a room in town over the dojo. She left little Dredmore here with us — not that we minded, because we loved him like he was our own, and the older kids were happy to babysit. She came back a year later, and the first time I tried to touch her, she threw me head over heels and damn near broke my back. So from that day forth, we declared a truce. Corey knows she can always call this place her home, and I haven't laid a hand on her that way for over ten years."

"Now, tell him the whole truth," Corey prompted. "It wasn't just about the sex. You used to beat me, too, just like you still do all the others. I'm warning you again, Mickey: Viviangela's going to leave you someday if you don't start treating her better."

"Vivi can pack a pretty good wallop herself," Mickey protested — but he did hang his head and look contrite for a few seconds. Then he resumed his narrative.

"I never have heard any talk of Corey having a boyfriend — or a girlfriend either, for that matter. I do feel hurt that she's doing things with strangers that she won't do with me. But Corey likes to mess with people's heads, and she says her massage business, seeing all those politicians, gives her a better chance to change the world than anything else would."

"But surely," Mark said, "there are other ways to change the world besides running a massage parlour!"

Mickey shrugged. "Depends on your point of view, I guess. Corey would have a hard time making it through any academic program. Vivi and I did our best with the home-schooling, but she can still barely write her own name.

"But she once saw a TV documentary on Felix Kersten, and he's been her hero ever since. He was the personal masseur of Heinrich Himmler, the notorious Nazi. After World War II, the Dutch government appointed a commission to investigate Kersten. Do you know what they concluded? Kersten had saved so many lives through his influence on Himmler that his service to humanity was without precedent in history."

"Still, if Corey really isn't into sex, why…?"

Corey spoke up. "Most of my clients aren't really into sex, either. To them, going for a good massage is just a leisure concept that suits their station in life. Oh, sure, most of them do want to get off while they're there. But mainly they just want to be pampered and made to feel good after they've worn themselves out playing the big tough macho man all day.

"But if anybody does want something more specific, we do our best to accommodate him — or her. Two of our ladies are working on research projects for their doctorate in abnormal psychology, and they love to get the kinky ones."

"I'd be happy to take those cases myself, any time," Mickey offered, twirling his thumbs. Then he turned to Mark and continued, "See what I mean, Mark? Corey sees all those bigwig politicians, and she sends them home feeling good. Then, a few days later, right out of the blue, the idea pops into their head to change some asshole law and make it more sensible.

"I don't know how she does it. I can rearrange people's heads myself, so she must have picked that up from me, but Corey knows how to make them love it and even pay her for it. — Well, she's really getting paid for the other thing, but you know what I mean."

"When I do it, even if it's something they desperately need — something that's going to save their life or their health or sanity or marriage or keep them out of jail — all I ever get for it is resentment and hatred. One guy that I'd saved from gambling away his life's savings showed up in the middle of the night and burned down my garage! I know I ought to just leave 'em alone to go to hell in their own way, but when I see somebody in bad shape and know I can help, I feel a moral obligation to intervene."

"Yeah," Zonker chimed in, spotting a chance to get even for the mushrooms, "Mickey's like a guerrilla therapist, and you can spell that whichever way you like.

"Now, imagine you need a heart transplant, only you don't know it yet. But Mickey knows it. So one day when you're walking down the street, going about your own business, he jumps out from the shadows and drags you into a back alley and performs that heart transplant for you. Only he does it with a hacksaw and no anaesthesia.

"Next thing you know, you're crawling back out of that alley, all sore and bleeding — and with somebody else's heart. It probably works a lot better than your old one did, too. So Mickey can't understand why you don't show more appreciation for the services rendered."

"You see what I'm talking about?" said Mickey, as though Zonker's words had vindicated him. "That's why I don't have any friends my own age. Oh, I have followers aplenty — legions of lieutenants stand ready and waiting — but no real friends. I have these children and a few old folks in town that are willing to put up with me for a few hours at a stretch. But most of my contemporaries feel too threatened by me. It would be even worse if I didn't drink; that evens the playing field a little. Viviangela here is the only peer I have, and most of the time she hates me, too."

Viviangela burst into tears and left the table. Mark heard a door slam in another part of the house. Corey got up and followed her.

Character References

At a wave of Mickey's hand, Dredmore and the other adolescents ambled off into a back room. Seeking an opportunity to empty his bladder, Mark rose with the others, but Mickey peremptorily motioned for him to sit back down. Mark felt a brief moment of panic to realize that he was here stoned, alone, at Mickey's mercy — together with a moment of relief to realize there would be no witnesses to his inevitable humiliation.

"You may have some potential to become a friend, Mark," Mickey mused. "Although, frankly, I doubt it. You come across more like a self-centred asshole."

Mark was flabbergasted. "You're calling *me* self-centred!" he exclaimed indignantly.

Mickey grinned. "Oh, I know I'm an egomaniac. I'm too intelligent not to know my own strong points and shortcomings. But a genius has to express himself or he'll go insane. I do care about people. These kids can tell you how different I am from most of the folks they run into."

"What gives you the right to call me self-centred? You hardly know me!"

Mickey smiled. "Glad to see you starting to show a little spunk, Mark! Tell you what, why don't you give me some character references? I feel like I'm entitled to a little information, seeing as how you have designs on my foster daughter. Who are the people that know you best?"

"Percy and Lana," Mark said, after some deliberation. "The people I work with."

"Fine. Please feel free to bring your *friends* along next time you come up. How are they for looks?"

"Lana's a real fashion plate, and Percy's your average skinny punk with hardware on his face."

"They into swinging?"

"I doubt it. Lana's an ice princess, and Percy's still a virgin — or was, until he met Corey. She gave him a freebie a few days ago." Mark could not keep the bitterness from his voice.

Mickey shared the sentiment. Another dark look passed over his face. Then he said, with suspicious heartiness, "Well, if your Lana's a cold fish, too, then you may understand my frustrations with Corey."

"Oh, Lana's not my lover. She'd like to be, but I'm just not interested."

"You amaze me, Mark." Mickey rocked back in his chair and clasped his hands behind his head. "How can a person not want to have sex with someone they have any positive feeling for?

"I have felt a deep and abiding passion for every living thing in my vicinity for as far back as I can remember. Our German shepherd didn't appreciate my advances when I was a child, but by the time I was nine or ten, I had made love at one time or another with most of the other kids in my class. And nobody's ever shown me any reason to tone it down. If ImmuJolt hadn't come on the scene when it did, I'd probably be dead of some STD by now.

"Ever wonder where ImmuJolt came from, Mark? Most people think it was cooked up in the research labs at the Centre for Disease Control. They never told the press how a bottle of ImmuJolt appeared at their gate one morning, along with a notebook of instructions for its manufacture. Where do you think that came from, Mark?"

"I'm sure I don't know."

"It was one of those lucky accidents," Mickey mused. "Actually, it was inspired by a chance remark that Corey made on a different subject entirely. Funny how life works. Science is the last thing on Corey's mind. She'd picked up some cheap medallion at the thrift store, and she was convinced it was giving her weird dreams. Well, she was telling me about one of them one morning, when something just clicked in my head. Within a year, I'd cooked up and tested my first batch of ImmuJolt.

"Know why the Commies have never cracked the formula? The damned stuff's based on kudzu and pokeberries — two weeds that everybody in the South used to be dying to get rid of! What do you think of that, Mark?"

Mark rallied his courage. "I think you're lying, Mickey."

Mickey roared with laughter, spilling his beer. "You know something, Mark? I think I like you after all. What makes you so sure I'm lying?"

"Because you're living in this rundown shack. The formula for ImmuJolt would have made you rich."

"Ah, you do have some sense of reason, after all! Mark — I *am* rich."

Riches More Than These

Mickey burst into song: *"I got life, brother, got my hair, got my toes, I got my liver!*

"Well," he rubbed his scalp and chuckled ruefully, "I've still got most of my hair, and the liver's hanging in there. Remember that head hair correlates inversely with testosterone, next time you admire your own shaggy mane in the mirror!"

Again Mark attempted to rise to pee; again Mickey motioned him back down.

"No, I wasn't speaking metaphorically, Mark. Now hear this: I. Am. Rich. Not nearly as rich as my old man, may he fry in hell, but I have enough money that I'll never have to work a day in my life for anyone else, and I don't even accept my citizen-shareholder dividends. TANSTAAFL! They're one of the ways the government keeps tabs on folks. Don't think for a moment that only the Commies and Corpses spy on their own citizens!

"I have enough money to run this little halfway house and educational centre for runaways. I know it looks funky; I like it that way. I get enough people at my door begging for help right now. I'd hate to have to start turning more of them away."

"I take it, then, that you have an inheritance," Mark said.

Mickey smiled darkly. "Not exactly," he said, each word a knife-edge dripping with bitterness and malice. "Let's just say that my old man provides me with a generous stipend, in return for which I stay out of his hair. Well, except for occasionally transferring some funds out of his bank account to places where they'll be put to better use. And I plot his downfall."

"And just who is your old man?"

"I'm not ready to tell you that, and you wouldn't believe me if I did. Let's just say that I came by my personality quirks honestly. I must admit that it has been a lifelong struggle to keep myself out of mental hospitals and jails, but now that the New Libertarian Democrats have lowered the age of consent to thirteen and decriminalized drugs, I figure I'm home free. That was largely Corey's doing, by the way, hard at work near the Capitol."

"It's hard for me to believe the local folks leave you in peace."

"Leave me in peace? Hell, I have them scared shitless! You see that drawbridge across the moat? There are three other bridges between here and town, and I'm set to blow up every one of them at the touch of a button.

"Did you see that thing in the front yard that's grown over with kudzu and honeysuckle vines? That's an armoured tank. I still have the ammunition and I keep it gassed up. Every year or so I take it for a drive down the hill and back up, just so they'll know it's still here.

"You see that Uzi hanging on the wall behind the geraniums? I've got four more like it, plus a couple of AK-47's.

I'm the only one that knows where the ammo is kept, and Viviangela has custody of the firing pins. Those things are here for our own protection. Not that I've ever had to use them, except once in a while to scare away poachers or local adolescents. I let off a couple of rounds into the air over their heads, and that's the last we see of them.

"But it's all based on a truce between me and the locals. I don't bother them, and they don't bother me. I pay my taxes, and every now and then I make a contribution to the Fireman's Ball or the KKK Bust Insurance Fund or some other local charity. I'm polite to everybody I meet, so long as they don't mess with me.

"Thanks to my marriage to Viviangela, I've been adopted into the Confederate Indian Nations, so legally I'm no longer subject to Confederate jurisdiction, anyway. And the C.I.N. isn't going to come up here to bother me — not while Vivi's mom sits on their Council of Elders. So that means all we have to worry about are the Plant Inspectors, and nobody likes to enforce those Commie regulations anyhow.

"But I haven't gone into town much the last few years. I don't feel safe outside my own territory, and I don't like to drive. Viviangela or one of the others takes the Harley down for groceries every few days. I must confess that I have increasing difficulty keeping the damned thing in an upright position." Mickey belched and opened another bottle of beer.

Black Box

"Does Corey often bring her clients here to meet you?"

"Hell, no!" Mickey looked directly at Mark. "This is the first time it's ever happened. Had me wondering if she might not be sweet on you after all, but I can't see any sign of it. She probably just wanted me to meet somebody who could back up her outlandish stories about astral travels."

"I asked her to teach me what she knows," Mark ventured. "But she seemed to think that might not be possible."

"Damned right, it might not be. Corey is a case unto herself. Mark, people are my main love in life. Certain select people, mind you; I don't have much use for humanity in the bulk. But I know the whole range of human experience from top to bottom. I can usually read a person as soon as I set eyes on them.

"But I can't read Corey, and I've known her for most of her life and almost half of my own. She's still a black box to me, Mark. On the level where I usually read people, Corey's just not there. I seriously think she might be what they used to call an idiot savant."

"Corey's no idiot!"

"Metaphorically speaking, you understand. She does have some abilities that ordinary people don't have, but there's also something missing." Mickey peered shrewdly at Mark. "Perhaps you'd like to get rid of yours, too?"

"Mickey, I don't know what you're talking about. Corey is a beautiful, fascinating woman. She gave me the best sex of my life without even taking her clothes off. I've watched her change into a wild beast and scare off half a dozen armed wildlings in the night. Without her help, I could never have found my way to the Astral Plane, or whatever it is. While I was in that zone, my surroundings kept changing so much that I soon lost my bearings. But Corey knew her way around well enough to find me and take me back with her. It may be some kind of transition zone between Realities, because since then I've been experiencing the lives of other people in other worlds."

Mickey was shaking his head in disbelief. "I'm sure Corey will confirm your story, but if you want my own opinion, she must have had you in a hypnotic trance. Corey is a trained hypnotist, you know."

"Maybe so; I'm in no position to argue that. But those experiences have kept on happening even when Corey isn't around. I've had one almost every night since that first session. They scare the shit out of me, so if I can't learn how to control them, I want them to stop.

"And there's one other thing that's been bothering me," Mark continued. "Are you familiar with the Reverend Christopher Rose?"

Mickey guffawed. "When I was still a kid, I went to sleep in front of the TV set one Saturday night and woke up the next morning to one of his sermons. I couldn't find the remote, and I felt like my mind was going to be sucked right out through that tube before I could summon enough willpower to crawl across the floor and turn the damned thing off."

"Well, you were lucky you made it in time. That man's dangerous. I may have made a serious mistake. I told you before, I met Christopher Rose in that transition zone just before Corey came for me, and he was *not* happy to see us. I could tell that he and Corey knew each other, but she refused to tell me anything about him."

"He's probably one of her clients," Mickey said. "Professional ethics, and all that rot."

"That's what I figured, too, at first," Mark said. "But Corey told me that Rose has been at this game a lot longer than either of us, so of course that made me curious. Last night I went to one of his revival meetings.

"Percy and Lana and I went as reporters — we work at *The Third Speckled Bird* — and I managed to get us seats in the front row. He saw me there, Mickey, and I'm sure he recognized me. He started leading this Voodoo ceremony, and everyone in the audience except me started coming together into this group mind...."

"And you were able to resist that? I may have underestimated you, Mark. A mob's intelligence can be measured by the average I.Q. of its members, divided by the number present."

"Sure seemed that way. Percy and Lana got sucked right into it. When I tried to get them to leave with me, one of the bouncers tossed me outside and locked the door. For all I know, the next time I see them, they'll be spouting Love and Truth like good little Rosebuds."

"The man does have charisma," Mickey allowed. "But now you are intriguing me, Mark. I would like to learn more about this Christopher Rose. You can bet your bottom dollar he's up to something. Maybe he's a benefactor to humanity, as Corey fancies she is, but that's not something we can count on. The man had enough influence to sway a national election. I happened to like the way he swayed it, but our tastes may not always coincide. Anybody who can do that is dangerous, no matter what his motives are.

"Mark, old buddy, I want you to bring your friends up here next weekend, so they can tell me firsthand what he did to them."

"Well, sure, but they won't know any more than I do about what's going on behind the scenes. I can't even be sure they're going to show up for work again. They looked pretty far gone the last time I saw them. We might need to call in a deprogrammer."

"I'll be able to find out more than you'd expect, unless he's made them into zombies by now. Making zombies used to be the dark side of Voodoo; Dredmore found an old book about it called *The Serpent and the Rainbow*. But that process would be too expensive to use on nuisance people, let alone a whole congregation. It was usually done for revenge, to make an example out of somebody that had turned the whole community against him. They had to take up a collection to pay for it. Zombies didn't even make good slaves after that much brain damage. It would have been easier just to grab an ice-pick and give the villain a frontal lobotomy, but I guess they knew more about poisons than brain surgery.

"Here, Mark, have another beer."

This was his golden opportunity!

Mark replied, "Mickey, I'm sorry, I'm not used to drinking so much, especially after all those mushrooms. I need to take a piss. Where's the way to your toilet?"

Mickey gestured toward the front door. Reluctantly, Mark stood up and walked outside onto the porch. While they'd been engaged in conversation, he hadn't been aware of how stoned he was, but now the midday sun stabbed his dilated pupils and the multitextured green world smashed against his open senses like a slap in the face. He teetered on the edge of the porch and peed onto a patch of kudzu. No wonder it looked so healthy!

As Mark reached to close his fly, Mickey leaned over his shoulder and reached around to lay a large, hairy hand over the one fumbling with the zipper.

"Don't be in such a hurry, Stranger."

Mark escaped in the only direction open — he jumped down into the patch of piss-covered kudzu.

Mickey held his belly and laughed uproariously, while the ferrets clattered at his feet and Kundabuffer barked menacingly.

Disoriented with alcohol, psilocybin and terror, Mark felt like it took years to scramble back onto the porch and start brushing himself off, glad now that he'd kept the old custom of tucking a monogrammed handkerchief into one pocket. He felt like the Incredible Shrinking Man, and would rather have been the Invisible Man. He hoped this episode was not going to be the first in a series of unwanted sexual advances. Mark had mastered the knack of fending off physical advances from women, but Mickey had enough of a psychological and strength advantage to feel like a threat.

"I— I— I wasn't expecting you to do that," he said inanely, as though he were the one who needed to offer an apology.

"Life is full of surprises," Mickey said jovially. "Well, then, come on inside, and we'll see if we can't find somebody more to your liking.

"Later on I'll take you for a stroll around the premises — there's a lot more here than what you've already seen. In the South tower, I have the kids turning out some computerized art programs with subliminals that are gonna shake the foundations of this society.

"By the way," Mickey winked after Mark had regained an upright position, "for the sake of decorum, I would advise you to zip up your fly."

Chapter 9
Let Sleeping Gods Lie

The Profit and the Lyin'

How many more billions had the last day brought? He had stopped keeping track years ago, leaving those trifling matters to his accountants. Gilbert Carson pulled the strings of the Conglomerate that controlled most of the planet. He had long since accumulated so many dollars (and Euros and yen and rubles) that twenty wildly extravagant playboys couldn't spend even the interest in a single lifetime.

By all the signs, his own lifetime would soon be drawing to a close. Given the circumstances, it might be for the best that he would be leaving no legitimate heirs.

Gilbert Carson examined the sagging skin of his face in the bathroom mirror. The mirror's frame and the plumbing fixtures were solid gold. He wiped away steam from the glass to better see his reflection. Even fresh out of the hot tub, his face showed the geometric patterns of a dried-up desert lake. He used to see them on his trips to Africa.

Damn! No safari hunting was permitted now even to Company officials, except on those silly wildlife ranches, where a man could shoot a tame rhino, maybe take out a couple of business associates in the bargain, and then stuff himself on the carcass. If he were rich enough, he could buy the horn, too, and have it powdered as an aphrodisiac.

Carson, of course, was rich enough. But rhino horn hadn't helped his problem any more than the other remedies had. Prostaglandins gave him migraines, horny goatweed caused heart palpitations, L-arginine had triggered a case of shingles that even ImmuJolt couldn't suppress, and now the doctors had told him to lay off the *sildenafil citrate* before it made him go blind.

But wasn't that what they used to say about masturbation?

Soon, They kept telling him, very soon now…. *Damned lying bastards!* Very soon now Gilbert Carson would be dead of old age, and then there would be no one left to remind Them of that terrible secret bargain.

Not that he was in a position to cause Them much trouble, anyway. His position as Uber-CEO of the Companies and Corporations was now in name only. Younger, quicker rising stars had eased him into a luxurious corner office, provided him with a voluptuous personal assistant, and suggested that it was time to write his memoirs.

By now all the systems he'd set up were operating almost automatically, each module able to function independently of the others. The process of converting Earth's food production capacity from feeding human beings and their pets and livestock to supplying special-order GMO fodder for Them had taken on a momentum of its own.

How many shipments had They already picked up from supply stations at those areas blind to satellite photography? Surely by this time They had taken enough to feed a small planet — which was exactly what They needed to do.

Soon, very soon now, They would start waking up the Sleepers and moving in to take command. Carson shuddered at the thought. It might be better to die first, after all.

No! He clenched his gnarled, speckled fists. If a man has already sold his soul, he should at least collect his payment. But … how?

It was becoming clear that They had no intention of coming through voluntarily. He had been a gullible fool when They had contacted him so many years ago, offering him the one thing that could still tempt the wealthiest man on Earth: Immortal Life.

And to earn it, all he had to do was to sell his own planet.

Well, hell, why not sell it? — he owned it, didn't he? Hadn't he bought and paid for it, fair and square?

Companies Love Misery

Back when he had stopped monkeying around behind the scenes and taken the reins in earnest, two billion people had been living on the verge of starvation. He had put a stop to that, making sure that every human being on Earth had their minimum nutritional requirements. Then he provided them all with shelter and clean water.

That had been simple enough, once he'd made it clear to the Commissioners who was in charge. There was no need for any more of those silly wars that had once kept the production game going. Gilbert Carson had raked in all the Monopoly funds, becoming the sole economic survivor on Corporate Island — and in this role as "King of the Corpses," Gilbert Carson took care of his own.

Carson prided himself on this trait. To the best of his knowledge, not one of his bastard children had been left without means of support — not even that obnoxious redheaded brat who had shown up in his office at age 12 to scream obscenities and accuse him of driving his mother to an alcoholic grave.

Hell, that wasn't his fault! When the bitch had let herself get pregnant, he had offered to let her keep her job, even offered her a salary increase, just like he had done with all the others. But she wouldn't have it. She had stormed out the door without even the courtesy to put her desk in order before she left. It wasn't his fault that she had gone back to her home town and turned to prostitution, too proud to accept his help.

But Carson liked to think he'd made up for it with the boy. Every year without fail, he sent a generous money order to the brat c/o General Delivery in Clayton. It was always picked up and cashed, and what thanks did he get? Not even a greeting card now and then!

Too bad, in a way — of all his progeny, Mickey was the one who reminded him most of himself. Carson had tried to befriend the lad for the first couple of years after his mother died. He had even paid in advance for tuition and lodging at a good boarding school. But the school had soon burned down, and Mickey was at first presumed a casualty of the fire. Most of the public didn't believe the tabloid rumours about the students' drunken orgy with exotic flammable drugs, but Carson did.

Wonder how Mickey is doing these days?

Carson hadn't been in touch with him for over 15 years. The boy hadn't been showing a lot of promise the last time their paths crossed — married to that Indian slut and barricaded in his Blue Ridge Mountain fortress like some hillbilly Sultan. It was hard to keep an eye on him in the backwoods of the Confederacy, completely off the Grid. He probably thought Carson hadn't noticed the tiny sums being automatically transferred out of his various bank accounts to unlikely places whenever a financial transaction didn't come out to an even number. Millions of fractional cents from a trillionaire's account quickly add up to a huge sum.

Bandit though he was, Mickey had shown more initiative than any of Carson's other offspring. Yes, it was about time to look him up again.

Carson would soon need to make a trip to Atlanta to negotiate with the Centre for Disease Control about increasing their ImmuJolt exports. He knew the CDC had been testing some other products that hadn't been put on the market yet. Maybe they had something that could help him stave off the Reaper for a few more years.

But mainly, he would be going to Atlanta because They had ordered him there to take care of some unidentified people who had been interfering in Their work. How was that even possible? Not even Gilbert Carson had found a way to interfere, and nobody else on the whole planet suspected a thing.

The Companies had control over all the communication systems outside the Confederacy, and surveillance even inside it. International commerce and communications all passed through the same system. Nobody could have possibly put the clues together. With the Confederate rebels diverted by their Victory Garden nonsense, nobody yet realized that the Earth had stopped producing more than a few basic food crops. Even those few had been genetically modified and were being grown in vastly greater quantities than the human population required.

Living conditions and environmental degradation had been so bad before the Big Bang that it had been easy to make a case for a plant-based diet. Carson didn't feel bad about that. Most folks were still better nourished than they had been before Company consolidation.

The bulk of Earth's grain and bean production had once gone to feed livestock consumed only by the affluent. Eliminating most of that livestock had not only reduced the amount of animal suffering, water pollution and greenhouse gases, but it had freed up plenty of plant food for people — and for Them besides. Nothing was wrong with that kind of wholesome arrangement, where all parties benefit.

But the next step would be more distasteful. Carson had begun trying to figure out some way to beat Them at Their own game. After all, he had gained control over one planet, so why not two?

At some point in the near future, human population pressure was going to trigger the Change to planetary consciousness. They were counting on him to make sure the Earth would be in a state of misery and chaos at that moment. The resulting stress would result in a rigid hierarchical collective structure that They could easily control from the top down.

They had contacted him in the first place because the benefits of ending war and hunger had almost counteracted the misery caused by the loss of freedom under Company dictatorship. They needed him to make sure that world conditions would take a sharp turn for the worse before the Change gained momentum. Trying to seize control of a more loosely structured collective consciousness would be like herding cats — or nailing Jell-O to a wall.

Carson hadn't dared refuse to cooperate with Them, and the promise of Immortal Life had been an attractive bribe. But he hadn't expected steering the world toward misery to be so *difficult*. In fact, he had assumed that mass misery was the world's natural condition, and that he would only have to refrain from any more heroic interventions.

In recent months, They had become more and more critical of his work on Their behalf. Despite all the rationing and restrictions, life on Earth had become entirely too comfortable for too many people, and They held Carson to blame for it.

At first he had taken the position that he could keep people almost as upset by feeding them news stories about fictitious threats and calamities as by creating real disasters, and it was a lot more cost-effective. The Nefilim had accepted that tactic for a while, but now they were pushing for him to come up with some catastrophe that would cause widespread suffering without significantly decreasing the population. That was going to be a real challenge.

They had also begun warning him repeatedly that only if the Change went through as planned would Gilbert Carson receive his reward.

By now, Carson had few doubts that he would indeed get his reward — not the one he had been promised, but the one he deserved.

Damn! damn! damn! Was there nothing he could do to stop Them?

The gibbering terror that suddenly overwhelmed him was unbearable. Gasping for breath, he quickly injected himself with a sedative and mood elevator. He kept prefilled syringes in every room of the house for just these occasions, but it was getting harder and harder to bring his faculties back under control. White-knuckled, he gripped the edge of the marble washstand and breathed deeply while waiting for the drugs to take effect. Then he pulled himself together and rang for his attendants.

Two charming Asian beauties were immediately at his door. They draped him in soft towels, rubbed him dry and accompanied him, one on each arm, to his bedroom.

Sleeping celibately with young virgins was one way that old men had traditionally tried to slow the aging process. Carson had been spending his nights with young girls for as long as he could remember, but the celibate part was fairly recent and involuntary. He had been so mortified at first that he had slept alone for several weeks and contemplated suicide.

But now he saw the situation in a new light: He was just taking part in a time-honoured ritual to restore health and vitality.

Thank God for life's small pleasures!

Off the Grid

"Oh, my God," Mark moaned, clutching his aching head. "Great Goddess! Isis, Astarte, Diana, Demeter, Kali, Mother Mary, Jesus, Buddha and Mohammed! Where are you all when I need you now?"

Mickey chuckled by his bed, probably thinking that Mark was reacting to the announcement that Corey and Dredmore had gone back to Atlanta without him. He glared at Mickey.

"Well, hey, I'm sorry," Mickey said, in a tone that sounded anything but regretful, "but we tried and tried to get you up, and Corey has appointments to keep at work tonight."

Sunlight was streaming through the curtains. Mark's watch read 4:00 Monday afternoon.

Well, of course it was! It had already been daylight by the time he had passed out. Had all those things really happened yesterday? He kicked the ferrets off the foot of his bed and looked around for the green-haired girl who had been beside him when he drifted off, but she was nowhere in sight.

He had left his mobile phone at home. A budget model, it had an annoying tinny sound and tended to disconnect in mid-conversation.

"Where's your telephone?" he asked. "I need to call my office."

"Sorry," Mickey said, looking smug. "We don't have any phone service up here. We're in a communications dead zone. Haven't you noticed? We're not even on the Grid. Everything here runs off solar or propane."

"What? How come?"

"Mostly it's just the geography of the mountain range. But computer surveillance systems have been screening all conversations for key words and phrases since the 1970s. Even an inactive phone can be used to eavesdrop on conversations, and you don't want to know about a webcam! Who needs to worry about that stuff? My old man might get an urge to look me up someday, and I don't want to make it too easy for him to get a fix on me. I've even tried to camouflage the rooftops to confuse satellite photos."

"Your old man." Mark sat upright and stared straight ahead. "Your old man. Well, you have good reason to worry about your father, Mickey. Hell on wheels! I know who he is now, and I don't envy either of you."

"Is that so?" Mickey folded his arms and rocked back on his heels, his belly straining against the belted folds of his leopard-spotted fake-fur bathrobe. "Well, this had better be good, because nobody in this house knows that except me and Vivi and Corey. So tell me, Mark, who is my old man?"

"Gilbert Carson."

The expression on Mickey's face was gratifying to behold. He collapsed backward into a cane-seated rocking chair.

"I had another dream," Mark explained. "Or whatever they are. I had another one, Mickey, and in this one I was your father. I don't mean that I saw him in the dream — I *was* him, thinking his thoughts. I saw his face in the mirror. And either your father is stark, raving mad, or we are all in more trouble than you could even imagine."

"I might have known he'd be stirring up something," Mickey muttered. "Even at his age. What's the old bastard planning this time?"

"You're not going to believe this, let alone like it!"

"Try me."

"Mickey, your father has made some deal to turn the Earth over to extraterrestrials. Now he's having second thoughts.

They promised him physical immortality, but now he thinks they lied."

"The hell you say!" Mickey leaned forward in his chair. "You were right; I can't swallow that story. If he really was having those thoughts, most likely the old coot has just gone crazy. In a way, I'm sorry to hear that. It'll take the pleasure out of my revenge."

Mark was taken aback. "What are you trying to say? What can you do to a man who owns half the planet?"

Mickey gave a knowing little smile and said nothing.

"Be reasonable!" Mark persisted. "The man's dying anyway. And he's dying in the knowledge that he's not only sold his soul and sold his own planet, but he's never even going to collect his payment. What could you possibly do to him that would be worse than that? Your father is already living in Hell!

"You may get a chance to see for yourself soon enough. He was thinking about coming here to look you up."

Mickey got up and stood at the window, gazing out through the edge of the closed drapes, with his face concealed by their folds. His long silence gave Mark an opportunity to get dressed and comb his hair.

Then Mickey turned and said, "Okay, I'm all ears now. What's that you were saying about extraterrestrials?"

Chapter 10
Food for the Moon

Change Control

The Nefilim cluster gazed over the lunar horizon at the crescent of Earth with anticipation and appetite. Patience was a natural attribute for them, so they had no sense of hurry, even though many generations of bodies had shed their shells while this mission had been in progress.

But time had become almost a meaningless concept. Most units of their species had remained in suspended animation inside their planetoid vessel since the expedition had first left its home star so long ago. The consciousness of their genetic organism was now adapted to astronomical time, not body time.

It had been long ago, yes, but not so long that their collective memories had lost any texture. Their dying star had become a pale ember in the sky. Moving slowly from the cold, they had been forced to retreat into the centre of their hollowed-out planet, using its own material substance to warm themselves with a central sun. After even the planetary substance had run short, with the protective shell alarmingly thin, they had captured a series of asteroids for fuel.

Then the terrible decision had been made — the decision that spelled life or death for their species. One of the larger planetoids had been prepared as a vessel, and as many bodies as possible had been dehydrated and stored in a state of suspended animation. Only a few monitors remained awake to observe, and to age.

Leaving their own barren husk of a planet behind, and moving at a speed at first excruciatingly slow but continually accelerating, the Nefilim had set forth in their planetoid to seek out a new star and a new world to sustain them.

The journey had taken eons. Though the monitor units had been slowed to a fraction of their normal metabolic rate, they still had to be replaced periodically, so the Nefilim biomass was gradually diminishing. In spite of its accretion of cosmic dust and debris along the way, their planetoid starship was much too small to sustain the awakened species even for a short time.

Several star systems had been investigated, but none of their planets had proved suitable. But at last they had come to the blue-green wonder that now hung in the sky before them.

Colonizing it had not been without challenges. For one thing, another race of starfarers had already laid claim to it, seeded it with life, and nurtured this life to a level of intelligence that bordered on self-awareness.

The Nammu had issued territorial warnings in no uncertain terms, so launching a straightforward occupation had not been possible. But they had grudgingly tolerated the Nefilim's presence on the Moon, so long as they took only the small amount of Earth biomass required to sustain their monitor units. The Nefilim had even been allowed to enhance their own dangerously depleted DNA with Earth's genetic material.

But now that Earth was approaching a change of state, the Nammu had issued an ultimatum. The Nefilim were about to be evicted! And they had no intention of leaving peacefully.

They had immediately begun stockpiling more supplies for their own Awakening, aided by an Earthling traitor in a position of power. They had promised the fool Immortal Life, but his essence was far too brittle to be absorbed into the collective mind of his own kind at their time of Change.

The Nefilim did not share the Nammu's ability to regenerate individual bodies. Their own Spartan existence made this practice seem like a frivolous misuse of valuable resources.

However, they could place the human in a state of sleep that would be as good as eternal. His immobile form would be esteemed by the Nefilim forever, as the one who had facilitated their restoration.

But first that pesky Nammu Watchguard and his agents had to be put out of commission.

The Nefilim would not make any aggressive moves until the Change was well underway, for even without Nammu assistance, human beings in their pre-Change state presented a serious danger. But soon their growing population density would forcibly trigger the Change, and the new collective consciousness of the planet would awaken in one of several possible forms. Which form it took would depend largely on how much danger was sensed at the critical point.

The amorphous, multivectored hedonistic assemblage would be useless for Nefilim purposes, and having those units underfoot would be a nuisance. Even worse, their childlike qualities would elicit protective parental behaviours of the Nammu in a way the gestating individual stage had not.

So the invading Nefilim must attempt to trigger negative emotions. They needed to induce a rigid, hierarchical collective form more like themselves, devoted single-mindedly to the survival of its own genetic organism. The Nammu customarily abandoned or even aborted any planet whose intelligence accidentally took this path, which they saw as a tragic evolutionary wrong turn. But the Nefilim could co-opt that hierarchy for their own purposes by seizing control of its leader.

They intended to use that human agent to recruit others in positions of power to influence the course of the Change. If the collective organism felt sufficiently stressed and threatened, it would congeal into a stiff hierarchical structure. Any surviving humans would become perfect slaves to prepare the planet for Nefilim habitation.

The leadership levels would retain some key characteristics of the earlier developmental stage. They could easily be enticed to work for the Nefilim while imagining they worked for themselves, even despising and exploiting the very masses that they were biologically designed to protect.

Already the Nefilim had engineered a slow changeover to the native foodstuffs that they found easiest to assimilate. New expanses of desert had been prepared to receive the Nefilim's own favourite food plants, which could condense moisture from the atmospheric gases. Once the Nefilim had taken full command, it would be necessary to dramatically alter the atmosphere and climate and eliminate most of humanity. Several contingency plans had been prepared for that purpose.

But in the meantime, they needed to keep the population high enough that the new collective organism would retain its structure. It could not start over in a different form, but it could cease to function.

They had not yet managed to find the secret resting place of the chief Nammu Watchguard, but they had succeeded in draining his power sources enough to put him temporarily out of commission.

The gentle Nammu had no taste for warfare. Once the takeover had been accomplished, they would probably just quarantine the star. The Nefilim would then have millennia in which to plan their next move after this planet, too, had been sucked dry.

The Nefilim did not indulge in ruminative thought, but they did keep the circumstances of their existence constantly in the foreground of their awareness, comparing these with their needs and goals. With rustling chitin and eagerly waving antennae, the Nefilim monitors gathered hungrily in the dome to await the next vessel from Earth, bringing Food for the Moon.

The Plot Thickens

"Mark! *Mark!* Please snap out of it and talk to us!"

Mark opened his sleep-encrusted eyes the merest crack. No Nefilim were in sight, only Lana and Percy. He was back home again, safe in his own bed — or as safe as any human being could be during these times.

Percy was standing at the foot of his bed, looking worried, while Lana sat on the bed beside him, cradling his head in one hand. The stinging of his cheeks let him know that she must have just slapped him in the face with the other hand.

She handed him a cup of hot coffee, which he held in shaky hands with gratitude and some embarrassment. So they had found his secret stash, had they?

"We were so worried," Lana said, as Mark propped up in bed to drink the coffee. He hated black coffee, but this time he didn't feel like arguing the point. He needed the caffeine!

Now Lana's hand was resting on his knee. "It's taken us almost 15 minutes to wake you up. When you didn't show up for work on Monday and didn't answer your phone, I didn't know what to think. I could've used your help to talk some sense into Percy. He still hasn't recovered from Saturday night.

"Then, when you didn't come in this morning, either, and still didn't answer your phone, I called Jennifer. She told me you'd gone with her to Clayton and she'd had to leave without you, but that one of the kids had promised to take you down to the bus station when you woke up.

"We decided to come by here to make sure you were all right, and as soon as we got to your front door, we could hear you crying out in your sleep. Your landlady was standing on the porch. She was about to call the police; she said you'd been carrying on that way for almost four hours. She unlocked your door for us. Mark, what happened to you?"

"I was planning to ask you the same question," Mark said. "But I'll answer yours first.

"I just got back from a dream trip to the Moon. This time I was looking at the Earth through the eyes of some alien extraterrestrial lifeform — and a hungry one, at that. It's an insectoid hive consciousness, not even remotely human, though it has stolen some snippets of our own genetic material."

"Oh, Mark, what next? Maybe we ought to get you to a psychiatrist before these dreams get any worse. Do you think Jennifer would know how to stop them?"

"I've never thought to ask. I'm not sure I want them to stop now. They're scary as hell, but I've been learning some important stuff."

"Right," Percy said sarcastically. "About space invaders."

Mark was dismayed to see that Percy's pentagram had been replaced by a gold cross with a dark crystal in the centre — a smaller replica of the one worn by Christopher Rose. But best to take one thing at a time.

"Hold on, Percy. I know it sounds crazy, but you have no idea how real it all seemed! I don't have any words to describe this last experience. I was in the mind of something truly alien."

"Well, look, Mark," Lana said reasonably, "even if the dreams are real, why should you put yourself through this every night when there's nothing we can do about it?"

"I'm not so sure that we can't do anything. The aliens do have a human helper. They're in league with Gilbert Carson."

"Who's that?"

"Lana, I'm surprised at you! One of my first jobs as a journalist was to research the hidden powers behind the

Companies. Gilbert Carson is not their official CEO, because he'd rather have one of his stooges take the risk of getting assassinated. But he's the one pulling the strings. He controls the food and water resources of the whole world outside the Cotton Curtain, and he's the bastard responsible for imposing those plant licensing regulations on the Confederacy."

"Let's kill him!" Percy said immediately. Seeing Lana smirk, he quickly amended, "Uh, maybe we could just arrange for Christopher Rose to have a long talk with him. No soul is so far gone that…."

"Can it, Percy," Mark warned. "I'm in no mood for either preaching or assassination plots."

"Carson may be as evil as you think," Lana said, "but we can't kill him just because you had a bad dream. Even if we wanted to, he's probably guarded day and night, and we wouldn't make it far in Commie territory. It wouldn't take them long to find out that we're not chipped."

"He'll be coming to Atlanta in a few weeks," Mark said, "to negotiate with the Centre for Disease Control. And he's going to drop in to pay a surprise call on his long-lost son in Clayton."

"Isn't that the place where Jennifer took you?"

Encouraged by Mark's forbearance, Lana now had one arm draped around his shoulder. Her other hand was kneading his thigh in an over-familiar way probably intended to seem reassuring.

"You got that right." Mark shrugged off the trespassing extremities and reached to retrieve a pair of knickerbockers from the nightstand. He pulled the pants on under the covers. "By the way, Jennifer's real name is Corey, and her foster father is Gilbert Carson's bastard — though Michael Arthur will say that he's his own bastard. You'll be happy to hear that he wants me to bring you both up to meet him. He wants to ask you some questions about that revival meeting with Christopher Rose."

There! The trap was set. Let Lana get a dose of her own medicine. It would be fun to watch her and Percy trying to fend off the advances of that no-class lech.

Maybe, if they could stay sober for long enough, they could even think up some scheme to save the planet.

Percy fingered his new cross and closed his eyes reverently. "Praise the Lord," he breathed. "It's a miracle!"

Chapter 11
A Man of the Cross

We Have to Do the Change

Lord, Lord, let it be over soon. The man now known as Christopher Rose stood at the sink backstage, washing his hands. *I didn't know what I was asking for.*

How long had it been now, how many centuries? Though he had been going into the Cauldron for rejuvenation once a generation, his brain and body weren't what they used to be. He still had the outward appearance of a vigorous man in his 50s, but his next rejuvenation was long overdue. Some problem with powering up the equipment, the Kingfish had told him.

Maybe it wouldn't even be necessary. Maybe the job would soon be finished and Christopher Rose would be allowed to die in peace.

He had no desire to experience the fruits of his labour. Losing himself in a collective consciousness seemed like a fate worse than death to Christopher Rose, who surely commanded the best-developed ego on the whole planet. Four centuries of life would have seen to that, even if he had not spent most of that time in the unenviable position of Earth's foremost human Custodian.

He had lain awake nights for decades, trying to think of some alternative course of action. The Kingfish had told him about the possible developmental pathways, and given him a direct experience of each one.

He still hadn't wanted to accept the truth.

"Why must we Change?" he had raged. "Why can we not go on as we are, ever growing in wisdom and power?"

But the Kingfish had shown him that that was not an option. The life-form that ceases to develop soon begins to degenerate. If the Change did not occur when the time was ripe — if, for instance, some disaster again reduced the population below the requisite numbers — the species would try again, and yet again, each time with a less cohesive result. But in the end it would wither and die, like a fruit tree that has been pruned back too aggressively and too often.

No, best that his species go on to fulfill the destiny encoded in its genes. But its new phase would have to begin without its midwife, Christopher Rose.

The Kingfish had been disappointed by his choice. It felt that his wisdom and experience would be invaluable to the emerging World Spirit. But it had promised to respect his wishes.

Without its intervention, Christopher Rose was much too old to be absorbed into the new collective organism. He would be allowed to end his life in his own way when the time came. If he were to die before the Change began, one of the earlier Custodians-in-waiting would be resuscitated to take his place. But that unfortunate newbie would be woefully out of step with the technological advancements of the last few centuries, and would find the modern dialects incomprehensible.

If only he could consult with the Kingfish now! Rose knew that developments had been diverted from their expected course even before the Big Bang. It was probably the doing of those damned Nefilim.

The gentle Nammu had rarely encountered a species that carried its predatory nature over into the collective stage. Christopher Rose had warned the Kingfish that the Nefilim wouldn't continue to respect their warnings. His own primitive solitary mind could comprehend the Nefilim danger better than the Nammu could.

In the past, he had always been able to alert the Kingfish at once when any problems arose, but in recent years his attempts to contact the Nammu Watchguard got no response. Something had clearly gone wrong. But how could he help, when he didn't even know where the Kingfish was physically located?

His mind flashed fondly to that Jennifer child, who had lied to him for the whole time he had known her, concealing her Gifts. She was clearly a direct descendant. How had she found her way to the transition zone? If she turned out to be a Custodian, too, there could be others that he didn't know about. Perhaps if their talents were combined, they could find the Kingfish.

But with that upstart reporter now on his trail, he couldn't risk going to see Jennifer again. That was a pity; her massages had done wonders to soothe his tired old bones, with their centuries of accumulated aches and pains.

He thoughtfully fingered the huge gaudy cross that hung against his chest. The pink scar beneath it was proof that the Cauldron could not heal all wounds. The radiation burn had seared so deeply into his flesh that there hadn't been enough pigment left to regenerate.

He had fashioned that cross himself. He had fulfilled every alchemist's dream by creating gold in his own laboratory, so very long ago, using toxic quicksilver and uranium ore. He would have soon died of mercury and radiation poisoning, had the Kingfish not contacted him through the ancient crystal he'd set in its centre.

That gold cross had represented the culmination of his life's work, he'd thought then; the crystal was just a shiny trinket. Little had he known how trivial that would seem in retrospect. His real work had only just begun. But displaying that keloid scar had kept him out of slavery more than once, during those terrible years when the dark-skinned peoples were oppressed.

His congregation was out there now, awaiting him. He no longer believed the fairy stories he told to make them happy — but still, he did make them happy, and that was all that mattered. He was systematically planting the seeds of joyful collective experience, for the emotional tone of the species at the time of Change would determine which path was taken.

The Companies had inadvertently done some of his work for him by ending the petty wars and competitions that had caused hunger and suffering for so many. But the appearance of the ImmuJolt formula had been a mixed blessing. It shored up psychic defences along with the physical ones.

While the Nefilim were circling up there like vultures, it might be best to keep those defences in place. But the Change could not be postponed indefinitely. When the time came, he would do what must be done.

In the meantime, the show must go on!

Rose fluffed up his grey-and-copper Afro, sprayed it with a product that would fluoresce under the stage lights to create a halo effect, and stepped forth to address his flock.

He Knows When You Are Sleeping

"Well, yes, I did get sucked into it for the evening, and it was a wonderful experience. For the first time in my life, I felt like I totally belonged, like I had finally come home. It caught me so off guard that I would have followed Christopher Rose without question for as long as it lasted. Unfortunately, when I woke up on Monday morning, I was back to normal."

Lana concluded her story and puffed on a hand-rolled tobacco cigarette, while Mark and Percy glared with disapproval.

"Amazing!" Mickey exclaimed. He was sober this weekend, but that wasn't the only thing he found amazing. "Even without the belief system, you were caught up in the group mind on your first exposure."

"Yes, but without the belief system it didn't stick. My family were nonreligious; Percy was brought up in the Church."

Uneasily, the others gathered around the spool table in Mickey's kitchen shifted their eyes to Percy, who was smiling beatifically and stroking the two ferrets on his lap.

"Yes," Percy confirmed. "I have always believed, and I was blessed."

"And blissed," Lana observed.

"The Kingdom of Heaven is at hand for those who have eyes to see."

"In one evening," Mickey marveled. "You say this happened to him in one evening! Even the Moonies used to spend several days indoctrinating new members."

"Well," Mark ventured, "Percy probably didn't present much of a challenge. He never was what you'd call an intellectual."

"The Mind is the Great Tempter," Percy recited.

"Percy," Mark said with exasperation, "I have explained to you that Christopher Rose himself doesn't believe that bullshit. He just says it to make people happy because, for some reason, if people stay happy we are all safer from those Bugs on the Moon."

"Right," Percy retorted, "Bugs on the Moon. And you sit there making fun of *my* beliefs!"

"Enough!" Mickey ordered. "Mark, I don't know what to believe at this point. But after this latest dream of yours, I think the fastest way to find out would be to go straight to the source. We need to shanghai Christopher Rose for questioning."

Corey was shocked. "Kidnap the Reverend? Mickey, I won't stand for it!"

"Figure of speech. We just need to have a long talk with the gentleman, so we have to somehow persuade him to see us. Mark has already failed at his attempt to get an interview, but supposing we just happen to be in a back room at Valhalla when the Reverend has his next appointment with you...."

"He won't be back," Corey said sadly. "He used to come twice a week without fail, unless he was out of town on tour. But since that first night when Mark and I met him on the Astral Plane, he hasn't been in to see me once. He didn't even call to cancel his standing appointments." She looked accusingly at Mark. "Christopher Rose was one of my favourite clients. Such a gentle, wise old man, and carrying so much pain! I did what I could for his body, but his spirit always eluded me."

"He never talked to you?" Mickey asked.

"Oh, yes, he talked — but never about himself. He wouldn't even tell me how he got that scar. He made up some story about being 'touched by the Lord.'

"I think he gets his pleasure by helping others, because he used ask about my problems. By the time I met him, my own life was in pretty good shape, so I used to make up stories so he could offer me advice. Then after a while he stopped asking, and just told me about the places he'd been and people he'd known before the Commies and Corpses took over."

"Well, one thing's sure," Mickey declared. "I'm never going to set foot in the door at one of those revival meetings.

"Wait, I've got another idea! Corey, I know you take videos of all your sessions. You haven't ever shown me any with Christopher Rose, but you must still have them somewhere."

"What? You take videos of your clients?" Mark was outraged.

"Mickey suggested that I start doing it," Corey explained, "for my own protection. That way I'd have something to hold over the politicians in case I ever get into any legal trouble. Also, the videos help me to improve my massage techniques and teach the new girls how to handle clients. Anyhow—" she suppressed a smile "—Mickey likes to watch them."

Mark felt a wave of nausea, mortified to think of Mickey voyeuring at the intimate session that had changed his life. His distress must have shown on his face.

"Don't worry," Corey assured him quickly. "He hasn't seen yours. Mickey likes the kinky ones, and I usually let the other girls handle clients like that."

"Well, then," Mickey said, getting up to pace back and forth across the kitchen floor, rubbing his palms together in anticipation, "we'll copy some scenes of you with Christopher Rose, editing out your face. And then we'll send that video to the Reverend, along with our request for an appointment."

"I don't like the sound of this," Corey said. "Christopher Rose has been a good client. It wouldn't be right to betray his trust. Anyhow, he's a powerful man and we could get hurt."

"But Corey, we have to talk to that man! If even half of what Mark has been dreaming is true, we need to find out immediately. Haven't you ever seen any of those alien beings yourself, when you visit this place you call the Astral Plane?"

Corey shook her head unhappily. "I never go very far down the side paths. They look so dark and scary, and the farther you go, the weirder they get. I usually just go to the central chamber and wait for instructions."

"Instructions from what?"

"I don't know. There's a big crystal in the chamber that communicates with me through my own crystal." She touched her medallion, and Mark noticed that the stone in its centre resembled the one in Christopher Rose's cross. He couldn't identify it, however.

"Words and pictures form in my mind," Corey continued. "I can tell they're not my own. Sometimes they are riddles that I can't understand, but most of the messages are pretty simple: 'Go there; buy this; do that; say such-and-such to so-and-so.'

"It always seems to work out for the best, so I just go along with it. I don't need to be in the central chamber if the message isn't too complicated. I can hear it wherever I happen to be.

"But when I ask questions myself, I don't always get any answers. It may be some kind of computerized navigation device that has only a few instructions programmed into it. I don't think it's conscious the way we are, yet it's been a good guide for me. I used to think it was my Guardian Angel. Now I don't know what to think. But I still trust it, because it's always given good advice.

"I told Mickey about a dream it sent me once, and he invented ImmuJolt. It told me to go into the massage business, and I've been happy and successful doing that. I don't know what I'd do if it stopped talking to me at this point. I've come to depend on it. So if Christopher Rose does have anything to do with it, I don't want him mad at me.

"Mickey, I won't let you have those videos! In fact, I'm going to delete them as soon as I get home."

"Oh, Corey — please, Coretta, do it for me," Mickey begged shamelessly, kneeling by her side and taking her hands between his own. "Please, Corey. It's so important!"

Corey sighed and rolled her eyes. "Mickey, you're wasting your time with that act. You can't have those videos." She pulled her hands away from him. "However, I will try to contact Christopher Rose myself and ask him to give you an appointment."

Mickey leaped to his feet. "Hot diggety, now we're cookin'! C'mon, mama, let's party!"

He flicked on the stereo, filling the house with foot-stomping Zydeco music, and yanked Lana up from her chair.

Lana was primly dressed in a lacy white cotton frock and a straw hat with daisies. Mickey himself wore nothing but a bath towel, over which his belly shook lewdly. Lana hesitated and cast a worried glance at Viviangela, who had been doing the dishes and was now leaning against the counter with her arms folded and a frown on her face.

"You might as well go ahead and humour him," Viviangela told her. "He won't give you any peace until he gets his way." She turned around and resumed her task at the sink.

Mickey and Lana proceeded to entertain the group with their own unique and vigorous style of Dirty Dancing. Mark watched the mismatched couple with a mixture of amusement and incredulity. Soon he felt the green-haired girl tugging hopefully at his hand and allowed her to lead him away to her room.

From time to time throughout the rest of the afternoon and evening, he could hear music punctuated by cries of pleasure echoing through the house from distant corners.

Chapter 12
Songs of Whales and Kokopelli

Interspecies Romance

Joy of the meadows! Joy of the sea!
Joy of the winged ones, flying and free!
Love for the four-footed, walking on the ground,
Love for the two-footed, dancing round and round,
Love for the fins and the feathers and fur
And Pachamama's green garment —
Sing praises to Her!

Around and around and around until the Universe merged into a sky of concentric circles, and the two merged belly to belly and were One, and the sets of two made a great circle and were One, and the circle of Two-Foots on the shore linked spirits with the circle of finned ones, and this double circle looped to infinity, leaping higher and higher into the great Void above the waters, pausing in midair for a moment of quivering ecstasy, and then came the splashdown, rousing senses to fresher peaks anew....

Dear brothers and sisters of land and water!

Cetacean voices crooned erotic rhapsodies for their lovers, while cruder human tones echoed and amplified their rapture. Being of one Soul and one Spirit, the Two-Foots sought the Beloved beyond their own species, and this tender courtship promised to be the overture of a lasting passion.

The Morning After

"Mark, you have less cause to be jealous than any man I know," Mickey declared unsympathetically, looking like the cat that ate the canary. "An interspecies orgy! Romance on a grand scale! That's something I've fantasized about all my life, and now it turns up in one of your dreams."

Mickey sat at the breakfast table, still wearing only his bath towel, his massive thighs straddling the thatched seat of his wooden chair. Viviangela was perched on one knee and Lana on the other, their faces the very picture of contentment, with their arms intertwined behind Mickey's head as he waxed eloquent.

"Just lucky, I guess," Mark growled, carefully averting his eyes from Percy and Corey, who sat thigh-to-thigh on the other side of the spool-table. Percy was swooning before her worshipfully, oblivious to the fact that Corey's own attitude seemed more maternal than romantic.

Mark could hardly stand it. He could bring himself to show only the barest minimum of courtesy to his green-haired companion of the night before. To his relief, she seemed to have no further interest in him, either, and was now aiming her flirtations at Dredmore.

Oh, Jennifer — oh, Corey, how could you? When you could have had **me**?

Mark could not conceive of any Universe in which Percy would have more sex appeal than himself. Yet, here was the evidence for all to see. He hadn't been so miserable since his dog died.

Mickey was rambling happily on about the merits of orgies for cetaceans and humans alike.

Mark abruptly pushed himself away from the table, ran back to bed, and pulled the covers over his head. It was worth a try — perhaps if he could sleep and awaken one more time, this too would prove to have been only a dream!

Biker Chick

A few hours later, Mark was startled awake by the sound of a noisy engine. He peered through the curtains in disbelief. There in the driveway was a huge motorcycle, a veritable tank on two wheels. And by the sound of it, it was not powered by methanol, hydrogen or electricity; no, the monster actually burned gasoline! Not only that, but it was cruising around without a muffler. Were all the traffic cops on holiday, or what?

He watched the two riders dismount. One was a beautiful blond woman. The second was a gnomish little Native American man, short and stooped. That explained it, then — the Confederate Indian Nations were subject to a different set of laws, even when it came to road traffic.

The gnome liberated a duffel bag from the back of his bike and slung it over his shoulder as he hobbled toward the drawbridge. Viviangela went dashing out into the yard to greet him.

Mark remembered where he had seen this man before: in the waiting room at Valhalla! Another mystery could be explained now. This occasion might make it worthwhile rejoining the human race temporarily.

The ferrets had stolen his socks while he slept. He ran a comb through his hair and then, as nonchalantly as he could manage, ambled barefoot into the kitchen.

He was just in time to see the gnome reach into his bag and take out a ruffled and disgruntled-looking chicken. It was a handsome bird, deep black with golden hackles and saddles, and a single bright blue sickle feather highlighting its tail. It fluffed itself up, preened its shoulders, strutted around a few steps, and then lowered its head and charged straight at the nearest ferret. Its target happened to be Mickey's favourite, a blackfooted creature by name of Grizzell Greedigut.

A brief but noisy skirmish ensued, until Mickey grabbed the broom to separate the two animals. The unfortunate ferret, its coat puffed up to twice its normal size, hurtled to the top of a bookcase, from which it clattered its displeasure.

The chicken paced back and forth beneath it, dragging its wingtips and keening ominously. Then it alighted on the back of a chair and let out a ragged but triumphant crow.

"Damn it, Koko," Mickey complained. "How many times have I told you to keep that killer chicken away from my ferrets?"

"Ain't she somethin'?" Koko acknowledged admiringly. "Her daddy was the finest fightin' cock in Oklahoma. Pellucidar was bred straight from a line that my great-granddaddy smuggled in from Burma after World War II. Illegal as hell — her ancestors are all extinct by now, so of course she's not on the list of Patent Approved Lifeforms.

"What St. Money has done to chickens is pitiful to behold, Mickey. Most of the ones on the market now will grow up deformed unless you feed 'em some brand-name scratch mix. They're lazy as lizards and almost as stupid. But not this baby — she'll eat anything that don't eat her first! It's the fightin' blood that makes her such a good layer, too. She lays an egg for me almost every day.

"Pellucidar is a good ol' bird. She sleeps at the foot of my bed every night, and when we're on the road, she stays right by my side, inside my sleeping bag. If she hears anything messin' around outside our camp, she sounds the alarm. This bird goes everywhere I do, and that's that! She's the best friend I've got. Look here how much she trusts me."

Koko scooped up the chicken, turned her upside down in his lap, and began stroking her throat. The hen lay still as death, feet in the air and neck outstretched beneath his fingers.

The blonde didn't seem offended to be playing second fiddle to a chicken, but Mickey hooted with derision.

"I'll bet she shits on your bed, too — I don't care what her pedigree is, Pellucidar's still a chicken. I don't want her making a mess in my kitchen and terrorizing my ferrets. She is not spending the night in this house! I want you to put her outside right now."

"Yeah, so your alligator can eat her? The hell I will! Who are you to be criticizing my chicken? You sleep with ferrets yourself."

"Oh, Mickey," Viviangela said reproachfully. "Do you have to fight with my brother every time he comes to see us?"

"Hey," Mickey said apologetically, "it's not that you're not welcome here, Koko. In fact, I am deeply grateful for all the risks you have taken on our behalf, and I want you to feel free to stop in any time you feel like it. But can't you put that bird in a cage or something?"

"How would you like to be put in a cage? She's already spent several hours inside my bag on the way up here."

Mickey shook his head ruefully. "Pellucidar may be a good layer, but she's still the meanest biker chick in the state of Georgia! Here, Koko, have a beer."

What's in a Name?

The gathering mellowed out after Koko accepted the beer. He took off his shoes and shirt and settled into a chair near the stove. Mark politely refrained from commenting on the mosaic of tattoos that extended from shoulder to shoulder across both his back and chest, drawing attention to the little man's spinal deformity — but Percy was a stranger to such tact.

"Man, oh, man," he said admiringly, "what great tattoo work! Where can I get one like that?"

Koko smiled. "No way you can, pal. This tattoo goes along with my special song that I got when I was initiated into the Confederate Indian Nations."

"I didn't get any song," Mickey observed resentfully.

"What do you care? You and Vivi don't even use the names they gave you."

"We sure as hell don't — not after I found out they mean Big Head and Long-Suffering Woman!"

"Hey, that ain't my fault. Everybody gets a name that matches their own character. And likewise, it ain't my fault they don't have enough songs to go around. We're lucky any of 'em survived at all. It's only fair that the natural-born, full-blooded Indians should get the ones we do have."

Koko hastened on apologetically, "I don't mean to say we don't consider you a full member of the C.I.N., but you still ain't Indigenous by birth. There ain't even enough songs for all of us. My sister didn't get one either, did you, Vivi?"

Viviangela shook her head in agreement.

"What's so special about those songs?" Percy persisted.

"They carry the history and folklore of our people. Most of the tribes in this part of the Confederacy were marched to Oklahoma on the Trail of Tears. Any folks that stayed behind had to pass for White and teach their kids to do the same. For the sake of survival, we lost our language and most of our tribal history. Our way of life had been just as advanced as the Whites, maybe more, but the settlers wanted our land. Never thought there might be a fortune in oil and uranium under the ground out in Oklahoma! But by the time folks got settled there, most of the elders had already died.

"Over a century ago, several different tribes got together at the Ghost Dance and tried to piece together what knowledge they'd been able to save. But it was already getting hard to tell how a lot of the stories and customs had started out. Some of 'em had been mixed up with Bible stories from the missionaries, or the teachings from other tribes.

"That's why I went to Oklahoma for my Initiation. They did a better job of keeping the teachings and traditions than the ones that stayed behind here. We're still finding old burial mounds in Georgia and Alabama based on stories told by the tribes in Oklahoma.

"By the time the Second Civil War was over and the tribes had banded together to form the Confederate Indian Nations, our history was just like the Tower of Babel. The New Age Wannabes had taken it and run with it. Cherokee lore got mixed in with the Celts, Islam and Tibetan Buddhism, and some bands were even claiming to be the Lost Tribe of Israel.

"Somewhere along the way, my own song got translated into English, so I can't even be sure which tribe it used to belong to, let alone how to sing it in the original language. But that don't matter now. From here on, the C.I.N. are sworn to stand together as one tribe and one nation."

"How does your song go? Will you play it for us?" Percy requested.

Koko took out his pennywhistle and played an eerie melody, while Mickey and Vivi accompanied him on bongo drums and guitar, and Mark valiantly rattled a tin of dried beans.

The others continued to mark the time after Koko had laid his whistle down and begun to chant:

"He sleeps, he sleeps, he dreams inside the stone,
The Old One, the Keeper who watches the seed,
Who watches the changes, the ice come and gone,
Who watches our people and knows what we need.
The Earth will grow barren, the animals die;
The trees will be slaughtered, the rivers run dry.
Then the Dreamer will waken when seasons are ripe.
He'll rise from the waters and send out his Call.
From every direction, of every type,
Our people will gather, one family, all!
The Dreamer bears gifts from the finned ones above,
And the Earth will grow green with rejoicing and love."

Proprietary Rights

"Somebody must have mistranslated that last part about the finned-ones above," Percy said. "We don't have any flying fish in these parts. But something about that song really grabs me. How do those words go again? *He sleeps, he sleeps…"*

"Stop!" ordered Koko. "That is *my* song. No one else may sing it."

"Well, I'm sorry! I didn't mean any offence by it. Do you mind if I look at your tattoos again?" Koko obligingly rotated his torso to afford a better view.

"Oh, yeah, I see now. This round thing here right over your hump—" Percy stopped, reddened, and then rushed on with embarrassment "—must be the stone, and this tadpole thing here in the middle must be the Sleeper. But what are all these other lines and dots?"

"Nobody remembers," Koko said sadly. "It may be some kind of map."

"How wonderful to be the bearer of such an old tradition," Lana said admiringly. "Could you sing it for us one more time?"

As Koko complied, Lana sat on the floor and leaned her head against Mickey's knee. Compared to Koko and the blonde, those two no longer seemed like such an unlikely pair. Nevertheless, Mark still had it in him to be surprised when the green-haired girl abandoned Dredmore and started making eyes at the misshapen little Indian. She cooed with delight when he reached into his bag and presented her with an embroidered scarf.

A reminder bell sounded in the back of Mark's mind. Tomorrow would be a workday! In fact, today was supposed to have been one, too. And here sat the staff members of *The Third Speckled Bird*, getting soused in questionable company, not even reachable by mobile phone, with nary a thought of work in their heads.

A couple of weeks ago, Mark would have been sorely troubled by this observation. By now, he felt only mild curiosity to note this odd turn of events.

But he did spring to attention when Koko reached inside his bag again and began pulling out little paper packets of contraband seeds. Seed-smuggling across the Cotton Curtain was one of the few crimes still taken seriously. St. Money's private security goons often didn't leave offenders alive long enough to stand trial.

Chapter 13
A Rose by Any Other Name

Sharing Spirits

Christopher Rose was visible through the open door as the small party arrived at his office, located at the end of a long corridor in the back of the Druid Hills Afro-Pentecostal Church. Though they knew Corey had already spoken with him, they had been surprised that the Reverend had agreed to meet with them on Wednesday, the same day Mark called to set up the appointment.

Dredmore had made a breakneck drive to Clayton to pick up Mickey, and found him still coming down from his mushroom trip of the night before. But he had sobered up enough to accompany Mark and Percy to the church after they'd finished work at the *Bird*. Lana was evading the meeting by working late, and Corey and Dredmore were just beginning their own work hours at Valhalla.

No receptionist had intercepted the visitors as they entered the church through unlocked doors and found their own way to the sanctum sanctorum at the rear, almost half an hour early.

Wearing an ankle-length gold-and-brown dashiki, Christopher Rose stood looking out the window. A small, tasteful Moving Picture based on an African savannah hung over his desk, and a portable stereo was playing Baroque chamber music at high volume. He appeared to be unaware of their presence.

The party paused awkwardly at the doorway. Then Mickey raised both palms and gestured for silence. His footsteps on the carpeted floor were inaudible as he mischievously tiptoed up behind Christopher Rose and laid a heavy hand square on the Reverend's shoulder.

Showing no startle reflex, with the smooth, fluid motion of a martial arts master, the Reverend wheeled around to embrace Mickey. His eyes were half-closed and a beatific smile spread across his face as he rested his chin atop Mickey's head. With the fingers of one hand, he beckoned the others to step closer. Mark and Percy warily approached the other two in front of the heavy wooden desk.

That's mahogany under that glass, Mark thought. *Must be an antique.* Even the Companies didn't tolerate rainforest imports anymore.

Released from the embrace at last, though the Reverend kept one arm draped over his shoulder, Mickey turned sheepishly to face the others. There were tears in his eyes and goosebumps on his hairy forearms. He and Rose had the postures of a small boy and his father coming back from a ball game.

The Reverend reached for his zapper and lowered the stereo volume to a pleasant background level.

"My son, I don't know who you are," he said in a soft baritone voice, "but you are obviously one of my own kindred."

Mark was relieved to see that Mickey wasn't so swept away that he let this statement go unchallenged.

"Ah... I don't think so," Mickey protested mildly.

The Reverend chuckled. He walked to a cabinet behind his desk and opened one of its doors. "You all look like you could use a good stiff drink!"

He uncorked an unlabelled large bottle of clear liquid and poured shot-glasses for them all.

"Now, do be careful," he warned. "This is vintage pre-Bang whiskey that one of my staff smuggled down all the way from

Hyder, Alaska. It's 190-proof — almost twice as strong as the stuff you're used to drinking."

"We're not used to drinking whiskey," Percy said weakly.

"Well, then, so much the better! No, no — don't drink it yet; you'll need a chaser."

Rose stepped into an adjoining room and filled some drinking glasses from a pitcher in the fridge. He distributed the sets of small and large glasses to the group, and raised his own shot-glass in a toast.

Percy's face wore an expression of religious ecstasy at the honour of taking communion with his idol at such close range. Mark was less enthusiastic. This whole scenario had uncomfortable overtones of his own first encounter with Mickey. It was clear what was about to happen, and Mark knew that he would not be among the finalists in any drinking contest.

"Be careful," the Reverend continued. "The secret is to get it down in one gulp so that it won't burn your mouth. Let's drink to the good fortune of our fair planet — Gaia, Mother Earth, Pachamama! Now that Corporations have the legal rights of Personhood, shouldn't we grant the same to Her?"

He downed his own drink quickly, and the others followed his example. Immediately, Mark and Percy were sputtering and coughing in their haste to quench their burning mouths with cold water.

But Mickey proved equal to the challenge. His eyes twinkling, he swished the alcohol back and forth over his gums, finally tilting his head back to let it trickle down his throat.

"Ahhh!" he exhaled gustily. "Mighty good mouthwash."

The Reverend refilled their glasses. "As I said, my boy," he repeated proudly, "you are one of my own."

Guiltily, Mark disposed of his own second drink into a large potted plant, palming the shot-glass to conceal its emptiness. He mimicked drinking along with the others, and then the Reverend filled the glasses a third time. Percy was beginning to lose his balance.

One more toast followed, and Mark again doused the unfortunate plant. Percy clasped his hands over his mouth and dashed off down the hallway in search of a washroom. He was clearly out of the action.

The Reverend and Mickey beamed at each other in satisfaction. Then they both looked suspiciously at Mark. He flushed.

"Young man," the Reverend said sternly, "I hope you will be willing to replace that Amaryllis."

Mark grinned. "No problem. Better it than me!"

"Well, then!" Having proved his point, the Reverend poured one more round for himself and Mickey and put away the bottle, now almost empty. "Let's step out back, shall we, and conduct this discussion in the gazebo under that sugar magnolia."

Alchemical Revisioning

Mark and Mickey followed Christopher Rose through a sliding glass door out into the courtyard and sat side-by-side in one of the double-seated gliders inside the gazebo, while the Reverend sat facing them. A cool breeze blew across their faces, scented of roses.

Mark noticed Percy hunched over and throwing up on the grass near the hedge. The glider's motion soon made Mark feel queasy, too, though he'd swallowed only a few spoonfuls of the Hyder brew. But he was determined not to be dealt out of the action after all he'd been through.

The Reverend stretched out his feet toward them, put his hands behind his head, and opened the discussion.

"Jennifer said that you had an urgent message for me." He looked at Mark. "I suppose I should have known I'd be hearing from you again."

"The Nefilim are getting ready to strike," Mark said boldly. Given the man's dark complexion, it could have been an optical illusion, but Mark could have sworn he saw the Reverend blanch.

"How much do you know about the Nefilim?" Rose asked him quietly.

"They're a hive consciousness. Their home star burned out eons ago. Most of their species are still in suspended animation inside the Moon. They need a new planet, and now they want the Earth. They can't invade it yet; they have to wait for the Change. But they're getting impatient."

Christopher Rose sighed — an old, tired sigh.

"I know there may be other Custodians, but I have never met one. In all these years, you are the first people I've met who could help me shoulder this burden. Oh, I did try a few times to share what I know, but the results have always been ... unfortunate. I stopped trying long ago."

"Just how old are you?" Mickey asked.

"The Kingfish — that's my own name for the amphibious Nammu Watchguard who looks after this planet — first contacted me in 1615," Rose replied. "I was an up-and-coming European alchemist named Johann Andreae. I didn't know that I was dying of the toxins produced by my own experiments; I thought I was on my way to fame and fortune. The Kingfish set me straight and directed me to a hidden cavern where I slept in a vat of gel until my body was repaired, except for the scar under this pendant. It's the same size and shape, but it's a replica; the original was dangerously radioactive.

"Later he wanted me to travel to the New World. I thought he must be mad! In those days, most Blacks in the New World lived in abject slavery, so what could I possibly accomplish? But he kept insisting until I finally agreed. I did owe my life to that creature, and I regarded him as almost supernatural.

"Children, those first few decades were pure hell. I never fell into slavery myself, but I had to witness such terrible things and live in such fear! For much of that time I hid out among the Native Americans.

"Eventually I became courier for some of the Founding Fathers, and the Kingfish advised me as to how to sway their thinking at the critical moments. But despite all my best efforts, it was only a few generations before Civil War broke out. I had tried to swing Northern opinion toward purchasing all the Southern slaves instead of fighting a war. Slavery wasn't the only issue, but most of the old Southern economy had been based on it, so they were determined to defend it.

"The Nefilim were already laying the groundwork for Company takeover, but I didn't realize yet that they even existed. The Kingfish was saving that piece of information for later.

"After the War, I was heartsick when conditions went from bad to worse for the first half-century. I took refuge in the nearest Cauldron, where I was finally allowed to meet the Kingfish face to face. And my first sight of that good creature filled me with loathing! It had the appearance of an amphibious horror that sickened the gut.

"I vowed to retire as Human Custodian, and I went down to Louisiana to live with a community of former slaves who had been adopted by a local Indian tribe. On my first trip to New Orleans, I met the Voodoo Queen, Marie LaVeau. She was already an old woman by then, but she still had all her magick! Marie was the only woman I ever met who came close to understanding me and accepting my story.

"I was getting so old and arthritic myself that I started to rethink my decision to accept a natural human life and death. You have no idea how unpleasant it was to be a mature adult in the world before dentistry!

"I contacted the Kingfish again and begged him to take Marie into the Cauldron and rejuvenate us both. But he told me she didn't have the right bloodline. The Nammu rejuvenation techniques only work on people who carry certain genes introduced into our species through a member of the French royalty. I trace my own ancestry back to King Solomon of Ethiopia, but some Merovingian blood must have crept in, or I couldn't be in this position. There was a time during the Renaissance when Blacks and Whites mixed as equals, and I am grateful to have lived long enough to see those times return.

"Yes," Rose concluded serenely, "I have lived long enough. I am so glad to meet you today, my son! When I can speak with the Kingfish again, I am going to ask him to accept you as my replacement. Lordy, lordy! Nobody knows how weary I am."

"What are you saying?" Mickey demanded. "Are you expecting me to get up there and preach to that bunch of idiots? No way in hell!"

"No, no," Rose soothed him. "That won't be necessary. The preaching is just something I do to amuse myself in a constructive way while I wait for further instructions. The congregation's simple joy helps to raise the emotional tone of the planet, and that will help to ensure that the Change takes a favourable course."

"Well, Michael Arthur doesn't take orders from anybody, human or space alien!"

The Reverend smiled fondly. "Forgive me, son, I don't mean to mock you — it's just like seeing my younger self all over again. Michael, did you say? Goodness gracious, we haven't even been properly introduced."

"Mickey. My friends call me Mickey. And this is Mark."

"Well, don't worry, Mickey, I'm not going to force you into anything. In fact, I am deeply concerned that something may have happened to my Nammu friend; I haven't been able to contact him for years. We could get by without him if those Nefilim weren't hovering around, but if what you say is true, Mark, our situation could be serious indeed. Just how did you come by your information, young man?"

"I… travel… to different places in my sleep. I become different people and see things through their eyes. I'm sure some of the places I've been don't really exist on Earth at this time." Mark described some of his night visions.

"You're right," Rose agreed when he was done. "You appear to be visiting alternative futures. The Change will be a critical time for our planet. We could become some version of either the Nazis or the Happy Blob. Forgive me if I can't sound too enthusiastic over either of those alternatives.

"But if anything happens to prevent the Change altogether, that would lead to the slow degeneration of our species and of the planet as a whole. Pachamama has her own program for development, and the day of the individual is almost done."

The Reverend hurled his shot-glass against a lamppost, shattering it.

"We don't have to just roll over and accept those choices," Mickey began excitedly. "We may be able to work out some way to let the rest of the world go through its Change while we save ourselves out from the process."

Christopher Rose looked at him with sad, bleary eyes. "Perhaps we could," he said. "But is that the way you want to spend the rest of your long, long life? On the outside looking in?"

"We could leave the Earth entirely! We could get the Nammu to take us to the stars."

"Somehow I fail to see how that would solve the problem. We'd just be on the outside looking in at a completely different species."

"Sure it would, Reverend! As soon as I sober up, I'm going to prove it to you."

Now that Mickey was feeling the full effects of his whiskey, Rose seemed to recognize that it would be pointless to argue with him.

"Can you help us find the Kingfish?" he asked Mark.

"Isn't he at that place you call the Cauldron?"

"There are Cauldrons at several concealed locations around the planet, but there is only one Kingfish. He intended to summon others as the time of Change approached. But I have only seen him once, and that Cauldron was at a Ground Zero site during the Big Bang. He may have been killed — but I don't think so. When I returned, the Cauldron itself was still intact, but most of the equipment had been moved out.

"The Kingfish occasionally commandeers weaker people, like your young friend throwing up over there, to perform manual tasks, and then substitutes a screen memory to account for the missing time. He can use many people in that way, but he can only communicate with people like us."

Mark noted that the word "us" had been directed at Mickey, and apparently did not include himself.

"Well, Jennifer has some connection with him, too," Mark offered. "Why don't we do a triangulation with dowsing rods?"

The Reverend leapt out of his swing, pulled Mark to his feet, and embraced him. "Brilliant idea, young man!" he exclaimed. "That is definitely worth a try. I have to lead another revival meeting this evening, but I'll talk to Jennifer about getting together later in the week."

"Wouldn't it work better if we took the readings from places several miles apart?"

"He's right," Mickey declared. "Jennifer is our most talented dowser, and she can do hers from Clayton. Unless this Kingfish keeps moving around a lot, one person might even be able to take all the readings in sequence."

"We'd probably get better accuracy if several dowsers take several readings from different locations. My son, we may be onto something big!"

Now ignoring Mark, Christopher Rose continued to address his comments to Mickey:

"Say, I wonder if you would step into my basement. I have a fabulous ancient variety of tomato plant in my hydroponic system; the tiny fruit is golden and divided into sections like an orange. Never thought I'd live to see those traits come around again! You know, people used to be afraid to eat tomatoes."

Leaning on each other for support, Christopher Rose and Mickey wobbled back toward the church, while Mark, as now seemed his destiny, brought up the rear.

Chapter 14
An Evening of Quiet Felony

Time on His Hands

A couple of relatively uneventful weeks had passed.

Mark sat on an overturned bucket amid the fabulous hydroponics that lined the walls of the subterranean level of the Druid Hills Afro-Pentecostal Church. He was using a small wooden scoop to transfer kudzu seeds from a large burlap bag to small paper packets.

Also at the task, in a small circle around the bag, sat Lana, Percy, Dredmore and Koko, on whose knee dozed a contented Pellucidar, her head tucked under a wing. From a nearby armchair, Christopher Rose pored over a map and beamed his approval on the operation.

"It sure was nice of you and Mickey to help me get this seed project going," he said appreciatively.

"Hey, no problem," Koko said. "You're the one helping us out now. We've been trying for years to figure out how to get these crops started in the Sahel. Dredmore was gonna try to make something happen through his Rasta friends over in Ethiopia."

"Yeah," Dredmore said. "The Commies gave special permission for Sunfest to be held in Addis Ababa next year. Rastas there are sort of like the Confederate Indian Nations here; they got their own thing going and don't respect no outside authority. I expect the Commies are scared of getting an *Obeah* hex put on them, 'cause they don't bother the Rastas too much, long as they keep up the ganja production and don't play no political music in public places.

"The Rastas are more free to travel than most folks, 'cause the Commies think they're usin' us as intelligence agents. But it's them that's bein' used by us. You oughta hear some o' the stories that get told!" Dredmore chuckled.

"But this here seed-smugglin' is a dangerous business. I'd sure hate to get my friends over there involved in somethin' that could bring the Commies down on their whole tribe. I like it better the way you've got it planned, Chris."

The Reverend Rose smiled with pleasure to hear himself addressed with such friendly familiarity. "Yes, I do believe this strategy will be for the best. The Church has an extensive underground network all over the planet. Even after the resettlement massacres, the population in Africa is too scattered for the Commies to keep track of everyone. Some tribes are so isolated they don't even receive ImmuJolt allotments, and still have to provide their own food and housing.

"Not long before the Big Bang, there was a movement underway to re-green the Sahel using water from the underground rivers and aquifers. They'd made a good start at a Green Belt, but that work was interrupted before much could be accomplished. But the old solar-powered irrigation pumps were sturdily built and designed to be repaired with locally sourced, low-tech components. With luck, many could be put back into operation.

"All we have to do is to use some small drones to scatter these seeds over a wide enough area at times when they'll receive enough rainfall to get them started, and Mother Earth will take care of the rest. The desert will bloom again. This kudzu is capable of changing the entire ecosystem, the entire climate."

"Sounds dangerous to me," Percy said. "What about the ecosystem already there? Kudzu can get out of control fast, and it doesn't even take carbon dioxide out of the air; it makes more of it."

"Son, not much is still living in those desert areas anyway. Old rock paintings showed people swimming, but in recent decades it's become so hot and dry and barren that the sands are almost sterile even of microbial life. The only plant life left is around the oases, and many of those varieties originated in other parts of the world.

"But the soil in the Sahel is still fertile. It was a lush and green place once, so it can become one again. This kudzu has been crossed with hops, so it won't increase the carbon dioxide levels, and it can go a long way toward reclaiming the deserts. You know how you can feel the temperature drop and humidity rise when you walk past a vacant lot here in Atlanta? If just one small patch of kudzu can do that, think of the impact of hundreds of square miles! Once we get it established, it will just keep on spreading, changing the climate as it goes."

"Not only that," Dredmore told Percy, "but it's useful, too. Already we're making biofuel and fabric from it. Every part is nutritious. The Japanese use it to thicken soups, and as medicine to make the blood more alkaline. You can weave the vines into baskets, or braid them to make furniture. You can feed it to your livestock, or chop it up and use it for fertilizer or compost. It's a nitrogen-fixer that enriches the soil just by growing there."

"What if it won't grow?" Percy asked, changing his concerns like a true pessimist.

The Reverend laughed. "Can anybody here tell this young man the formula for growing kudzu?"

Dredmore grinned. "If the ground be covered with concrete or pavement, you got to find a little crack to drop the seed into. Then you jump back quick before you get hit in the eye!"

"It could become a problem when the time comes to get rid of it," Lana mused. "Kudzu can smother out huge oak trees. It can destroy old houses and even whole forests."

"No problem in Africa," Dredmore assured her. "Growing conditions are less favourable there, and there are more wild grazing animals. A lot of people still keep goats and cattle. All you have to do is tether a goat, or put a fence around it, and it'll clear the kudzu out of an area in no time. A goat will eat it right down to the root."

Koko scowled. "Brother Rose, I have a feeling our friend Mickey didn't tell you the other part of his plan."

The Reverend raised his eyebrow. "Oh? Is there more?"

"What we have here is not just ordinary genetically modified kudzu crossed with hops. Mickey has developed a strain that's responsive to electrical impulses."

"Is that so? I remember reading about some research being done on that before the Big Bang."

"Once it's all growing the way we want it, it's going to become the relay transmitter for a worldwide broadcast system. We'll be able to jam the whole Commie communication network."

"Not to mention our own," Dredmore added. "But we figure the Confederacy can get by without it longer than they can."

"Dear me." The Reverend rubbed his chin thoughtfully. He did not look particularly alarmed. "Mickey didn't inform me of this detail. I wonder if it will work? The Africans might not appreciate that part of his plan. They do love their mobile phones."

"Most likely it will work," Dredmore assured him. "Mickey knows his science."

"But does he see the implications of organic communication circuitry? Children, you can't imagine the hours of human labour that go into making one of those little gadgets you use so casually." Christopher Rose gestured to the digital watch and calculator that Percy wore on his wrist.

"Shall I give you an idea how much? In spite of all our grievances, the Confederacy still imports most of these gadgets from the Companies instead of making them here ourselves. It's not just that the rare minerals are found mostly in Africa. The whole Congo has been torn apart to bring us the coltan that goes into mobile phone batteries, and it requires slave labour to turn out electronic products at a price people can afford. We used to think technology would mean that machines and robots would do all the work, but just as often it means that people have to work like machines."

"I take it that you don't wear digital watches, then," Percy said.

The Reverend reached into his trousers and pulled out a pocket watch.

"I've had this timepiece for a century and a half, and it's still ticking away. But if something does break, I'll need to have the replacement parts made by hand. These days it's almost impossible to find a watchmaker, whether blind or sighted."

Chapter 15
Father and Child Reunion

Remedial Studies

The next few weeks passed for Mark as in a dream. Corey was making an effort to fulfill her promise to pass on her knowledge. He had been camping out at Valhalla almost every weeknight. While Corey was busy with her clients in another part of the studio, she sometimes had him read for her into a recorder. For most purposes, she relied on text-to-voice software or handheld talking scanner pens, but these didn't do well with handwritten correspondence or journals.

Between appointments, Corey and Dredmore instructed him in the arts of breath control, martial arts and Ericksonian hypnosis. Mark was also encouraged to practice massage on any unassigned staff members. They appeared delighted to advise him on the special ways of pleasuring a woman through touch — but he had been chagrined to discover his ignorance. He'd never stayed long enough with any woman to master her unique sexual operating instructions, which were often so different that each female might have belonged to a different species.

With Corey's mentoring and weeks of practice, he had finally learned to fold his legs into the Lotus pose, and she even allowed him to wear her own medallion during meditation. He kept hoping to start receiving messages through it, but so far that hadn't happened. Mark treasured the time spent with Corey during these teaching sessions, but nothing that he'd been learning or observing at Valhalla fell within the realms of the paranormal.

He cringed to recall that he had never taken any interest in the lost arts of dowsing or table-rapping when his own Granny had entertained the rest of his family with sessions that they'd all treated as rainy-day parlour tricks. Her dowsing rods had never found any oil or water reserves, but they could zero in on lost metal objects. She could easily coax any heavy dining table to balance on one leg, waltz across the room, or rap out answers to simple questions. The table dispensed no higher wisdom than you'd expect from a piece of wood, but it was like the proverbial singing pig: the marvel was not that it was done well, but that it was done at all.

But no one had ever bothered to capture one of those sessions on film or video. Even when a handful of visiting rocket scientists had seemed mightily impressed, the simple country folk magic passed down by little old white ladies from the foothills of Appalachia hadn't much interested their modern grandchildren. Younger generations wanted their own Magick to be accompanied by transcendental Altered States!

Mark was popular enough with the ladies at Valhalla, but Corey herself had had no further sexual contact with him — nor with Percy, which Mark found some small consolation. She assured them both that they had a special place in her heart, and that she would love them always — as a sister. But if they wanted to spend more quality time in her presence, they would have to start behaving more like men and less like puppies.

They got the message. Mark pushed his passion down into the deepest, most hidden chamber of his heart. There it throbbed away so painfully that at times he wanted to double over in agony and could barely stand erect.

Their group Circle ceremonies had defaulted to new leadership, but somehow the team of three still managed to get *The Third Speckled Bird* published on schedule, even if its quality wasn't up to their old standards.

Lana and Percy had begun spending much of their free time in the church basement with Christopher Rose, helping with his various projects to undermine the Companies, distribute illicit heritage food plants to the far corners of the globe, and incite goodwill and high spirits among the masses. Percy was still firmly convinced that Rose was, if not the New Messiah, at least His Prophet, albeit perhaps an unwitting one.

Mark had once approached Rose about the possibility of a Magickal Apprenticeship, but the Reverend had turned down the suggestion in no uncertain terms. He said that anyone without the natural Gift might cause untold harm by blundering around on the Probability Plane. It would be like trying to take part in a rough ball game when you couldn't see the ball.

Partly because of this warning, and partly at the urging of Percy and Lana, who feared he was heading toward a nervous breakdown, Mark had adopted the habit of casting a protective Circle around his bed each night. His troubling dream excursions into Alternate Realities had almost ceased.

On most weekends the three *Bird* staff members drove the *Hummingbird* up to Clayton. They had solved the overcrowding problem by clearing out the small storage compartment behind the front seats and were now taking turns huddled up in it uncomfortably during the trip.

Mickey and Viviangela had started teaching them the secrets of computer piracy, as well as the techniques for modifying ordinary artwork and videos into Moving Pictures. They made a point of always incorporating a few subliminal suggestions, either to encourage the viewer to buy the next art disc, or to incite sabotage of Company systems.

Lana was allowed to perform a scarf dance for one such art-loop. The image was altered until her human form was unrecognizable, with only the colours and patterns of motion remaining. Mickey then merged that image with an equally indecipherable movement sequence derived from an orgy that he had recorded earlier. The resultant abstract was completely tasteful, yet so pleasingly erotic that Corey decided to test-drive the program in the Luxury Room at Valhalla. Lana herself had even managed to program a passable art disc, a simple Nature loop of fractal ferns with matching music.

Mickey had kicked out all five of his original adolescent house-guests shortly after the visit from Koko. He said he had gotten up one night for a drink of water and found them out in the yard performing some kind of perfectly synchronized wildling mime ritual.

"I can't help it," he said sadly, when Mark asked what had happened to his young green-haired friend. "I know it's irrational, but that stuff just gives me the creeps. I won't allow it on my property. Don't worry, those kids will be okay — they all know how to fend for themselves now."

The following weekend, Corey presented Mickey with two big-eyed waifs who had shown up at Valhalla in search of employment. It was love at first sight, and Lana was displaced from his knee for a time. She privately confided to Mark that she was glad of the opportunity to have Viviangela all to herself.

Vivi was teaching Lana how to work with modelling clay, and Lana had started schlepping around wearing a tattered kerchief and filthy overalls. She had stopped wearing makeup and painting her nails. In fact, she had cut her fingernails off, right down to the quick. "They get in my way," she explained.

Mark was privately appalled by the physical transformation in this woman who had been such a masterpiece of fashion art. But she seemed so much happier that he couldn't bring himself to criticize her appearance, even after she started showing up at the office in this unkempt condition. They rarely had any drop-in visitors, and most of her interviews and sales work could be done by phone or electronic mail.

By unanimous consent, the ***Bird*** offices were now closed on Mondays instead of Saturdays, so that the staff members could time their Clayton visits to coincide with those of Corey and Dredmore.

Mark realized that this magic carpet ride on other people's karma could not go on forever, but he pushed that thought to the back of his mind. Experiencing so many changes in such rapid succession had cut him loose from the moorings of his old Reality.

Frustrated as he was over his failure to win Corey's heart, he remained caught up in the new land of wonder and mystery that she had laid open to him. Despite his initial resistance and all evidence to the contrary, Mark had fallen under the hypnotic spell of Mickey's boastful self-confidence and his attitude of being Emperor of a Universe in which ordinary rules did not apply. So the next turn of events caught them all by surprise.

Bridging the Generation Gap

Dredmore and Percy were attending a special Sunday morning service with Christopher Rose in Atlanta, where Corey's shapeshifting was meant to be the star attraction. So only Mark and Lana were present at Mickey's house when the unmarked black helicopter came down.

Mark had almost forgotten the dangers facing them, but Mickey had had his automatic weaponry at ready for weeks. He had also been holding regular emergency response drills and target practice sessions. The two new youngsters thought it was great sport to be playing with things that go ***bang!***

First the helicopter circled the house, hovering near each of the towers as though trying to spy in the windows. Viviangela and Lana had been busy in the Third Tower making a statue of Pandora, and Lana used a slingshot to send a big wad of clay out an open window toward the copter. It splatted against the windshield. The single passenger, a wizened little old man, shook his fist and shouted something unintelligible.

There wasn't a lot of open ground area inside the moat, so the copter was forced to land outside it, crushing ornamental flowers and sending dirt and plant debris flying in all directions. The drawbridge had been drawn partway up by the time the two occupants had disembarked.

With Grizzell Greedigut perched on his shoulder, Mickey stood just barely outside the doorway. Behind him, inside the house but fully visible, his two young protégées stood holding shotguns and looking much too eager to shoot something.

From each of the three towers, Mark, Lana and Viviangela now aimed a military assault weapon through narrow, metal-reinforced slats in the walls. Bullet-proof plates had been hurriedly lowered to close off the main windows.

The helicopter pilot and the old man exchanged uncomfortable glances. They appeared to be armed only with small Citizen Handguns — the kind the New Libertarian Democrats handed out free to people who lacked the initiative to master any weapon more demanding. But Gilbert Carson also had a long, narrow carrying case strapped over one shoulder.

"What can I do for you?" Mickey boomed courteously from the doorway, with his voice electronically amplified.

"Mickey, my son!" cried the old man, throwing his arms wide and staggering a bit from his unbalanced load. "Don't you recognize me? It's your father!"

"Father?" repeated Mickey in a puzzled tone. "There must be some mistake. I have no father."

"Goddamn it, you impertinent ingrate, this is Gilbert Carson, the source of your livelihood. If you don't allow me to come in and talk to you, I am not only going to discontinue your annual allowance, but I am going to have you prosecuted for transferring funds out of my bank accounts."

"I am wounded to the core that you would think me capable of such a thing. I don't suppose you can mention one piece of hard evidence that could be used against me in a Court of Law?"

"Evidence? We have videos of those young computer pirates you sent down to Atlanta, taken right at the public terminals while they were punching out their instructions."

"That doesn't sound like me at all," Mickey noted.

"We traced them back to the Clayton bus depot!"

"Well, now, that does narrow it down a bit. What is the population of Clayton, do you suppose? How many people pass through the town every year? These mountains do attract their share of tourist traffic."

"Mickey, don't play games with me. We know those kids were living with you."

"Well, then, perhaps you should come in and take a look around, just to satisfy yourself that no one of that description is on the premises. Of course, I do take in lodgers from time to time, but I don't keep in touch with most of them after they've gone on their way, and I certainly won't be held responsible for anything they do after they leave here."

"Put down the damned drawbridge so I can see for myself!"

"I'll be happy to oblige. But first, I would like you both to put down your guns and leave them on the other side of the moat."

"Dammit, Mickey, a man has a right to bear arms!"

"In public, yes. Here in the Confederacy, it's our civic duty. But in my own house, I make the rules. Do you want to come in, or not? What's that thing you have on your back?"

"For God's sake, Mickey, have some pity on your old father! I'm bringing you a present!"

"Hmmph! Okay, that can come over with you. But please put the guns down where I can see them, at least a hundred feet from the drawbridge."

Scowling, the visitors complied with his request.

Mickey went to lower the bridge himself, since his young companions found the cumbersome pulley-and-crank apparatus hard to operate. He put on a show of struggling with it, taking longer than necessary. No sooner had the visitors crossed over than he began to raise it again.

Carson was sputtering with indignation.

"What's your problem?" Mickey asked mildly. "You said you wanted to come inside."

"You'll pay for this, you rapscallion!" But the old man's voice held a hint of fatherly pride, as he and the pilot strode toward the house.

"Uh-uh!" Mickey ordered. "Your friend stays there by the bridge. Kids, you keep your guns on him. Carson, you can come inside, but I don't want you bringing reinforcements."

"You must have taken your Boy Scout training to heart, Mickey. I've never met anyone more prepared for guests."

"Let's just say that this visit was not entirely unexpected," Mickey told him, and grinned at the old man's horrified expression. "Oh, yes, I have my own intelligence network; never think I don't. Well, you can come on in now."

He called upstairs: "You-all might as well come down here and join the fun! But keep your weapons with you."

Then, mercifully, he turned off the voice amplifier.

Beware of Creeps Bearing Gifts

After leaving his "gift" just inside the doorway, Gilbert Carson was taken on a more-or-less complete tour of the household, bypassing only sensitive areas such as the munitions closet, seedling flats and the root cellar with its emergency escape tunnels. He expressed effusive admiration for the statuary and Moving Pictures.

Eventually, Mickey began to affect a show of cordiality. He offered his father some homemade ginger beer, and even sent a bottle outside to the helicopter pilot sweltering in the sun.

Carson took a seat by the spool table and began to wax sentimental under the influence of alcohol.

"Mickey, son, I know I haven't been the best father to you, and you may have reason to feel bitter toward me. But I have come to realize some important things late in life, and one of those things is the loss it has been to me to have had so many offspring, and yet never to have had a real family.

"As you must know, Mickey, I'm approaching the last years of my life, and if I haven't chosen an heir, your shiftless half-brothers and -sisters are going to be battling it out in Court for so long that most of my estate will end up in the hands of the lawyers. They've been groomed for this moment all their lives; I'm well aware that their mothers refused to terminate the pregnancies in hope of someday laying hands on my fortune. Well, so far as I'm concerned, they have no right to it. I've always provided them with enough to meet their needs.

"Mickey, you're an arrogant man, and a scheming man, and a lazy man, and even a violent man, but you are not a greedy man. That puts you way ahead of the others in my book. I have experienced first-hand the consequences of greed, and I will suffer my regrets until the day I die. Since you have expressed absolutely no interest in my fortune, and since I believe you to be the one most capable of managing it, I am offering to train you as my successor."

Mickey stared at his father, dumbfounded.

"Now, that is the damndest thing I've ever heard," he said finally. "I'm sorry, old man. Some people call me an egomaniac, but I've never had any desire to rule the world. I just like to control my own immediate surroundings, and what you see here inside this moat is all that I feel up to handling."

Carson seemed unsurprised by these words.

"I would like for you to take a few days to think over my offer. As a token of my trust in your abilities, I am passing on to you the most prized object in my possession." He retrieved the long narrow carrying case from the doorway and presented it to Mickey, held formally with both hands. "Please, open it now."

It was amateurishly made of plain unfinished wood, secured only by a buckle and three hinges — not at all the way you'd expect a rich man to transport a valuable object. Mickey took it by one end and looked at it suspiciously, shaking it and rotating it in his hands. At last he sat down, balanced the case on his knees, opened the latch and peeked inside it.

Then, as if it had contained a cobra, he leapt to his feet, causing the carrying case with its contents to fall to the floor and his chair to topple over behind him. The ferret Grizzell Greedigut ran for cover. Mickey's fists clenched and unclenched repeatedly.

"How dare you try to do this to me, old man! *How dare you!*"

Carson's surprise was comical.

"But— but— you must not understand." He bent down with arthritic difficulty and picked up the case, lowering himself to a seat and laying it open on the big spool that served as a table. It was lined with blue velvet padding that cushioned a spear. "I remember how taken you were with that Samurai sword I gave you when you were a teenager, and this spear is infinitely more valuable. It is a very ancient historical object."

With both hands, he lifted out the spear reverently for all to see. Its shaft was made of sturdy new wood, but the point and base were obviously very old. In fact, they seemed to have been broken and then repaired and reinforced with a crisscross of fine wires of gold, silver and copper. Between the two halves of the blade, a nail was wired into place.

"Do you take me for a fool?" Mickey ranted. "I've seen pictures of the Spear of Longimus. It has passed through the hands of dozens of tyrants down through history. Adolf Hitler was obsessed with it! I'm not a superstitious man, but this thing must be filthy with bad karma. I should have known you would have stolen it as soon as the Commies came to power."

"I did not steal this spear, Mickey. I bought the museum."

Collateral Damage

"Well, you may have bought the museum, but you can't buy me! I don't think much of the way you and your Commies have been running things, and if you're expecting me to step in now to clean up your mess, you've got another think coming. How far do you think I'd get before one of your rivals had me killed? And if they didn't, the Nefilim would."

Gilbert Carson sprang to his feet in tipsy terror. "How did you find out about the Nefilim?"

"I know a lot of things you don't think I know, old man. And let me tell you, out of all the human beings on the face of the Earth, the Secret Chief of the Commies and Corpses is the last person in a position to stop them now. You should have thought of that before you made your bargain. The Nefilim own you, body and soul. Now that they've reneged on their part of the agreement, I guess you're hoping they'll let you weasel out of your contract and spend your last years in peace if you hand your first-born son, which is probably *me*, over to them to take your place. You've got a lot of nerve!"

By now Mickey was bellowing at full volume, six inches away from the face of his cowering father.

Gilbert Carson retrieved his spear, popped back into the case and scurried to the door.

"You won't get away with this," he hissed between his teeth. "A son should show some respect for his father! I was only trying to help you."

He halted in the doorway and appeared to notice for the first time a pen-and-ink sketch of Corey hanging on the adjacent wall.

"Who is this woman?" he asked suddenly.

Mickey smiled in self-indulgent fantasy. "My best lady-friend," he replied smugly.

Carson hastened out of the house almost as though this last piece of information had been the most frightening of all. He stopped at the edge of the lifted drawbridge and stared down at the alligator in the moat.

Mickey stood in the doorway with his arms folded. "Going somewhere?" he chuckled.

The old man was literally dancing in his fury.

"Oh, all right, if you feel that way about it," Mickey said. Slow as molasses, he began to lower the drawbridge, stopping it a couple of times in mid-air to pretend the rusty mechanism had got stuck. Finally he halted the bridge about three feet above the far bank.

"Oh, shucks," he lamented. "That's as far down as I can get her. Guess you'll have to jump!"

As though on cue, Grizzell Greedigut jumped from the windowsill back onto Mickey's shoulder.

Hurling imprecations in seven languages, Gilbert Carson followed his pilot (who was trying hard not to laugh) back over the bridge, allowing the younger man to lift him down on the far side. They picked up the handguns they had left on the ground.

"Hey, you forgot something."

Mickey hurled the spear case across the moat. It landed at Carson's feet, popped open, and the spear bounced out onto the ground. As Carson bent to gather up his desecrated treasure, Mickey waved to him cheerfully.

"Y'all come back, now!"

Gilbert Carson's face was a study in rage and impotence. With surprising strength and a grimace that was dreadful to behold, he hurled the spear straight down into the moat.

Then he snatched out his handgun and, like the trained marksman he still was, took aim and fired. With a shriek of pain, Grizzell Greedigut fell off Mickey's shoulder and lay twitching in the dust, with half his head missing.

Kneeling beside the ferret, the blood-spattered Mickey gave a long wordless wail of grief and horror.

"Kill him!" he yelled to the others. "Shoot the bastard now! Don't let him get away."

The visitors went racing back to their helicopter, with Carson making remarkably good time for such an old man. Mickey's command was answered only by a couple of stray shots from the family newcomers, clearly aimed to frighten rather than kill. Much as they disliked Carson, nobody else was willing to kill a man or down a helicopter to avenge a ferret. If the truth be known, the spoiled and ill-mannered Grizzell

Greedigut was not a popular member of the household, and no one but Mickey would be sad to have him gone.

When he realized that nobody else was going to open fire on Carson, Mickey raced for the armoured tank. While the pilot was starting up the helicopter, Mickey clawed his way through the foliage to its interior.

The tank's engine sputtered reluctantly to life. The huge gun-barrel creaked as it rotated through the vines, and opened fire just as the copter was lifting off. The sound of shattering glass echoed back from the mountainsides, but the copter did not falter in its flight and was soon out of sight behind the tall oaks and pines that surrounded the homestead's small clearing.

Mickey got out of the tank and went back to gather up Grizzell Greedigut for a ferret funeral.

The Short Arm of the Law

Mickey was turning under the last spadeful of dirt while the others, trying to look sad, stood in a semi-circle holding pails of marble pebbles to lay over the tiny grave, when a police car pulled up in the driveway.

The very picture of hospitality, Mickey fully lowered the drawbridge and strode across to greet the officer.

"What brings you here today, Sergeant Johnson?"

The young policeman shuffled his toes in the dust and looked sheepish. "I hate to disturb you, Mr. Arthur, but our department just got a call from Gilbert Carson...."

"You don't say? He was just up here and shot one of my ferrets. Isn't there some law against coming onto other people's property and killing their animals?"

"Of course there is. Do you want to press charges?"

"I haven't decided yet. I have plenty of witnesses."

"I don't doubt that you could win your case in a fair court of law, but it might cost you a lot to pursue it. Carson could drag it out for a long time."

"Hmmph! So what did the old geezer have to say for himself?"

"I'm sorry, Mr. Arthur — he reported some unauthorized greenery on your premises. Specifically, sunflowers and smoking cannabis. I have the search warrant right here."

"I can't deny it; there they are." Mickey gestured to the South side of the house.

The cop walked over to inspect the offending vegetables.

"Goodness gracious! You do have a green thumb, don't you, Mr. Arthur?"

"Not really; it just takes some attention and hard work." Mickey did not mention that he had done little of that work himself.

"Never seen better," the cop said, admiringly. "I really hate to do harm to these fine plants, but I'm sure you recognize the position we're in."

"No problem, no problem, I understand completely. If you don't mind, though, I'd rather do the honours myself. We don't want any herbicide spray on the premises; we garden organically."

With the same shovel used to bury the ferret, Mickey quickly and efficiently dug up the offending greenery, making sure to keep a large ball of dirt attached to the roots of each plant. Then he went into the woodshed and returned with several large cardboard boxes, into which he stacked the plants carefully.

"There you go, officer. These ought to keep long enough for you to get them back to the station-house, where you can make sure your boys *destroy* them properly."

Mickey wheeled the plants to the police car in a child's wagon and placed them carefully into the trunk. The young cop beamed with pleasure at this unexpected gift.

"Uh, Mister? I just want to make sure.... You do keep up your bust insurance with the KKK, don't you? I'm afraid we're going to have to slap you with a fine."

"No problem, no problem; I'm fully insured and it'll be taken care of. I hope this Carson fellow hasn't been causing any problems for your boys."

"Well, Mr. Arthur, now that you bring it up, I do get a bad feeling about that man. First he wanted to charge you with attempted murder, but when he explained the circumstances, I told him that in my opinion you had just been standing your ground and protecting your property.

"Then he wanted to charge you with unauthorized possession of military equipment, but I told him you had bought that stuff at a surplus auction right here in town, and all your permits were up to date. So finally he settled on a complaint about the plants here. But I don't think he's done with you yet, not by a long shot. And if he ever takes a mind to go after you with the big guns, I don't know if we can do anything to help you.

"We don't like the man any better than you do, and we respect the fine work you're doing to uphold the values of the Confederacy with your Victory Gardens—" the officer nodded toward the plants "—but we can't offer you much protection against somebody like Gilbert Carson, and neither can the KKK. He's got too much money and power on his side.

"So if I was you, I'd play it safe for a while. If you've got any other contraband lying around, or any, ah, questionable hobbies that could be taken the wrong way, I'd suggest you get rid of 'em right quick — you know what I'm saying? No telling what his next move is going to be."

"I see what you're getting at, officer, and I do appreciate those words of wisdom."

"You can pay your fine at the Courthouse next time you're down in town, and they'll give you a receipt. Have a nice day."

Mickey waved cordially as the police car drove off. Then he wiped his sweating forehead and sighed in relief. The wooded acreage in back of the house was liberally peppered with every shade-tolerant illegal perennial that Koko had been able to procure for him since his marriage to Viviangela.

"Tomorrow," he said, "you kids had better plant us some more decoys."

Oedipal Alligator Blues

By the time Corey, Dredmore and Percy arrived around sundown, the tension in the house was palpable. Mark had remained in the background during the events of the day, not daring to draw attention to himself. Everybody else also did their best to stay out of Mickey's way. He was still alternately moping over the loss of his favourite ferret and raging over the effrontery of his father.

To add to his disturbance, he had noticed a few inches of the spear handle protruding upward from the centre of the moat near the drawbridge, and had discovered that the alligator Kundabuffer was missing. Apparently Carson had claimed two casualties, and the reptile had stayed under the water to die. No one had attempted to retrieve the body yet; one burial a day was enough.

"Oh, Mickey," Corey said, when she entered the house and saw his face. "What happened?"

Just outside the open door, her dogs sniffed nervously around the little mound of marble stones covering the ferret burial site. She whistled a warning to prevent them from digging up the carcass.

Corey and Dredmore listened with quiet sympathy while Mickey recounted his recent traumas.

Percy was more vocal in his support. "I think you had the right idea, Mickey. The first time I heard about Mark's dream, I told him that old man needed killing!"

"Nobody knows that better than I do," Mickey agreed. "But still and all, what can I do? Much as I don't like to claim him, Gilbert Carson *is* my father. I think that's why I missed him with the tank artillery, even at such close range. What would it do to a man's insides to kill his own father?"

Trying to take his mind off the subject, Corey said, "Speaking of old men, I had a really weird old guy show up at Valhalla a few days ago. He's been coming back almost every night since then. He always gives me a huge tip, and he leaves a chauffeur in a big black limousine waiting outside during his session. Some folks think our car is extravagant, but this one is bigger than some street shelters.

"I feel uneasy about that man; I can tell he's carrying some terrible secret. I may not accept any more appointments with him, because he's turning into a real hassle. He isn't satisfied to have me massage him. He's no longer capable of getting off sexually, but he still keeps pestering me to let him 'do something for me.' Faking orgasm is not my style, so I told him straight out that he would just be wasting his time, because I've never had a sexual climax in my whole life.

"Well, would you believe it, that just got him more turned on! In fact, he offered me a king's ransom to come and live with him. Of course I turned him down, but I wish I could understand his motivations. If I thought I could help him, I'd keep trying, but seeing somebody like that takes a lot out of me. After every session with him, I've had to go meditate and take a shower before I felt clean enough to see another client. The last time he came by, I told him I might have to stop working with him, and that I would give him my decision the next time he called. Some of my other girls would be happy to put on a sex show for the tips, but he's got his mind set on me. I feel almost like I'm being stalked.

"This may sound like a silly thing to worry about, but I pride myself on my ability to work with all my clients in a compassionate and constructive way. I can even handle clinical sociopaths who have a black hole where their heart's supposed to be. It's been a long time since I came across somebody who just creeped me out."

If she and the others had been less agitated, Corey would have never indulged in such a long monologue without monitoring the response from her audience. But her emotions had finally wound down enough for her to notice the expressions on the faces turned her way.

"Why are you all looking at me like that? — *Oh, shit!*"

"It's him!" Mickey said. "It's got to be him."

"The Nefilim were planning to send him to Atlanta," Mark recalled. "He probably had to charter a helicopter to drop in on us here."

"Corey," Mickey said, "think very hard. I want you to give me a complete physical description of that man."

"I can do better than that," Corey said. She reached into her handbag. "I brought you this video of his last session. I was hoping you could help me figure out what his problem is."

Mickey snatched up the video and popped it into his viewer. A few seconds later, he was leaning forward and shouting, his face livid:

"It is him! *It's him!* Corey, do you know who that man is? You've been seeing my father!" He seemed almost on the verge of apoplexy.

Outnumbered

"Good grief, Mickey," Corey said, "calm down! What are you getting so worked up about? We're not blood relatives, and your father is just another client to me. I don't even like the man."

"Good!" Mickey said. "I'm glad you don't like him, because I forbid you to see him again. Do you hear me? I absolutely forbid it!"

Corey stared at him in astonishment. "Mickey, get a grip! Since when do you get to tell me what I can and can't do?"

"I mean it, Corey; I'm serious. That man is dangerous. I'm telling you for your own good: Don't ever see him again."

"Now, hold on just a minute. If he is Gilbert Carson, then I do need to see him. We need to find out as much as we can. If I can get him to tell me how he's getting supplies to the Nefilim, we may be able to figure out some way to stop them. At the very least, I might be able to influence Carson to ease up on some of his administrative policies in a way that could benefit the whole Confederacy, as well as all the lands beyond the Cotton Curtain."

Mickey rolled his eyes skyward. "And people say *I* have a big ego! Coretta, please be reasonable. That man is nothing but trouble. Whatever he has in mind for you, nothing good can come of it. I want you to stay away from him."

"Mickey, it sounds to me like you're just jealous. I'm sorry I am not as susceptible to your charms as others are, but you should realize that your father can offer me nothing sexually.

He can't even get it up anymore! Whatever decision I make about him will be for my own good reasons — and it will be *my* decision, not yours."

"Goddamn it, Corey," Mickey began, lunging toward her. An instant later, Corey had thrown him flat on his back. Her dogs stood over him, growling.

"Don't you ever try to lay hands on me like that again," Corey said. "When are you going to learn that it doesn't pay to treat people that way? Come on, Dredmore, let's go back to Atlanta."

She grabbed her handbag, whistled to her dogs, and headed out the door.

Dredmore paused to stand over Mickey's prostrate form. "Bloodclot, mon, you oughta know by now you can't pull that shit with Corey!"

"Get out of here!" Mickey commanded savagely. ***"Get out right now!"***

"Well!" commented Viviangela from the sidelines, as the door slammed shut. "I guess you told them."

Mickey began another lunge in her direction, but Lana cracked her bullwhip in front of him.

"Uh-uh," she said quietly. "You don't get to hit Viviangela while I'm around."

Lana stood her ground grimly, clutching her bullwhip, while Mickey kicked a hole in the plywood door and then put his fist through an interior wall.

"You and Percy might as well take the *Hummingbird* back to Atlanta," she told Mark. "It looks like I'm going to be needed here in Clayton for the next few days."

Chapter 16
Abduction

Moon Shots

Gilbert Carson paced the floor in rage, overlooking the city below from his hotel suite high in the Glass Towers. This was the last straw! He'd had enough mistreatment from all concerned. With his courage bolstered by a cocktail of pharmaceuticals, he reached his decision.

But first he would deal with those damned lying Nefilim! He couldn't get out of his mind something that girl Jennifer had said, about how lucky he must feel to have the power to do some real good in the world.

He was soon on the phone to his Director of Corporate Security. He used only the lowest priority scrambler and decoder circuit, to avoid alerting outside attention to the conversation.

"Sir?" the man said incredulously. "The *Moon*, sir?"

"Yes, God damn it, the Moon!"

Carson knew the Director had been selected for his position partly because his personality profile had shown him to be unlikely to obey stupidly destructive orders, no matter who issued them. Even the Companies did not want to risk a repetition of the Big Bang.

Yet, in light of all the space debris floating around out there, some sort of space military capability had to be maintained. Astronomers had briefed Carson thoroughly about the likelihood of meteor collisions with the Earth within the next couple of centuries. They could be of such magnitude that even Earth's ruling elite might not be safe within their deep underground hideaways or orbiting space stations.

Similar fears may have motivated the apparently senseless rush during the late 20th Century to develop the "Star Wars" technology, useless for defending against international foes, but possibly helpful for deflecting incoming meteors if they could be detected early enough.

But there was no need to make things needlessly difficult by telling the public the truth. Most people were happier to believe that all nations' capacity for nuclear warfare had been completely dismantled. Fortunately for the future of humanity, there were no human colonies on the Moon yet, so the Director could probably be bullied into obedience.

"This is Top Secret," Carson hissed. "Under the Rainbow!" That was the verbal code to convey authority to carry out a directive immediately, without waiting for the customary approval of the Board.

"But, sir — to bomb the *Moon?*"

"The dark side only. We have no stations there yet. Five years ago, I handed you a sealed Black Box. I want you to open it now. The combination is 23-dash-M-O-O-N-X. It contains a map of the dark-side lunar surface. Everywhere there's an X, I want a bomb detonated, the most powerful ones we have. Is that clear?"

"Yes, sir, but—"

"Please, Director. This is deadly serious. You must not delay. Enemy forces are already setting up lunar bases. If we don't act at once, it could be too late."

"Enemies? Surely not the Confederates...."

"Worse than that!" Gilbert Carson reached for a convincing lie. He knew that the truth would only convince the Director of his insanity. "The Nazis are back! They've been operating out of secret underground bases in Ecuador all this time, and now they're preparing to take over our entire planet. They've even infiltrated the Companies' own Board of Directors."

"Oh, my God! Then we should also target Ecuador."

"No, no, their Earth bases are still poorly equipped and unarmed. They have moved their base of operations to the Moon and will be launching their attacks from there. There isn't a moment to spare!"

"Yes, sir, I shall give the orders at once."

"Please use the auxiliary computer power system and run the necessary programs yourself. Do not involve another person if you can avoid it, and do not, I repeat, *do not* interface with the Grid in any way."

"Understood."

"Thank you, Director. May God be with you, and with us all!"

"And to you also, sir."

Carson could hear the despair in the other man's voice, and he heaved a sigh of relief as he broke the connection. There were times when the powers of a dictator came in handy. He had summoned the last vestiges of his humanity in this tardy attempt to repair some of the damage he had done.

But that internal battle had laid waste to his spirit, and his brief flare of integrity had already burned itself out. His next impulse was born of pure selfishness.

He leafed through a translated reproduction of an old text on Alchemy. He'd been studying the topic for decades. He had not wanted to accept the conclusions it led him toward, but by now he had no doubt as to what had to be done. The procedure would be difficult and distasteful on many levels, but his very life was at stake. Such an opportunity might never come his way again.

Jennifer was the only woman he'd ever met who could provide enough life force to revitalize his own. He would have that energy, come hell or high water. Preparations had been completed several days ago, and now he must act before the Nefilim learned that he had betrayed them.

But he still had a little time to spare. Rapid response had been another convenient military fiction. Even with computer calculations and robot technology, nuclear missiles with interplanetary capacity were cumbersome things that would take several hours to mobilize, aim and launch. In the meantime, he needed to cleanse himself first.

Speaking of high water, rationing was for the Little People; the rich could easily afford the surcharges! Gilbert Carson ran himself a hot steaming tub, added some bubble-bath and Epsom salts, and eased his creaking old body into the suds.

Emergency

Mark's eyes popped open. The room was still in total darkness. It was now in the wee hours of Wednesday morning. His mind traced over the outlines of this latest peek into someone else's Reality, and he felt an urge to vomit.

Immediately following the dispute at Mickey's on Sunday night, he and Percy had beat a quick retreat back to Atlanta in the *Hummingbird*, leaving Lana in Clayton to protect Viviangela.

Mark had been so shaken up by the day's events that he had neglected to cast his protective Circle on Sunday night after his return, but nothing untoward had happened. On Monday afternoon, he had phoned Corey to find out if she could shed any light on the domestic violence of the day before.

She assured him that hot-tempered rows were an everyday occurrence in Mickey's household. It was just that over the last few weeks, Mark and his friends and his night visions had created a more peaceful diversion from their usual conflicts. True, it had been years since Mickey had tried to get heavy-handed with her, but the poor man was stressed out from the encounters with his father and the cops, and the death of his beloved pets.

"Don't worry," she told Mark. "The next time we see them, it'll probably be like nothing ever happened. I've decided not to have any more sessions with his father, anyhow; that man gives me the creeps. Usually I can see through surface personality problems and character defects, and heal some of the hurt that caused them. But with Carson, I can't find much to work with."

Mark had spent most of Monday putting his home and yard in order, and then gone for a workout at the Breeches & Cutlass Club. By now his garden was a lost cause, since he had neglected to mulch it earlier in the Spring while there was still moisture in the soil. He was startled to realize how long it had been since he had spent so many hours at a stretch in his own sadly neglected home.

Monday night, almost as an act of faith, Mark had again slept soundly without the protective Circle.

On Tuesday, he and Percy had put in several extra hours at the *Bird*, since they were performing Lana's tasks as well as their own. Mark was so tired at the end of the evening that he had omitted his usual stop-off at Valhalla and headed straight home. This time it hadn't even occurred to him to cast a protective Circle — and now his carelessness had been rewarded by another nauseating trip into the mind of Gilbert Carson. Between the two evils, Mark preferred the Nefilim. At least they were loyal to their own kind, in accordance with their nature.

He made a dash to the bathroom in time to throw up. Then he splashed cold water over his face, wiped it down with a towel, and spent a few minutes getting himself together. It was about 3:00 a.m. Wednesday morning — too early to get up, but he dared not go back to sleep after what had just happened.

His mind cringed away from further memories of the slimy inner world of Gilbert Carson, but he knew they needed every bit of information he could dredge up. Bracing himself with a cup of hot coffee, he sat down to relive the dream sequence and jot down notes before he forgot. He hardly moved for almost half an hour. When he came to the end of replaying Carson's ruminations, he flipped back into his own Reality with a shock.

He'd better warn Corey right away, no matter what ungodly hour of the morning it was. He dashed across the room and, as he was reaching for his telephone, it rang. Dredmore's voice sounded shaky and far away:

"Mark, we need your help bad. I've just been shot, Corey's been kidnapped, and Christopher Rose is lying here dead. I've already called for an ambulance, but I need you and Percy to get over here as fast as you can and try to do some damage control. This place is a mess."

Over the phone, Mark could hear the sound of approaching sirens. Thinking as fast as he could, he called Percy, who lived only a couple of blocks away from Valhalla and could get there faster. Foreseeing some action ahead, he slipped on a pair of cargo pants and ankle-high hiking boots. He tossed an outdoor supply kit into his backpack, strapped on his Dress Bowie and hastened out the door. Fortunately, July was not here yet, so he still had custody of the *Hummingbird*.

By the time he got to Valhalla, the commotion was in full swing. Dredmore was being lifted into the ambulance. Now dizzy with blood loss and painkillers, he was no longer making a lot of sense. Percy was trying to repeat what Dredmore had told him to a patient police officer.

The crimes had taken place just as Corey was getting ready to lock up after a long night's work, and Dredmore felt certain that agents of Gilbert Carson had been involved. Her two watchdogs had been shot and killed. Corey herself had been injected with a tranquilizer dart and spirited away in a big black limousine by two thugs.

They had also attempted to kidnap Christopher Rose, who had been given an after-hours emergency massage as her last client of the evening. But Rose was larger and slower to respond to the tranquilizer. Before it had fully taken effect, he had managed to stab himself with a knife-blade concealed in the base of his big gold cross.

The police officer took down all the information sympathetically, but not without some skepticism. He had occasionally been a client at Valhalla himself, so he was on friendly terms with Corey, but the whole situation looked suspicious. It was clear that more had been going on at Valhalla than met the eye. But on the surface it appeared that the world's wealthiest man, who normally resided North of the Cotton Curtain, and the Confederacy's foremost TV evangelist had been competing over the attentions of a prostitute.

Though sex work was no longer illegal, it was still disreputable. The cop was worried that there might be clues that could lead investigators back to his own department, where a careful audit might show how often sessions at Valhalla had been charged to their Undercover expense account.

"This is terrible," the officer said, "just terrible. We'll do everything in our power to locate the young lady. But I should warn you that a large part of our investigative resources are going to be tied up in a more important case. The Centre for Disease Control *and* the main Coca-Cola factory were bombed less than two hours ago. Survivors say it could take a couple of years to get their ImmuJolt distribution back on track. It's going to damage our Confederate economy and become an international health crisis. Both production facilities were completely demolished, and several key researchers living upstairs were killed. "

Now that car commuting was outrageously expensive and environmentally reprehensible, large organizations often provided on-site housing and childcare for their staff. Corey and Dredmore themselves had lived in the same building as Valhalla.

"Carson did it!" cried Percy. "It must have been him."

"Be reasonable, now; the man can't be in three places at once."

"He's rich enough to hire people to do anything he likes," Mark said. "We want him arrested and charged!"

"Are either of you related to any of the victims? Even if you are, and if Gilbert Carson is still in the Confederacy, arresting a man in his position is not as simple as all that." The policeman folded his notepad and put away his electronic gear. "However, I have noted your charges, and we will do our best to locate him."

He had assumed a formal, bureaucratic tone of voice that suggested the police were not going to be much help.

After a trip to the precinct station for prolonged questioning, Mark and Percy drove the *Hummingbird* to Clayton. It was mid-morning by the time they arrived at Mickey's. The drawbridge was already down, and they saw by the motorcycle that Koko and his current lady had come visiting. The arrival of the quiet little *Hummingbird* attracted no attention, and Mark and Percy stood in the doorway for a few moments before they were noticed.

The household vibes were still heavy; Mickey was sporting several angry red welts across various parts of his anatomy. Lana, Viviangela, and the two young newcomers were also showing some bruises. Things seemed to be relatively amicable for the moment, however.

Mickey was pointing to the tattooed designs on Koko's bare back and proclaiming, with drunken fervour: "That has to be the Kingfish; see that tadpole? That's why we couldn't find the entrance. Our dowsing rods on Mount Arabia kept pointing straight down, the shortest distance, but see this line? The tunnel opens up way over here to one side."

"You're nuts, man," Koko told him. "There ain't no such thing. It's just an old Indian legend. I oughta know; it's on my own damn back! But I'll tell you one thing — just in case you're right, I ain't goin' near that place again."

Mickey looked up and saw Mark and Percy.

"Uh-oh," he said. "If it's Wednesday, this must be trouble."

Percy's brave front collapsed. "She's gone!" he blubbered. "He's dead!"

Pothole to Hell

A couple of hours later, the *Hummingbird* was heading back to Atlanta. It was a tight squeeze. Mickey, the largest of the three, was too drunk to drive, so he had to hold Percy on his lap while Mark drove. The luggage space, which might otherwise have had room for a small third person, now held an Uzi for Mickey and a handgun apiece for Mark and Percy, in addition to three backpacks and an assortment of emergency supplies. Proclaiming himself both a pacifist and a potential mass murderer, Percy normally refused to carry more than the minimalist billy-club, but he had relented on this occasion.

They stopped by the Clayton police station to tell Sergeant Johnson that Gilbert Carson was now chief suspect in a kidnapping and should be held for questioning if he turned up again. The cop had already heard about the crimes in Atlanta. He wrote down their additional information with all due seriousness, including Mickey's claim to be Carson's son, but pointed out that the Confederacy had no extradition treaty with the Companies. If Carson had fled North of the Cotton Curtain, he would be out of their reach.

"He's taken her to Mount Arabia," Mickey kept saying. "I know it! Don't ask me how; I just know it."

"I hope you're right," Percy said, "but we've searched over that whole area half a dozen times already this summer."

Mark, too, failed to see the logic of their destination, but he was grateful for a chance to switch off his brain and let someone else take charge. His own action plan had come to its end when he and Percy had walked through Mickey's door.

"Look!" Mickey shouted, as they approached the parking lot below the site of that fateful Beltane ceremony. "That's why we never could never find the entrance. It was underneath the pavement!"

But not any longer. Now the centre of the road had been torn open, and there was a heap of rubble surrounding what was clearly the entrance to a tunnel. A pick-axe and shovel lay nearby, but large rocks scattered many feet from the hole in all directions suggested that explosives had also been used. Thanks to the parking lot on one side, any vehicles that didn't drive straight into the hole could still swerve around it, but there hadn't been much traffic along that backwoods road even in the old days.

In modern times, the site was visited mainly by secret societies holding ceremonies, young lovers looking for privacy, and drunks looking for trouble by harassing the first two groups — plus a tiny smattering of family picnickers and botanists. (Flora atop the granite bubble was amazingly similar to that of the Sonora desert.) It had been years since the Highways

Department had done any maintenance on that road, and it would probably be a long time before anybody happened by to investigate the fate of any people who disappeared down that tunnel.

A big black limousine waited in the parking lot, with its driver sound asleep behind the wheel, his feet sticking out the open window on the passenger side. The rescue party quickly agreed not to disturb his slumber.

They parked the *Hummingbird* a few hundred yards away, around a bend in the road, and made some cursory gestures toward concealing it beneath some broken-off foliage. Taking their smaller weapons from the trunk, as well as a flashlight, a first-aid kit and an emergency tool kit, they raced toward the tunnel entrance.

There was a drop of about six feet to the floor below, but Carson had thoughtfully left a rope ladder in place for their descent. The passageway was so narrow that they had to walk single-file, and Mark was soon struggling with claustrophobia as the daylight from the entrance faded away behind them.

They hurried forward for what seemed like forever, but was only five or ten minutes according to the glowing dial of Mark's watch. At last they saw a light ahead, shining through some curtains.

As they burst through into the hexagonal chamber, for a moment Mark thought he must be back on the Astral Plane, hallucinating. They stopped in their tracks and stared around them in stunned silence.

Chamber of Horrors

The open area was about thirty feet across, illuminated by a dim glow from the walls themselves. Most of the objects in view were totally unfamiliar. Strange liquid sounds of hissing and bubbling were coming from a large partially covered opaque tank that extended the length of one wall to their left.

What they saw at the far end of the room would have made a good set for a horror movie. A large black tray about five feet long, trimmed with Oriental characters and inlaid with precious stones — bordered by what appeared to be not just mother-of-pearl but fresh ivory — was resting atop a narrow table. Under the tray, the table was draped with a purple velvet cloth, its hem embroidered with gold metallic threads.

The tray had been set up as a grotesque altar with a chalice made from a human skull. Beside the skull, a flame was burning dimly within a green glass flask that emanated a thin haze of malodorous fumes. The centrepiece of the altar was a huge green crystal that resembled the smaller ones in the medallions worn by Corey and Christopher Rose — and, in miniature version, many of Rose's followers.

Percy fingered his own cross pendant, looking back and forth from it to the weird altar.

"What *are* these things?" he chirped, so excited that his adolescent voice was cracking from the manly monotone that he usually affected. "Whose purposes could they serve?"

That question was answered when Mark pointed to the human form slumped against the wall on the left, near the tank. It stared straight ahead, completely motionless and apparently oblivious to their presence. It was Gilbert Carson, of course.

Mickey walked over and lifted Carson's gun out of its holster, then quickly searched the inert form for other weapons. Finding none, he cupped his hands around his mouth and called out: "Corey! *Corey!*"

"Over here," came her muffled voice. "Quick, before he comes back to his senses! He's injected himself with BellaTrix to get himself in the right frame of mind."

BellaTrix was a dangerous short-acting street drug. The user spent half an hour in a totally hallucinatory universe, and then snapped back to reality with a hard-on (if male) and a bad temper — if he snapped back at all. Some BellaTrix users died of heart failure or were rendered permanently insane.

Looking to see where the voice was coming from, the rescue team noticed the outline of hands and feet just beneath the purple velvet drape at each end of the "altar" table, with leather straps anchoring them to the table legs.

They raced over to the table and removed the altar tray to the floor. Mark lifted up one end of the purple drape to uncover Corey's face.

Now it became evident that she was bound to her own lightweight folding massage table with retractable wheels. Carson's thugs must have taken it during the kidnapping. The foot of the cleverly designed table had been folded down so that her groin was at the edge, her legs arching down at an uncomfortable angle so that her toes dangled only a few inches above the floor. The table was equipped with footrests for such positions, but Carson apparently hadn't understood how to use them.

But the other end of this table had acquired an even more sinister new feature. Corey's head was secured in place with Velcro straps, and suspended directly over her forehead, its metal frame clamped to the sides of the table, was a miniature guillotine blade.

"Oh, Corey!" Percy lamented. "What has he done to you?"

He hastened over and quickly detached the guillotine with the tools attached to his Swiss Army knife. But the leather straps binding her arms and legs were the sturdy commercial BDSM variety, padlocked into place and hard to cut through. Percy flung back the purple velvet covering her body.

"Oops!" he said. "Sorry." He laid it back into place.

Beneath it, Corey was totally nude, except for her medallion and an odd G-string-like contraption over her crotch, consisting of folds of red satin in the shape of a rose, with an opening in the centre.

"What the hell is that thing?" asked Mickey, lifting the velvet drape again to peer curiously.

Percy flipped out another tool from his survival knife and began to saw away at one of the leather wristbands.

"It's the latest model of OrgasMagic," he said. "I've seen them advertised in the sex magazines. Some of their designs are pretty weird; that's one of the nicer ones. It sends a pulsating electric current across the pubic floor."

"Hmmph!" Mickey said. "Never had any use for sex gadgets mysef. Anything they can do, I can do better."

He took out his own knife and began sawing at one of the leg bands, while Mark did the same with the other leg.

"I think his general idea was to use the OrgasMagic to force me to climax," said Corey, "and then at the crucial moment, he would slice off the top of my head and eat my brain. Something to do with giving him immortal life. The man is hopelessly deranged."

"Yeah," Percy agreed, "that guillotine blade isn't nearly heavy enough to cut open a skull."

A Dream Fulfilled

"Well," Mark said, "old Carson probably knew he'd never get another chance like this one. Now that these OrgasMagic gadgets are on the market, orgasmic virgins must be hard to come by."

"This is no time for bad puns," Mickey scolded. He looked up from his task with the leg band and lifted the edge of the purple drape to peer at the device one more time. "How do these things work, anyway?"

Percy, who had clearly done his research, eagerly gave the answer:

"Pushing the little blue button at the top left sends out a mild electric current that stimulates the woman sexually, and then the red button beside it on the right triggers her orgasm."

"Go ahead and do it," Corey sighed. "I know you've been wanting to give me an orgasm for all these years, Mickey, and if it will spoil my value for people like Gilbert Carson, I'm willing to go along with it. But I've been channelling my sexual energy into the upper chakras for my whole life, so it scares me to think of what might happen if we release it all at once."

"Corey, you should know better than to fall for that sex-negative superstition," Mickey told her. "Look at me; I've had several orgasms a day ever since I reached puberty, and I'm still going strong."

"Yes, but your sexual circuitry developed along different principles."

"Oh, Corey!" Mark got to his feet and leaned over the table to embrace her. "Please don't be afraid. You know we all love you." He was pleasantly aware of the OrgasMagic sandwiched between their bodies.

Suddenly, Mark felt himself being hurled aside. He lost his balance and fell to his hands and knees. When he looked up, Mickey had taken his place and was standing over Corey like some newly-conjured elemental force. Mickey flexed his massive biceps and squared back his shoulders in triumph — and warning.

"This is the chance I've been waiting for," he crowed, "for the last fifteen fuckin' *years!*"

Be Careful What You Wish For

"Mickey!" said Percy, scandalized. "At a time like this!"

"Shut up, Pipsqueak — she told me to do it."

"But not with you inside me," Corey pleaded. "Please, Mickey, I just don't feel right about it. We don't know what's going to happen."

"Hey, little girl, every woman feels like that the first time." By now, Mickey had found the opening of the OrgasMagic and had begun a rhythmic thrusting.

"And this really is the first time for you, isn't it, Corey?" he crooned. "This time it's going to be different. This time you're going to come for me, just like all the others."

"*No*, Mickey!" yelled Corey. But the OrgasMagic was already pulsing its current, and she began to writhe and moan. "Please stop! You don't know what you're doing. Something terrible is going to happen!"

"Just relax and enjoy it, baby" crooned Mickey. "This is *my* area of expertise now."

Mark and Percy watched with a mixture of horniness and horror. In an agony of frustration and self-loathing at his inability to challenge Mickey, Mark moved to the opposite end of the table, where Corey's head was still strapped down with Velcro.

"Don't worry, Corey," he whispered, "this will soon be over and we'll get you out of here." He placed a comforting hand on each shoulder and leaned his forehead against hers.

Mickey continued his thrusting, his enthusiasm mounting as he watched Corey's increasingly violent involuntary responses. When he could contain himself no longer, he gave a low growl and stepped up the tempo of his pelvic thrusts. His hand reached down to push the second button.

Corey began to wail, "*Oh!* Oh, Mickey, forgive me; *I can't help it!*"

Her cries became wordless and more urgent. Mickey began his ejaculation with a triumphant cry of ecstasy — which swiftly changed to one of anguish and horror. He jerked himself away from Corey and fell backward to the floor, where he lay in the fetal position, clutching his groin.

At the other end of the table, Mark's body went rigid with shock and he, too, collapsed in a daze. While his body was unresponsive as a dead weight, his consciousness continued to register the ensuing events.

Corey was still thrashing her torso and shouting, *"Take it off! Get that thing off me!"*

Percy flung back the velvet drape, revealing that the green crystal in her medallion had begun to glow brightly and shoot off sparks. He snapped off the chain and flung the medallion across the room. It bounced off the wall and fell into the tank of liquid, which was soon emitting bubbling, sputtering and crackling sounds.

Percy was too busy to notice. With new strength born of adrenaline, he had put away his own pocket knife, liberated Mark's Dress Bowie from its sheath, and was using it to chop viciously at the leather arm and leg straps. In this way, he quickly freed the sobbing Corey.

Mickey stayed curled on the floor at the foot of the table, uttering grunts and whimpers of pain.

Then a new voice was heard. Quavery and distressed, it spoke only two words: *"Oh, shit!"*

A Man Misunderstood

Percy whirled around and headed toward Gilbert Carson, who was gnawing his own fingers in distress.

"For all those years, I did as I was told," Carson lamented. "Immortal life, they promised me — *immortal life!* It's all I ever wanted, and now it's all ruined."

"Old man," Percy said, his cockscomb bristling as he leaned over the little tycoon, holding the blade to his throat, "selling out the Earth to aliens would be enough evil for one lifetime. But you really outdid yourself by bombing the CDC last night, and then trying to sacrifice this woman."

Carson looked shocked. "But I didn't! *I didn't!* I didn't even know about the CDC. I'm telling the truth! I'm not helping the Nefilim any longer. Why should I? They made my life a lie. They wanted me to kill that thing in the tank and bring them Jennifer and Christopher Rose for questioning — but I wouldn't do it! I knew that thing had been keeping Christopher Rose young somehow, but my own research teams might have able to figure out how it's done.

"I'm having the Nefilim bases bombed. We can only take out the ones on the surface, but it's the best I can do.

"I'm sorry about Jennifer. I don't know what came over me. But when I found this spell in an ancient text on alchemy, it seemed like my only hope. I never meant to hurt anybody. I just didn't want to die!"

Percy spat. "You really had yourself convinced that eating somebody's brain wasn't going to hurt them? Nobody wants to die, but you don't have to worry about me killing you. I wouldn't dirty my hands with it. You'll get more punishment by staying alive and thinking about what you've done. We've already guessed that you're the one that engineered the Big Bang."

"But I didn't — *I didn't!* Oh, the world has misunderstood me so! The Big Bang was the work of Christopher Rose.

"You think that man was a saint. Well, let me tell you, he's a cold-blooded killer. The Earth was right on the verge of the Change, and if it had happened then, it would have gone the way of the Nefilim, so Rose needed to cut back the population in a hurry."

Carson raved on: "Do you think the Nammu gave you ImmuJolt to cure disease? It was just meant to prevent pregnancies and keep the population down. You think the Nammu care about you any more than the Nefilim do? They just want to tilt the Change in their own favour.

"There's no counting how many tens of millions of people died in the Big Bang. Your sainted Christopher Rose is the biggest scoundrel in the history of this world!"

"Shut up!" Percy bellowed at Carson. "Liar! *Liar!* You're just trying to run down everybody else to your own level. I don't want to hear another word out of you. If you know what's good for you, you'll hightail it out of the Confederacy as fast as you can, because there are warrants out for you all over the state of Georgia.

"Well, don't just stand there shaking — *run!"*

Percy lay down the weapon and lifted up Corey into his arms.

"We need to get out of here, too. Corey, honey, can't you stand up yet? Here, wrap your arms around my shoulders and I'll carry you on my back."

Radiant with manly courage, Percy carried Corey out of the tunnel, with Gilbert Carson fleeing down it ahead of them.

The Kingfish Awakens

Then the half-lid to the tank of liquid began to open on its hinge. With a great effort of will, Mark managed to turn his head in time to watch a strange apparition being lifted out of the tank by a mechanized sling. It was slowly propped against the side of the tank until it was almost in an upright position, straddling the bottom of the sling with divided tail-flippers that could almost double as legs. It was taller than a man, and its upper flippers ended in tentacled appendages.

Moving laboriously, leaning on the tank for support, it stepped out of the sling and dragged itself along the wall to a row of pegs. From them, it removed a cape and a staff topped with a large green crystal. The cape had an iridescent fishscale pattern on the outside and was lined with some absorbent material. It secured the cape around itself like a bathrobe.

Next it took down a gold-coloured mask of a human face with a realistic black beard, which it slipped into place over its own inhuman visage. A turban completed the transformation. The resulting effect, while still obviously nonhuman, no longer evoked gut-reactions of revulsion.

Then it belted a rectangular control panel in front of the cape. A set of small finger-like tentacles fluttered over the panel.

"Be not afraid," a computer-generated voice said. "I am the Kingfish. I have overslept."

Ponderously, leaving a trail of dampness and using both the wall and the staff for support, the creature came to stand over Mickey. He was gaping in awe, astonishment temporarily overriding his pain.

The green crystal atop the staff began to glow, and the creature extended it toward Mickey's groin. His body spasmed, and an expression of vast relief came over his face.

"Thank you," he whispered, as tears flowed freely down his cheeks.

Then the creature dragged itself over to extend the crystal toward Mark's forehead. He felt something shift inside him and suddenly felt revitalized, alert and confident, with his mobility restored. Struggling to his feet, he automatically retrieved his Dress Bowie, left on the floor by Percy.

"Listen well," the mechanical voice told them. "These effects will last only a short time. I am sorry, my children. In ages past, I could have healed you in the Cauldron, but the Nefilim have so drained its power that now it can barely function even as my own resting place. This device can offer only temporary relief of pain and fatigue.

"I am aware of much that has happened on the surface. Memories of all those wearing the small green crystals are transmitted to a device synchronized with my own brainwaves. I could know, but I could not move, until the energy stored in Corey's crystal shifted the balance in my favour when it fell into my tank.

"Be not afraid," it repeated. "The Nefilim have an inflated estimation of their own power. They even overestimated Gilbert Carson's capacity for evil. The Earth is in no further danger. The Change is now on course, and it is happening on schedule. The cetaceans have made their own Change already, and they will play a conscious role in shaping the path of *Homo sapiens* and the other primates. Every sentient being of every species will be enfolded within the global mind eventually."

"I don't understand," Mark said. "I thought large populations triggered the Change. The cetacean population has been declining for centuries. Most types are still endangered."

"The Change is triggered by the total mass of conscious energy on the planet," the Kingfish explained. "It is irrelevant which species provide it. Vegetation, microbes and fungi also play their roles. Cetacean fertility has been impaired by the ImmuJolt waste discharged into your sewage systems and from there into the oceans. Their populations will reestablish themselves afterwards. While I remain awake, I can make adjustments to correct much of the damage already done by the Nefilim, and I shall signal for my people to send help.

"But our friend Johann — the man you knew as Christopher Rose — is gone forever. I feel sadness and regret, but he wanted to make certain that his knowledge would not fall into Carson's hands. He was old and tired, and the last task of his service had upset him a great deal. "

"What was his last task?" Mark asked.

"Destruction of the ImmuJolt production facilities."

Imaginal Bodies

Mark and Mickey gaped in astonishment.

"These are complex relationships," the creature continued. "A butterfly in its larval stage secretes a chemical to break down the old form so that the caterpillar can metamorphose into a winged creature. As the caterpillar spins a cocoon and enters the chrysalis stage, most of its body melts down into an undifferentiated protoplasmic soup. But a few specialized cells called Imaginal Bodies form stable coordinate points to provide a scaffolding to govern the formation of the emergent butterfly. As the moment of Change draws near, so too your own species must break down the protective barriers between individual minds. Groups like yours are the equivalent to Imaginal Bodies during the metamorphosis of your planetary organism.

"Viruses and bacteria continually transfer genetic material between species. Much of that seemingly inactive, surplus DNA that your scientists used to believe performed no useful function serves as a planetary gene pool. Species may become extinct, but their genetic material may express itself again when conditions are ripe.

"As human beings increased in number and other large species declined, more and more of that genetic storage function was shifted over to bacteria. After all, the Earth is one single genetic organism. Some call her Pachamama. You call her Gaia.

"Your species has never stepped outside of Nature. Your cities and industries are as natural to you as a hive is to a honeybee.

"The ImmuJolt formula was automatically transmitted through the communication crystal when the time was right. It has allowed the breakdown of barriers to proceed almost unnoticed with minimal threat to physical well-being. But now the time for Change has arrived. Even ImmuJolt could no longer completely suppress the signs of it, and without ImmuJolt, the Change will accelerate rapidly. It cannot be safely postponed any longer.

"Christopher Rose recognized the signs; I had described them to him long ago. But he was reluctant to take action, knowing that many human lives would be lost.

"Once the Change is complete, your species will quickly re-stabilize at a new level of vitality and will function as a single organism. It is unfortunate that the Change may be accompanied by a high mortality rate among individuals who are unable to align themselves with the new pattern. However this is unavoidable, and many of their memories will be preserved intact.

"We Nammu have been with you from the beginning, and we will do all we can to ease your passage. After the Change, we will be able to communicate with your people more openly, as we already do with the cetaceans."

Mickey said bitterly, "I guess that means our own days are numbered. Before long we'll either be dead, or we'll be absorbed into the Happy Blob."

"I cannot say what your own fate will be," the Nammu told him. "The Change most easily assimilates the young who have not yet reached sexual maturity, and the very old whose reproductive years have ended. For a time, both the old and the new patterns will coexist among your people, and great conflict will arise between the two.

"But the outcome is not in doubt. Whatever happens to you as individuals, you must never forget that you have helped to ensure the continued evolution of intelligent life on your planet. It was no small task."

"Exactly what are you?" Mark blurted out. "Where are you from? Why do you want to help us?"

"We Nammu are your neighbours from the star system you call Sirius. Our ancestors originally seeded life on your planet, and we have watched and guided its development from the beginning. Our own race is so ancient that we have passed through both our individual and collective phases. We are now at a third level of development in which the full consciousness of the Whole manifests through each individual, who goes forth to be of service at a certain stage of maturity.

"You might think of us as cosmic conservationists, equivalent to your own park rangers. I am the Chief Watchguard who regulates the outer forces impacting your star system. I was stationed here to ensure that your planetary lifeform would develop in a balanced and healthy way, without interference from predators like the Nefilim. Though we are clearly different from you, we do share much of the same genetic stock. In that sense, you are our children."

Sages, Fools and Tools

"What are you going to do about the Nefilim?" Mark asked.

"The Nefilim arrived at a later stage in your planet's development. They, too, had a hand in bringing forth your species, mixing in some of their own genetic stock. But they did not take the pleasure of an artist in creating beauty. They wanted to create slaves and workers, so that they might ravage yet another world as they already had their own. I think now they will look elsewhere."

"You're going to let them get away?"

"Predator have their place in the greater scheme of things. It is not our role to judge the rest of creation; we only tend our own gardens."

"Are you saying that Gilbert Carson will just be allowed to run free," Mickey demanded, "after all the damage he's done?"

"You fail to understand. Christopher Rose was a highly evolved man who served humanity in full self-awareness, even though doing so meant a continual struggle against his own individualistic desires and moral sensibilities. He was offered immortal life, but he chose not to accept it. His conscience was too torn by the deeds he had done in our service.

"Gilbert Carson, on the other hand, sought immortal life with such selfish passion that he was willing to betray his planet to attain it. His obsession brought him only misery. But despite his conscious intent to serve only himself, his lack of allegiance to the old structures of your society allowed him to function unconsciously as our best agent. Lacking any true sense of Self, he was most responsive to the suggestions fed to him by our communication devices.

"The lives lost during the Big Bang were more than offset by the elimination of large-scale warfare. The food that Carson diverted to the Nefilim was a trifling matter in light of the food and shelter that he provided for his own people. Though he was motivated not by compassion, but by pride in ownership, the citizens of your world are now in such good shape that no man, not even Gilbert Carson, has the power to divert the Change from its natural course.

"As you must know, Carson is not of sound mind. For most of his life, he has served to express the wishes and fears of the collective Self — first of your own species, then of the Nefilim and the Nammu. These functions overwhelmed his weak individuality almost completely. Michael Arthur, you have seen the pathetic shell of this man who thought to rule the world — your father. Would you have me add to his torment?"

Mickey made no reply, and the Kingfish continued:

"You declined Christopher Rose's offer to become his successor in the Work. That is well, for soon a fleet of Nammu will arrive to oversee the Change, and human Custodians will no longer be necessary. However, there does remain one last task that will require human assistance. Listen carefully, my friends, our time grows short.

"Do you see the four large sealed clay jars on the floor at the left of the Cauldron — the tank where I slept? You will see different bands of colour and symbols at the neck of each. Take careful note of them, for they contain the seed stock of past agricultural societies ranging over your entire planet. Your own civilization needs them desperately, now that the gene pool of your food crops has become so depleted.

"Your task is to distribute that seed to all parts of the world, and see that none of it is wasted.

"Each variant within the jar is vacuum-sealed in a translucent bubble that can be broken between the thumb and forefinger. The jar with the red neckband contains seed for hot climates, and the blue is for colder. The green-necked jar contains salt-tolerant varieties. Those in the yellow will thrive in arid climates.

"Please do not fail me in this, for even with the Nefilim no longer stealing your surplus food, you will need help in securing an ample supply to take you through the Change. There will be times when your current methods of farming will no longer be possible."

"Consider it done, Kingfish," Mickey said. "That's right down our alley.

"Good! Now, I have some remaining tasks that must be done as quickly as possible — I can stay awake only for a short time longer. My support systems are still not functioning as they should, but that will be corrected after help arrives.

"You need help also. I must send out a Call for some of your own kind to take you for medical assistance, and for others to come and conceal the entrance to this hiding place. They will retain no memory of having done so.

"You may leave the jars by the side of the road as you exit. I will have them buried and a rosebush planted over them, so that you can find them again after you are restored to health."

The Kingfish touched each of them a second time with the healing rod.

"This should give you enough strength to get back to the surface. You will fall asleep by the roadside, and help will arrive soon after. Take the jars now, and go!"

Acting without question, Mark and Mickey set the jars on Corey's massage table, lowered its wheels, and took them out through the tunnel. Since Percy had taken the flashlight, they had to use the tiny lights attached to their keys for the first part of their exit, but sunlight shining through the entrance guided them for the last part.

The rope ladder was still in place. Mark climbed up halfway first, and Mickey handed the jars up to him one at a time, to be carefully set on the ground. Mark then had to assist Mickey in struggling up the ladder, for their strength was failing rapidly.

Neither the *Hummingbird* nor the black limousine was anywhere in sight. They managed to conceal the jars in a roadside ditch before they collapsed in the weeds a short distance away. A gentle drizzle of rain began to fall.

"We'll both be covered with ticks and chiggers by the time they find us," Mickey complained.

"Probably will," Mark agreed. "Uh, Mickey — for the sake of decorum, I suggest that you fasten your fly."

The last thing he heard before he lost consciousness was Mickey's incredulous exclamation:

"My God, Mark — she burned it right off!"

Chapter 17
Sanctuary

You Can't Go Home Again

Mark came to his senses several weeks later in a padded Quiet Room. After a couple of abortive attempts to communicate his memories, he had maintained a prudent silence and meticulously correct behaviour for the time it took to convince the doctors that he was back to his normal self.

That was far from the truth. He felt the emotions of each person in his environment as if they were his own, and at times it was hard even to be sure of the spatial location of his own body. But the deception was a matter of extreme urgency. Mark knew that if he spent much longer in the psychiatric ward, he would lose himself entirely.

As it happened, the doctors released him to the custody of his sorrowful mother just in time for Thanksgiving. Of course, she had no guest room in her tiny widow's apartment, and the despair that permeated her existence was more than Mark could bear, especially now that he had become its focal point.

Her apartment was so overpriced that her employment pension and citizen-shareholder dividends combined were barely enough for her to live on, and his own savings account and citizen-shareholder dividends had been confiscated by the hospital. That left him with only the few dollars of emergency cash that she'd been able to spare for him. Mark knew that he would pay dearly in guilt and favours for any further help that he accepted from her.

Only one course of action remained open to him. A few days later, he packed up the few possessions that had been salvaged from his old life and stole out of the house before daybreak, leaving a note saying that he had been invited to spend the holidays with some friends, out of town and off the Grid.

It was easier to navigate the empty streets before dawn, and Mark steered a wide path around the few other pedestrians. In the absence of ImmuJolt, most were now wearing facemasks. By the time the city had come alive, he was standing on the steps of the building where Valhalla had once been. As he had feared, the doorbell buttons had no listing for the massage studio, nor for Corey or Dredmore.

He rang the suite that had formerly belonged to Valhalla, and spent a few awkward moments talking with the bleary-eyed woman who now ran a sewing shop from that location. She denied any knowledge of what had become of the people who used to work there, and he could tell that having to turn away former Valhalla clients was trying her patience.

Mark had already determined that they had no phone listing; likewise, there was no Atlanta listing for Percy or Lana. The old number for *The Third Speckled Bird* yielded only a disconnect notice, and its former office windows were dark. The police had been equally unhelpful.

Mark trudged over to Piedmont Park and sat by the lake for an hour or so, thinking. The Kingfish had told him to distribute those seeds, but Mount Arabia was a long way out of town. Mark no longer had his bicycle, nor cash for cab fare, nor other friends that he could hit up for favours.

He pawned all the rings on one hand for a little more cash and hitched a ride to Clayton, where he managed to talk two local residents into driving him partway to Mickey's house. They refused to take him the whole distance, so he had to walk the last long stretch of unpaved road uphill, carrying his belongings. But the exercise helped him to stay warm in the chilly wind that whipped up the slopes.

When he finally arrived at Mickey's place, his heart leapt with hope to see Corey and Dredmore's car in the driveway! But all was suspiciously quiet. The only sign of life was the chicken Pellucidar, who was pecking listlessly in the gravel and made only a perfunctory rush at him as he walked past.

The drawbridge was already down. As Mark crossed it, he noticed that the water level was a few inches lower. The shaft of the spear thrown by Gilbert Carson was still visible in the moat, now obviously embedded in a leathery reptilian carcass spattered with blue paint. Some catfish fingerlings gulped hopefully at the surface as his shadow passed over the water. With the gator gone, the moat must now be stocked with food fish. A paint-stained rag had been stuffed into the hole that Mickey had kicked in the front door.

With unaccustomed formality, Mark knocked.

At first he didn't recognize the sensuous red-headed matron who greeted him. But then he sensed a powerful energy field overlaying his own — happy affection bubbling up from a deep well of loneliness and sorrow. It felt familiar and reassuring, like a warm blanket. When he saw the woman's face light up and she reached out to embrace him, the truth hit home.

"Mickey?" he exclaimed incredulously, blushing furiously and struggling to get free from her clutches.

The heavyset woman grinned assent.

"Didn't even have to change my name," Mickey said jovially. "But I did have to lose about 60 pounds, and I'm still not down to where I'd like to be.

"Well, don't look so surprised! You were there; you saw what happened to me. What did you expect me to do? Sexual reassignment surgery can construct a pretty good vagina, but they still can't regrow a whole penis. Don't just stand there with your mouth hanging open — come on in. My God, it's good to see you again, Mark! I don't get much company anymore."

Mark entered cautiously. "I saw Dredmore's car in the driveway."

"Yes, he was kind enough to leave it here. He said I needed it more than he did. Dredmore's always been a good boy. Did you try to go back for the seeds?"

Mark shook his head no.

"Good; you wouldn't have found anything there. I had Dredmore pick them up for us. After the transfusions and stitches, he was only in the hospital for a few days. He tells me the seeds have already been distributed, so I guess our mission on Earth is done."

"How are he and Corey?"

"Oh, Dredmore's doing fine. The bullet did nick an artery, but apart from that it was just a flesh wound, and he wears the scar with pride. He's dropped out of University for a while, and he's playing drums in a reggae band and sharing a house with the other musicians.

"Dredmore's the only one who still keeps in touch. I was in the hospital for a long time, and he was the only visitor I ever had there. Not even Viviangela — she ran off with Lana, and I haven't heard from either one of them since the last time you were up here. When I got back home, all my ferrets were gone, and the State had put the kids in a group home."

Mickey's voice cracked, and she ducked her head away until she could regain her composure.

"I'm sorry," Mark offered tritely.

"Both of 'em ran away not long after that, and nobody knows where they are now. I worry about those girls. They weren't with me long enough to have learned how to make it on their own."

There was one glaring omission from this litany of sorrows.

"How's Corey?" Mark asked.

Mickey's eyes got a far-away look. "She was physically unharmed."

Mark felt a chill. "What does that mean?"

"Mark, she's changed. She isn't her old self anymore. She isn't *Corey*."

"What are you talking about? Did she crack up?"

"Some might say she had a nervous breakdown. She's still functional, up to a point, but she's just not the same person.

"She's married to Percy now; would you believe it? They're running a hardware store in Dalton, and ol' Percy's taken to the pulpit. He fancies himself to be carrying on the work of the dear departed Christopher Rose. Corey's not allowed to talk to me, but Dredmore brings me the news now and then.

"Look, there's no way I can explain it to you; you need to go see for yourself.

"We can drive to their house, and I'll wait for you around the corner. Maybe you'll have better luck than I did. You and Percy used to be friends; he never did like me."

"Can we leave right away?" Mark asked eagerly. "This has been preying on my mind for a long time."

"Sure," Mickey agreed, taking down a jacket from a hook behind the door. "No sense in putting it off.

"Let's add some water to the tank before we leave; this buggy's so big, I don't like to run her on anything but the hydrogen system. Why do all the young men want to tool around town in some huge car? I was satisfied just to have my armoured tank in the yard."

They started walking toward the car; then Mickey stopped, snapped her fingers in chagrin, and thrust the water jug at Mark.

"Will you add this to the car for me? I have to run back into the house. Forgot my purse!"

Road Trip

"The doctors told me I should still be able to climax," Mickey continued, as she started the car. "Not like before, of course; I don't have the equipment for that anymore. They gave me a little bump that looks like a clit, but it doesn't have much sensitivity — sexually, that is. It's pain-sensitive enough! Maybe it needs more time to heal.

"But they did manage to regenerate enough penile tissue to line the vagina, and the male prostate is analogous to the female G-spot. I've been trying to learn how to energize that area, but it's hard to judge its potential all on my own. I had to use a dildo for the first few weeks to keep the new orifice open, but I never did like sex toys. Never needed one before." She shrugged.

"When I first got out of the hospital and felt healed enough down there to risk it, the first thing I did was to go out to a singles' bar. Well, that was a terrible mistake. Even when I was decked out in a designer dress and expensive wig, it didn't take me long to find out that the kind of men interested in picking up a fat middle-aged woman with stubble on her chin are not my cup of tea!

"I did get a few nibbles at the Lesbian bar, but they soon decided they didn't like me for all the same reasons they don't like men. Then I thought about coming on to adolescent boys as a mother figure, but that just didn't seem right somehow."

"Why not?" Mark asked. "It didn't bother you before, when you were a man."

"I can't explain it. I felt confident in that role; this one is still new to me. Maybe I'll adjust eventually. I've already taken some acting lessons to get better at female body language. Now

I'm thinking of taking up belly-dancing. I need to learn how to move more gracefully."

Mark shuddered involuntarily, and then glanced around guiltily. But Mickey continued, giving no indication that she had noticed:

"I did meet some good people in the transvestite scene. They gave me pointers on how to dress and fix my hair and makeup, and a couple of them even invited me back to their place. We gave it a good try, but it was the same old story. A gay crossdresser wants a man with all his equipment, and a straight one wants a natural-born female.

"What's your own story, Mark? Where have you spent the past few months?"

"In a mental hospital. I just got out."

Mickey inhaled sharply in sympathy. "You didn't make the mistake of telling them the truth, did you?"

"Afraid I did," Mark admitted. "Of course, nobody would believe me. The doctors told me a crew from the Highway Department found us by the roadside and brought us to the hospital. We'd have died of thirst before another car passed by, but their surveillance drone had picked up the road damage.

"The police assumed that we'd been taking part in some occult ceremony on Mount Arabia and had overdosed on their sacred hallucinogen. They even suspected me of castrating you. Good thing there were no traces of blood on my Dress Bowie! By the time they sent any cops to check out my story, the road had been paved back over, and the Highways crew that had picked me up could only remember fixing a bad pothole.

"I think the authorities want to forget the whole thing. They sure didn't want to hear the part about Gilbert Carson — it was trouble enough to have him associated with the death of Christopher Rose.

"Corey and Percy must not have told them what happened underground," Mark continued. "The official story now is that Rose killed himself because Corey had rejected him to run off with Carson. Dredmore came after Carson in a rage, and Carson shot him in self-defence. Then he soon got tired of Corey and dumped her. You've got to admit that their story is more plausible than what really happened."

"Carson's dead too, you know," Mickey informed him. "He killed himself about a month after the kidnapping. It got about ten seconds worth of news coverage. Most powerful man in the world, and most people had never heard of him.

"Do you still follow the news? The President of the Confederacy has challenged the Companies' CEO to hand-to-hand combat during the next Olympic War Games, winner take all. What chance do you think they have against us, Mark? Those degenerates aren't used to doing their own fighting."

"They'll play dirty," Mark predicted.

"Well, they might at that. Man, the times are getting strange. Percy's shaved off that rooster's comb, and now he's preaching sermons on the radio and TV every Sunday morning! He's turning into a pretty good rabble-rouser, but he'll never hold a candle to Christopher Rose."

"How do you spend your days now, Mickey, without your family?"

Mickey sighed. "I do my artwork; I garden; I read a lot, when I can find my glasses. You'd be amazed how much time it takes just to keep up with the chores, when you're the only person on a homestead like this. I never realized how much of that work I was dumping on the others. No wonder they all left. I get pretty damned lonely up there. Every now and then, somebody I knew before comes by to look me up, but they never stay long and they never come back. They just can't handle the New Me, I guess.

"I realize now how strong I used to come on with my masculinity. I used to depend on intimidation and sexual charisma to get me through conflict situations and let me get away with mistreating others. That kind of raw sexual power just came naturally to me. I never had to work at it, and nobody had ever taught me how to control it. Viviangela was a good match for me in that way; she used to be almost my female counterpart. But raw sexuality has become a thing of the past."

"It was so much the heart of you," Mark said. "Surely there must be some of it left."

Mickey frowned thoughtfully.

"It's true that the urge is still there, but that's only a nuisance now that nobody responds to it."

"Just wait and see," Mark said encouragingly, seeking to ease Mickey's emotional distress and, with it, his own. "I'll bet before long you'll be able to use your sexual power as a woman just as effectively as you did when you were a man."

Mickey turned to look him full in the face. Their eyes locked for a second, and Mark suddenly realized where this conversation was headed.

Shaken, he wrenched his gaze away, so that Mickey could put her eyes back on the road where they belonged. Time to change the subject fast!

"Do you have any good music in this jalopy?"

"Mostly classical, I'm afraid," Mickey said. "I know that's not your usual taste. Hey, here's one you might like: *Carmina Burana.*"

She popped the disc into its player, and they drove the rest of the way in silence.

Being Normal

Mark's heart was in his throat as he walked up the steps to Corey's home. Mickey had dropped him off in front of her house and was waiting for him in the vehicle a couple of blocks away. He shuffled his feet uneasily during the long pause after he rang the bell.

When the door finally opened, at first he thought he must have the wrong house. Corey had cut and straightened her hair and was a good twenty pounds heavier. Instead of looking like a teenager, as she had before, she now appeared much older than her 28 years — almost middle-aged.

She was wearing tacky terrycloth house-slippers and light blue rayon slacks with a matching tunic top. A standard-issue gold cross pendant hung around her neck, and a matching set of gold and diamond wedding and engagement rings glittered on her left hand.

Mark had been bracing himself to receive a psychic blast of terrible unhappiness. To his surprise, this strange woman emitted only the faintest whisper of melancholy. She blinked at him uncertainly.

"Corey," he said tentatively, "don't you recognize me? It's Mark."

"Oh, Mark!" She gave him a quick, chaste side-hug, and then pulled back primly. "Thank the Lord you're all right! I worried so about you. We both saw what happened to Mickey. I know it was God's punishment for all the sins he committed, but still it makes me sad. I try my best not to think of those times. They're all behind me now and I've found a new life in Christ, praise Him!"

"May I come in?"

"Oh … yes, of course, please do come in."

Her house was 100% Middle Confederate. The wallpaper sported Confederate flags, rattlesnakes and falcons. The tabletop was contact paper over particle board, with a flowered design and a flimsy recycled aluminum frame. A little pot of dusty paper roses sat on the table, alongside a package of chewing gum and a bottle of EZ-Dozit. Two framed dollar-store prints of pathetic children with huge eyes hung by the doorway, and a life-sized picture of Jesus gazed reproachfully from over the sofa.

Corey sat down beneath it, angling her knees away from him and intertwining her legs to tuck one ankle behind the other. She plucked nervously at the armrest covers. Mark took a seat in the matching chair.

"Percy and I are married now, you know," Corey began defensively.

"Yes, I heard."

"We're really very happy. He takes good care of me."

"I'm so glad for you both."

"I can't remember much about how things used to be, but I know I did some wicked things while the Devil was having his way with me. But that's all over now that Jesus Christ has saved me. Now that I've been born again, I will never stray from His path again."

"Corey, please hear me. You were not an evil person. How can you even think that? You were wonderful! You were helping us to save the world."

"Don't be blasphemous. Only Jesus Christ can save us, and not even then unless we repent and accept him as our Saviour. Mark, have you repented yet? I know my son Dredmore hasn't. I've tried and tried to bring the Good News to him, but I can tell I'm not getting through. I hope he sees the light before the Day of Judgment. It can't be long now."

"Corey, please try to remember back to the time when we knew each other. Can't you remember that at all?"

She began to tremble. "Please don't make me go back to that time. That last day was so horrible. I tried to warn you to be careful. I knew somebody was likely to get hurt, but I couldn't allow the Devil to keep me in his power. But I never meant to hurt you and Mickey!"

She began to sob uncontrollably. *"I couldn't help it!"* she wailed.

Now Corey was broadcasting her pain with full force. Its intensity left Mark feeling stunned. He came to sit beside her on the sofa, putting one arm around her and patting her shoulder awkwardly, trying to comfort her.

"Corey, what happened was our own fault, not yours."

But she was no longer hearing him. She continued to sob, and her body contracted into a smaller and smaller fetal position. Mark was almost disabled by the waves of grief washing over him.

Then he heard footsteps approaching outside. The door was flung open, and now Percy's waves of fury created a complicated interference pattern with Corey's waves of pain and his own waves of fear. Mark was so overwhelmed by the emotional stimuli that he was unable to speak as he turned to face Percy. But what a different Percy! He was even wearing a tie. — A *tie*? To work in a *hardware store*?

Percy's face was scarlet as he confronted Mark.

"What are you doing to my wife?"

Forget About Her

Mark jumped to his feet guiltily. "I wasn't doing anything," he croaked inanely, his mouth dry.

"Don't hand me that story!" Percy was shaking with rage. "I remember what you were like."

Mark managed to muster some indignation of his own to push back the psychic blast from Percy. "What do you mean, 'what I was like'? You had a few faults of your own, as I recall."

"I looked up to you like an older brother," Percy accused him, "and you led me into some *terrible* habits!"

"I led you, bullshit! I was just nice enough to let you tag along after me."

"Well, now you've gotten rid of me, and I hope you'll be kind enough to return the favour."

"Percy, can't we still be friends? You must have known how much I cared for Corey. I never wanted any harm to come to her, and I'm not going to try to take her away from you."

"Yeah, Mark, we could all see how much Corey meant to you. You were screwing all the whores in Valhalla."

"Hey, just a minute now, that was her own idea. They were instructing me in Tantra."

"And then you just stood there and let Mickey rape her!"

"Well, hey, Percy, old friend, I don't recall you springing into action either."

"I wanted to, and I would have, if I'd thought I could count on you to back me up."

"ARRRGHHHH!" wailed Corey, rocking back and forth. "Please don't do this. *Please stop!*"

Percy bent down and circled Corey with his arms.

"Mark," he said, in a dangerously quiet voice, "I think you'd better leave now."

"Please, just tell me, before I go: How is she, really? Is she always like this?"

"No, she's okay most of the time. She's a little quieter than she used to be, but she's a married woman now, so that's to be expected. She does have some trouble remembering things, but electroshock will do that to folks. She has her feelings hurt very easily. She doesn't like to be around anybody but babies and animals — and me, of course. I don't think she could hold a job yet. She worked one day in the hardware store and went home in tears after a customer came in to exchange a tool.

"But she doesn't need to work now, thank the Lord; she has me to take care of her. I'd rather have her like this than doing the kind of work she was before. At least she's living a clean, pure Christian life now, like any normal woman, and our marital relations are good. That has to count for something."

"Is everything all right? I heard shouting and crying."

An elderly woman wearing a concerned expression stood in the open doorway.

"Yes, Mrs. Harris," Percy replied. "Corey just heard a piece of bad news. I think it would be best if you didn't ask her about it later; you can see how it has upset her. I can take care of her myself. This gentleman was just leaving — weren't you, Mark?"

"Yes," Mark agreed, backing toward the door. "I'm sorry that I had to be the one to tell her."

As the door closed behind them, Mrs. Harris accompanied Mark for a few feet down the sidewalk.

"Corey seems like such a nice girl," the lady offered. "But she's so timid and unsure of herself. She doesn't need to be — Percy is truly devoted to her."

"Yes," Mark said. "I can see that."

As promised, Mickey was waiting in the car.

"That didn't take long," she commented, starting the engine as Mark belted himself into the passenger seat. "How did it go?"

"You were right," Mark said with despair. "Corey is gone. This is somebody else."

"Who knows?" Mickey said, philosophically, as they started the drive back to Clayton. "The Corey we knew always did seem a bit unreal, almost like an autistic person using acting techniques to pass as normal. Perhaps this is the real Corey — a girl sexually abused by her father, who had a child by him, who never could learn to read or write, who earned her living in the sex trade — and who saw her first orgasm castrate her foster father. Who was, strictly speaking, raping her at the time."

Mark grimaced. "It sounds so crude when you put it into those words. Why didn't it seem that way before?"

"Because it *wasn't* that way. The Corey we knew then had transcended those primate tribal taboos and created a world where she could live on her own terms. Now that she's had her wings clipped, she's allowing herself to be defined by the Church and Society. Ain't Society wonderful, Mark? You know, most earlier governments would have had both of us locked up by now, if not executed."

Mark shook his head ruefully. "All my life, I've thought of sex as being good for my health and sanity."

"Just the same here," Mickey agreed. "Corey was so different from other people — especially me. I saw sex as the cure for all ills, and I was always frustrated because I was never able to share with Corey the one thing that gave my own life a solid foundation. All the rest of my life was built around that core of sexual gratification — any time, any place, with absolutely anyone that I damn well chose. Sexuality was what kept me connected to the rest of the human race. On most other levels, I had better rapport with the ferrets! How could I hope to understand someone who rejected that?"

"I don't think Corey rejected her sexuality," Mark said. "She just … handled it differently."

Mickey began shaking with silent sobs, her tears leaving a dark trail of mascara down her cheeks. She pulled the car over to the side of the road and hunched over the steering wheel, hiding her face between her forearms. Mark maintained a discreet silence for several minutes and finally asked, quietly, "Would you like for me to drive?"

"No, thanks." Mickey straightened up and dabbed her eyes with a lace handkerchief. "I'm okay now. You're in no better shape than I am. Let's stop at the first roadside motel we pass. It's already dark, and the roads are getting icy."

"Sure, Mickey, if you think that would be safer."

Mickey was silent for a long moment before she started the car again. She turned to Mark with a facial expression of soul-sadness.

"What's going to become of me, Mark? Do you think, if I could find Viviangela, she might take me back now that I'm a woman?"

"Viviangela?" Mark echoed, dumbfounded. "No, Mickey, I'd say that Vivi has gone her own way and you would do best to forget about her."

Mickey sighed, and they drove on in silence until they came to a motel.

Fledgling in The Redbird's Nest

The motel was called The Redbird's Nest, and its rooms were over a noisy tavern called The Stiff Upper Lip. Mark and Mickey assured each other that the racket would keep them awake anyhow, so they might as well go down and have some food and drinks.

Mark was dreading the psychic onslaught of so many customers flinging their emotional energy and germs around with drunken abandon. He was relieved to discover that, so long as he remained in Mickey's proximity, her own strong energy field helped to shield him from the others.

The Stiff Upper Lip was a typical motel dive, devoid of any attempt to create an interesting ambience. Mark and Mickey seated themselves at one end of the bar. As they were ordering their first drinks, Mark spotted the young hooker sitting at the other end. She was shivering in a cheap flowered minidress that clashed with her frizzy red hair, and didn't look a day over sixteen. Attention was directed toward her minimal cleavage by a large gold cross on a chain. At the centre of the cross was a greenish-black crystal.

Mark nudged Mickey and directed her attention to the girl. Mickey caught the girl's eye and motioned for her to join them. She approached warily, rightly cautious of any potentially kinky situation where she would be outnumbered.

"I'm curious, my dear," Mickey began, in her best motherly tone. "Where did you get that cross?"

The girl smiled with pleasure. "Do you like it? I found it at a yard sale a few weeks ago." The vibes she radiated were fresh and hopeful.

"Do you know yet how special it is?" Mickey continued.

"Oh, yes! You may think I'm makin' this up, but sometimes Jesus talks to me through it."

"Does he really? What does he tell you?"

The girl shrugged. "He's been teaching me all sorts of things. He tells me things that I ought to do."

"Such as…?"

"Well … he got me to stop doin' dope. He helped me get away from my pimp that used to beat me, and he helps me stay away from the cops, too. They don't care that I'm over the legal age of consent; they still used to find some excuse to bust me and then let me off in exchange for a freebie. Jesus taught me to love myself and take care of myself. And he helps me to understand things like how we're all just little parts of the Great Mother Earth. He says soon I'll be ready to go to Atlanta and start making some good money. He says I have work to do there."

"Did he tell you to come here tonight?"

"Well, yeah, he did. I don't usually work out of places like this anymore. I'm starting to get enough referrals that I can just wait for clients to call me. Are you the ones I was supposed to meet here? You're not really a woman, are you? I can tell."

Mickey sighed. "I'm afraid I am now, but you're correct that I didn't start out that way. What's your name, child?"

"Gwendolynne Matthews."

"Well, Gwendolynne, my name is Mickey, and my friend here is Mark. Look, I have a place in Clayton, way up on the side of a mountain. There's no telephone service, but everybody in town knows where I live. You are welcome to visit me anytime and stay for as long as you like, no strings attached. Think of it as a safe place, if you should ever need one."

"Why, thank you," Gwendolynne said. "You know, several other people have made me offers like that. They all want to help me get off the streets. But I figure I'm old enough, I ought to be making my own way. I've been doing this since I was twelve, and it wouldn't feel right to go back to being a kid again, with some older person bossing me around. My mama stayed too drunk to look after us kids, and she got mean when she drank. This way, I can make sure my little brother has food and warm clothes. I know some folks think what I do is wrong, but the way I look at it, if Jesus don't mind, why should they?"

"Indeed. Gwendolynne, I have no desire to change your life; I'm sure you know what you're doing. I simply wanted to offer you my hospitality."

"Well, I sure do appreciate it, Mickey, and maybe I will come by and pay you a visit someday. Now, if y'all will excuse me, I think that gentleman that just came in might want to do some business with me tonight. I hope y'all don't mind. It was nice talkin' to you."

"No, no, go on and do what you have to do."

Mickey waved the girl away and downed her whiskey sour with one gulp. "Bartender! Can I have a refill?"

The First Time

Mark awoke the next morning to the sound of snoring and was relieved to discover that he and Mickey had spent the night in separate beds. In the dim light, Mickey's nude form had the not-displeasing appearance of a sturdy female with some extra poundage — which, he reminded himself, was exactly what Mickey now was.

Without ImmuJolt to modulate his metabolism, Mark now had the worst hangover he could remember. Luckily, the motel had thoughtfully provided a small package of pain pills with aspirin and opium. He downed a couple of them, drank a bottle of tomato juice from the mini-fridge, and padded into the bathroom to have a shower. Then, wrapped in a towel, he sat for a while on the side of his bed, taking stock of his current situation and his options.

All his thoughts kept leading him in one direction, but at first he didn't want to accept it. After a time, however, he had come to his decision.

He pulled back the shades and allowed the sunlight to awaken Mickey. They gazed at each other with some embarrassment.

"Good morning," Mark said at last, with a brave smile.

Mickey raised her eyebrows sleepily and her hand patted the mattress, inviting Mark to join her.

Mark could feel his heart pounding as he walked slowly across the room and sat down on the bed beside Mickey. She rested a hand on his knee and closed her eyes as he sat watching her. He could see little patches of curly red hair across her breasts and torso, where the depilatory cream, laser and electrolysis had all failed to do their job completely.

She sighed deeply as Mark trailed the back of one hand down her body from chin to pubes. His other hand stroked her forehead — being careful not to dislodge the wig.

Suddenly, Mickey pulled him toward her with an astonishing strength and kissed him full on the lips. Her sexual and emotional hunger reverberated through every fibre of Mark's being, and he was surprised to find his body responding so readily.

Determined to play the aggressor, Mark pushed her shoulders flat against the mattress and began to nibble his way down one arm to the fingertips.

The next thing he knew, he was flat on his back with Mickey vigorously giving him a blowjob.

"Wait a minute," he protested weakly.

Mickey caught his eye and winked, but kept on with her task. Mark could feel his willpower going under, and he fought to regain control. He took her head between both hands and, with all his strength, forced it away from his cock.

"I said *wait,*" he repeated. "How are you going to come if you don't let me fuck you?"

Mickey looked abashed. "Your point is well taken," she admitted. "I will try to lie back and let you take the lead." A shadow passed over her features. "I thought I might have to be quick. I was afraid you wouldn't want me."

Mark threaded his fingers under the edges of the wig through the tangles of her real hair. He let one hand come to rest on the nape of her neck, and the other on her forehead. Then he guided her head to the crook of one arm and began to stroke his palms across her breasts.

"Mickey," he said at last, "who else could I go to?"

Understanding flashed between them, and their lovemaking turned gentle and sensuous. Not until they lay resting in each other's arms, their energy spent, did Mickey voice the thought for both of them:

"This was my first time as a woman!"

Chapter 18
Sacrifice

Keeping a Safe Distance

Mark rubbed his eyes sleepily as Mickey sat bolt upright in bed beside him. "Whazza matter?"

"Did you hear that?" Mickey ranted. "That's the third time that damned chicken has crowed this morning, right under this window, and it's not even daylight yet! How can you sleep through that racket?"

"No need to be in such a fowl temper," Mark told her. "She's just a lonesome hen going through a gender identity crisis. You should be able to sympathize."

"She's going through a damned meat-grinder," Mickey declared, gnashing her teeth in rage. "This is the last time that bird is going to disturb my sleep!"

"Aw, settle down, Mickey. You're the one who just woke *me* up. Pellucidar is the only animal we have left. It would break Koko's heart if anything happened to her."

"Koko's never going to set foot here again. We never did like each other. He only used to come around because I was married to his sister. Koko's the one who ought to get the axe for running off and leaving that bird here; I don't care if the cops were on his tail. I know she's what chased off all my ferrets while I was in the hospital. And she hasn't laid an egg for weeks."

Reluctantly, Mark got out of bed. Time to stoke the stove anyway, damn it. The house was freezing cold, and both he and Mickey had slept in their long underwear. He grabbed his parka off the bedpost, his toes felt around the floor for his moccasins, and he padded off toward the kitchen.

"Maybe she'll shut up if I throw a handful of corn out for her."

"NO!" Mickey bellowed. "We can't waste any more grain on feeding that bird. We've barely got enough food to make it through the winter ourselves."

Mark knew they were getting low on supplies. They hadn't made an expedition into town since their trip to Dalton over a month ago. The increased numbers of wildling street gangs they had passed had alerted them that the Change was gaining momentum. In the absence of ImmuJolt, there was also an alarming amount of coughing and sneezing.

Mickey had always maintained a large store of emergency supplies, but they had stocked up on supplemental food, medicine, and other necessities. Then Mickey had destroyed the three bridges along the road to the house after they returned.

Now they took their homemade ImmuJolt faithfully every day, in hope that it might help them resist the Change, or at least prevent a disease or infection. Occasionally they went to a less shielded part of the mountain to monitor the radio newscasts.

By this time, even kindergarten kids were going wildling when they were put together in groups of three or more, so most schools and day-care centres had ceased to operate. Education was now restricted to home-schooling and distance learning. But so many students were already being home-schooled that the public hadn't become alarmed yet.

Vast numbers of adults had begun going in for religious revivals and other forms of mob fanaticism, and Percy had risen to evangelical stardom.

Since many people had carried the viruses for HIV and other stealth diseases, formerly suppressed by regular doses of ImmuJolt, there were rising numbers of illnesses and deaths.

Hospitals had become used to seeing mainly injuries and the occasional birth defect or difficult childbirth. Younger doctors couldn't even diagnose many of the old-time diseases that were returning now, with immune systems weakened by shortages of ImmuJolt.

The tonic had been traditionally supplied by the Centre for Disease Control to the soft-drink companies. Though the secret formula had been made public as an emergency measure, relatively few households had managed to obtain all the ingredients and equipment, let alone follow the tedious and time-consuming instructions necessary to prepare it. Many people were buying or selling useless or toxic imitations.

But the rising mortality rate was more than offset by the rise in pregnancies. Orgies had become a fad, too. The Change had the younger generation feeling the love, but they weren't yet reconciled to the dreary practices of contraception, safe sex, or quarantine of sick people. None of those precautions had been necessary during their years on ImmuJolt. They were mystified and amused to see so many of their elders wearing facemasks in public places.

Satellite photographs had begun showing mysterious patches of green spreading rapidly across the Sahel Desert. Confederate newscasters joked that the phenomenon sounded a lot like kudzu.

And then there was the Moon — or there *wasn't* the Moon. Its sudden departure from the Earth's gravitational field had triggered earthquakes and volcanic eruptions around the globe, and had been taken as a portent of the End of Time. The last time they'd heard a newscast, the Moon was reported to be past the orbit of Jupiter and still accelerating on its way out of the Solar System.

Mark knew the Moon's departure meant the Nefilim had accepted defeat, but he doubted that the Nammu had expected them to take the Moon with them as they left. Like everyone else, he missed the Moon. Nights were so *dark* without it! The two small asteroids that the Nammu had recently steered into Earth orbit to help keep the protective geomagnetic field intact reflected much less light, produced far lower tides, and women could no longer predict their fertility cycles.

Mark swore as he stumbled over a stool on his way to the woodpile.

Mark swore a lot these days. So did Mickey. In fact, both had developed a personal litany of obscenities which they muttered continually whenever their mouth and mind were not otherwise occupied. Telling themselves that it might help them to avoid the Change, Mark and Mickey religiously had sex twice a day. But during the rest of their waking hours, when they couldn't avoid each other completely, they went out of their way to be as rude as possible.

There had nonetheless been several eerie occasions when they had found themselves walking in lockstep or even saying the same things at the same time. But they had learned that they could avoid such occurrences by staying pissed-off at each other. Given the personalities involved, this feat was not difficult.

End of Empire

"Damn it to hell, you arrogant shithead!" Mark shouted, slamming the stove door closed on the fresh firewood. "I'm not going to watch that bird starve to death. If you don't want me to feed it, you're going to have to kill it yourself."

There was a thud from the bedroom floor, as Mickey got to her feet.

"All right, then, I'll kill it," she snarled. "Where did you hide the goddamned axe?"

Their search through the dark tool-shed was a hazardous one, and Mark's hand soon developed a cramp from pumping the little flashlight generator. They had long since run out of fuel for their main generator, and the homestead had never been equipped to produce much of its own methane. There were solar panels, of course, and a small amount of thermovoltaic electricity. But this time of year, in midwinter, the little energy that could be gleaned was saved for the single light bulb that hung low over the kitchen table.

It was almost daylight before they could find the axe. Despite the cold, both were sweating and panting frosty puffs of air by the time Pellucidar was finally captured between Mark's heavy leather gloves. She squawked her indignation and pecked at him furiously.

Mickey backed away as Mark grinned and thrust the thrashing bird in her direction.

"This dirty work will be easier if we can calm her down first," Mark said. "Poor old girl; she didn't even get a last meal."

He squatted and turned the hen upside down on the chopping stump, holding her head still with one hand and her feet with the other. Mickey cautiously approached and squatted beside them. She began stroking the chicken under the chin as they had seen Koko do. It worked like a charm. Pellucidar soon lay limp as a rag doll, her neck helpfully stretched out across the stump.

Mark looked across at Mickey. "Well, this is your chance. Give her the axe!"

Mickey wore a distressed expression.

"Come on, Mickey!" Mark insisted. "She's not going to lie still like this all day. This was your idea in the first place. Look here, you said it yourself, we need to kill this bird. She's going to be our Christmas dinner. Aren't you tired of eating nothing but cornbread, blackeyed peas and collards? I'll pluck her myself and make us a nice stuffing. We can collect the fat for frying."

Mickey blinked several times and swallowed hard. She stroked the limp chicken morosely. Finally she said, in a weak voice, "I can't."

"Oh, hell!" Mark leapt to his feet and grabbed the axe. "Do I have to do everything around here? Get your fingers out of the way."

Mark raised the axe; then he paused. "Forgive us, little warrior," he said softly, "but I guess we do need some peace and quiet — and one good meal."

The axe seemed to fall in freeze-frame slow motion. A ray from the rising sun glinted off the blade, making an arc of light that traced its descent. There was one terrible blunted sound, followed by a moment of awful silence, before the headless body went flapping wildly across the yard, leaving a trail of red over the white dusting of snow.

Motionless with shock, the two gawked at the antics of the decapitated bird. Then their eyes met, and they knew the long dark night had vanished without a trace. The tyrannical Empire of the Ego was ended. The soldiers had laid down their arms and the slaves had run free, and there would be rejoicing forever — or at least for a day.

Standing in their longjohns in the dawn-sparkling snow, Mark and Mickey embraced as comrades, and as lovers, and as old adversaries grown weary, and they threw back their heads and laughed and laughed and laughed.

When its death throes were over, Mickey scooped up the black-feathered corpse by its feet. She dipped a finger in its blood and painted warrior stripes on first Mark's and then her own cheeks and forehead.

Then the two linked arms and walked back into the house, their steps matching in perfect rhythm, and they spoke in one voice:

"Let's get this bird in the oven! This is Christmas Eve!"

The Beginning

"Therefore, the man of understanding ... looks at the world and sees that everyone and everything has always understood. He sees that there is only understanding. Thus, the man of understanding is overwhelmed with happiness.... His heart is always tearful with the endless happiness of the world....

"Because you have already understood, you find it necessary to touch his hand. Since you love so much and are not understood, you find it possible to touch his ears. He smiles at you. You notice it. Everything has already died. This is the other world."

*~ Franklin Jones, **The Knee of Listening***

Author - Cherokee Freechild

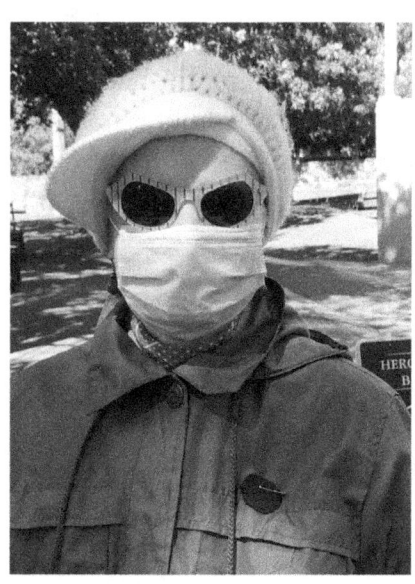

Cherokee Freechild grew up in the Deep South during the Civil Rights struggle. Oral history says her tiny hometown was founded by Cherokee families fleeing the Trail of Tears by passing as white. They succeeded so well that no trace of their language or culture remains, but her family did retain a tradition of Appalachian folk magic.

Cherokee's home addresses have ranged from Manhattan to Fairbanks. She has edited zines on UFOs, parapsychology, social justice and environmental issues. She was copy editor for *High Times* and staff writer for a management consulting company and several community newspapers. Not one of her sensitive legal, medical or government workplaces ever required her to pee into a bottle. (Where were the freedom-loving patriots when *that* got started?)

A zealous antipoverty activist, during the 1980s she produced and hosted weekly TV talk shows on food issues in New York and Atlanta. Then year 2000 rolled around, and world hunger hadn't ended yet. It's now a smaller percentage of global population, but that still leaves a lot of hungry people. Most of them live in places where it's hard to get accurate statistics, but some are sleeping in the streets of North America, mercilessly hounded by cops and security guards.

This novel was written in a log cabin "off the grid" in the BC Interior, as an entry for Ted Turner's "Positive Future" fiction contest. Its intent was to depict a global society where Southerners had become the Good Guys. That task proved harder than expected, even after bringing in space aliens!

Obviously, this novel did not win that contest. Even the winner had a dystopian setting; it featured a Socratic dialogue between a genius child and a talking gorilla about the folly of human society. Sour grapes: that seemed more like a screed than a novel! But many readers do like it, and it has even changed lives, so the judges made the right call.

Originally this book was meant to time out around 2012, which the Mayan calendar predicted would be the year of the Great Turning. That didn't happen on schedule, so the story had to be moved to an alternative timeline to maintain plausibility. Some cosmologists do say we're living in a simulation. And some members of the "Southron heritage" movement prefer Canadian spellings, which simplified the editing!

Cherokee is a certified yoga instructor and NLP practitioner. She has exhausted her counterphobic "bucket list," from firewalking to bungee jumping, but remains terrified of motor vehicles. After starting life with big goals, she has failed to find a suitable cult or commune, end war and hunger, maintain Cosmic Consciousness, or even control her temper. However, she did initiate an ongoing Atlanta chapter of Results.org, a citizens' lobby to create political will to end hunger.

Though nostalgic for Southern cooking and warm summer nights, she is waiting out the COVID-19 pandemic in Victoria, BC, with a housemate who spearheaded the Gay Lib movement in Western Canada. Her current causes are Guaranteed Livable Income, Dying with Dignity, and housing the homeless.

Cover Artist - Oberon Zell

Oberon Zell ("The Wizard OZ") is a renowned Wizard and Elder in the worldwide magickal community. Inspired by the science-fiction novel *Stranger in a Strange Land*, by Robert A. Heinlein, in 1962, Oberon co-founded the first legal Pagan church (the Church of All Worlds; incorporated 1968—**CAW.org**), and in 1967 he was the first to apply the term "Pagan" to CAW and the other newly-emerging Nature Religions of the 1960s and '70s.

Through his publication of *Green Egg* magazine (1968-present—**greeneggmagazine.com/**), Oberon was instrumental in the coalescence of the modern Pagan movement, which has grown to become now the 2nd-largest religion in America. In 1970, Oberon had a profound Vision of the Living Earth which he published as the earliest version of "The Gaea Thesis."

In the 1980s, living in a large Hippie homesteading community in NorCalifia, Oberon and his lifemate Morning Glory resurrected authentic living Unicorns, and led a diving expedition to New Guinea to solve the mystery of Mermaids. In 1990, MG coined the term "polyamory," and launched another significant movement. (MG died of cancer on May 13, 2014.)

A prolific and award-winning artist in several media, Oberon illustrates books and creates altar figurines and jewelry of Gods and Goddesses, mythical creatures, and magick symbols (**themillennialgaia.com**). He is the author of *Grimoire for the Apprentice Wizard*; *Creating Circles & Ceremonies*; *The Wizard & The Witch*; and other books. He is also Headmaster of the online

Grey School of Wizardry, which he founded in 2004 (**GreySchool.com**).

From 2015-'17 Oberon created and operated The Academy of Arcana in Santa Cruz, CA—a store, classroom, library, museum, and gathering space.

A world traveler to mystic sites for over 40 years, in 2018 Oberon spent three weeks in the Yucatan exploring Mayan ruins, and a month in Guatemala, presenting workshops on Quantum Consciousness and participating in Mayan ceremonies. In November of that year he attended the Parliament of the World's Religions in Toronto. In the summer of 2019 he spent a month in Ecuador, teaching and conducting rituals.

Oberon has appeared on numerous TV shows, and is the subject of a film documentary: "The Wizard OZ" (2017) **https://vimeo.com/215849774**. He is now settled at the Venusian Church Longhouse in Redmond, WA.

www.ingramcontent.com/pod-product-compliance
Lightning Source LLC
Chambersburg PA
CBHW071832020726
47502CB00004B/1325